UnCensored Ink

Banned Book Inspired Anthology

Edited by Amy Nielsen and Ian Tan

Wild Ink Publishing

Contents

Welcome

Here at Wild Ink, we are appalled and saddened by the censorship we see now and throughout history. To combat this intellectual outrage, we issued a call for submissions to speak truth to power: to tell book banners how dangerous their efforts are.

According to the American Library Association, there were more censorship attempts in 2022 than any year since the organization began collecting data twenty years ago. Additionally, 90% of censorship attempts today target lengthy lists of titles, some well over a hundred books. Prior to 2021, most censorship attempts targeted one title. And it should come as no surprise, with our country in an all-out culture war, books featuring BIPOC and LGBTQ+ characters and themes are at much greater risk of being censored.

No longer are highly educated instructors, media specialists, and public librarians entrusted to make selections for their readers that not only their readers can see themselves in but also books that challenge the status quo—books that give readers a different perspective. The very thing they were educated in. The very thing politicians were not. In some extreme cases, politicians accuse these same individuals of committing crimes simply by providing a title they disapprove of to a reader.

For authoritarians and their supporters, book banning is the floor. They've yet to define the ceiling. What other forms of creative expression will be next on their hit list—music, theater, paintings, sculpture? When we lose our intellectual freedom, we lose our democracy.

All people deserve to see themselves reflected in books. Also, as humans, when we read about someone else's life experience, it's how we develop empathy and compassion. Something this world could always use a little more of.

Amy Nielsen

Editor - UnCensored Ink

FOREWORD

Hey everyone,

I just have a few words to share before you begin this book. First, if you're not yet sure what exactly to expect (given the diverse composition of anthologies), you'll come across quite a few stances and viewpoints that many might consider 'political'.

If this discourages you from continuing—now hold on a second, don't close on me just yet—please know that much of writing throughout history is inherently 'political'. Or, more specifically, intended to comment on the wretched, unpleasant scenario of the world and its systems. Charles Dickens authored many British classics, including Oliver Twist and A Christmas Carol, in critique of the harsh work and living conditions that the poor were forced to endure during Victorian era England.

American writer and civil rights activist James Baldwin wrote essays, poems and novels that draw from a web of his life experiences, including his childhood in Harlem under a "brooding, silent, physically abusive preacher step-father," and what he witnessed in Paris. Poverty, discrimination, explorations of homosexuality and bisexuality... these all were part of his writings.

"Every poet is an optimist," Baldwin told Hugh Hebert at the *Guardian* when *BealeStreet* was published. "And yet, you have to reach a certain level of despair to deal with your life at all..."

And The Hunger Games? This trilogy that drastically changed the YA & dystopia genres from their debut in 2008-2010 and remain American household titles to this day? Author Suzanne Collins first got the idea because she noticed how "unsettling" it was to switch channels between a TV game show and footage of the Iraq War.

Heck, Captain America? A graphic novel franchise's literal human embodiment of America's ideals and beloved to this day thanks to Chris Evan's heart-filled onscreen portrayal? The character was originally meant as propaganda to egg on the US entry into WWII. One iconic issue even has him punching Hitler in the face. Yup, on the front cover.

I could keep going, but the point is that at its core, this anthology is really not that different from a lot of the literature we've been willingly and even enthusiastically consuming all this while. The world is a boiling pot of grungy unfairness and colorful natural beauty, and to pretend it's only one or the other is to tell the biggest fiction of all. And ironically, as writers by nature, we cannot do that.

The whole purpose of UnCensored Ink is to champion for the right for all stories to exist. Some of them aren't about banned books, per se, but those are the kind of stories that would be banned.Maybe not every story is for you, but we want to do our part so you can make that call.

Maybe some people veer away from stories like these because they can be heavy, and mental health already has enough anvils resting on it as it is. And I get that, truly. So I prepared trigger warningsfor those submissions that lean on the heavy side. I do want to encourage you to still give each one a shot, maybe with a trusted reading companion who can weather the intensity alongside you. And, of course, take your time. Don't power through something if you truly can't.

Lastly, I don't know how many of our writers will become this era's Charles Dickens or James Baldwin or Suzanne Collins. But thanks to the opportunity to work with UnCensored Ink, I know this era has a Maribeth Juraska, an Earl Carrender, a Riley Kilmore, a Christopher DeWitt, a Demi Michelle Schwartz, and a Helen Z. Dong.

A Bruce Buchanan. A Johnny Francis Wolf and a Vi Putrament. A group of Filipinos who joined our movement from the other side of the world. I wish I could name all the writers who contributed.

Poets. Parents. Educators. Librarians.Veterans. Gen X to Gen Z. Americans and non-Americans.

I am proud to have worked alongside these amazing people. And I hope you'll be proud to buy and read their stories.

Thank you.

Ian Tan,

UnCensored Ink editor & project coordinator.
www://ianlancethought.wordpress.com

-100-

Philosophy
&
Psychology

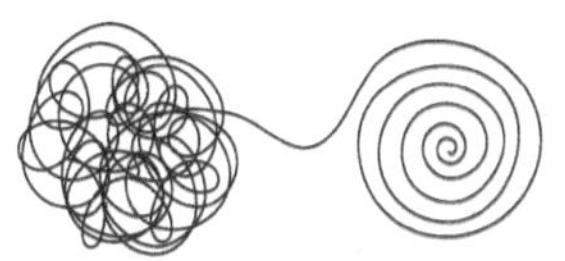

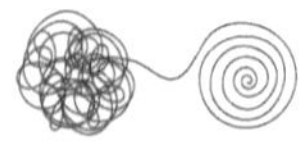

Every Book Its Reader: Viewing Self-Censorship Through Ranganathan's Library Laws

EJ Masters

There are a lot of different reasons we go to library school. Some people go to get the master's degree that will allow them to become a librarian or archivist, work in special collections, or a hundred other jobs. Some people go because they love books and reading and want to share that love. Some people go to be a school librarian. Some of us collect degrees like Pokémon cards. None of us go to *prevent* people from having access to books.

Librarians tend to be the front-runners when it comes to conversations about censorship and book banning. We create displays and book talks and reading challenges to get these books into the waiting hands of our patrons. We buy "I'm

With the Banned" t-shirts and bumper stickers. We stand up to book challenges and protect our community's right to access information the best we can.

More and more, something disquieting is happening behind closed doors when we compile lists of new books to add to our collections. When we decide which displays to make for the season and which authors to schedule for a visit. When we decide what the public will be able to access through our collections.

We all know pulling a book off the shelves is censorship. The black sharpie over certain words or illustrations: censorship. Actually, *burning* the books? Definitely censorship. We must challenge censorship in all forms, even if the call is coming from inside the house.

But what about when the book just... isn't purchased in the first place? When we don't add it to the colorful display in the front window? When we keep it on that "special" shelf behind the desk, away from the general public?

Soft censorship and self-censorship *are* censorship. When we choose not to purchase a book because the fear of backlash or challenges loom over the title or subject matter, we are censoring. The books and materials we choose to add to our collections are the books and materials our patrons have on offer. They simply cannot choose something that isn't available to them. Most librarians are familiar with Ranganathan's five laws of library science, but let's examine those through a lens of censorship:

1. **Books are for use**. Your patrons cannot use books that do not exist in your collection. Are those books shelved or designated in a way that allows your patrons to safely access them? We may be tempted to mark our 2SLGBTQIA+ books with a rainbow sticker for easy identification, but that may put a patron at risk of harassment or worse and prevent them from checking out the book at all. We may have a special shelf behind the circulation desk with "more mature" topics, but how can any of us know what another person is emotionally ready to read? I have elementary students whose home lives would be considered "too mature" for their peers to read about, but for whom those circumstances are their everyday life. We must let our patrons use the books and make their own choices.

2. **Every book its reader.** The emphasis here is on the *book*. How can that book, that life-changing, life-*affirming* book, find its way into the hands of its reader? Is it being shelved prominently? Is it part of a display? Is it being recommended? Not every book is for every reader, but every book is for *someone*. Do we truly have the freedom to read if we don't have books about a wide variety of topics? We know, and have seen time and time again, that the right book placed in the right hands at the right time can change a person's life; it can transform them from an apathetic shelf-browser to a devourer of words. Maybe that one graphic novel isn't

for you, my school librarian friend. Maybe it's for your student.

3. **Every reader their book**. Every reader has the equal right to get the book of their interest. Does your collection reflect that right? Every August when I do my library orientation, I have my students make a word cloud of books and topics they'd like to see in our library. It's a great way to find gaps in the collection and discover new community interests. The interests of my student body are wide and varied, and part of my job is to provide information and books about as many of those topics as I can—especially those things I'm not interested in. That unconscious bias of simply preferring Fantasy novels can make a huge impact on my purchasing decisions, which is, in itself, a form of soft censorship. Your library is for an entire community, and your collection should reflect that.

4. **Save the time of the reader**. Many people don't even know where to begin when they walk into a library. There are too many options, too many shelves, and the intimidation is real! Save their time and have new and exciting things for *all* readers readily available. Will it save the reader's time to have to request a title through interlibrary loan because your library (or system) was soft-censoring that topic or title? Relying on other libraries or library systems to stock the books your community needs saves no one's time and prevents your

patrons from finding what they need. The harder it is for a reader to find their book, the less likely they are to try again the next time—if there *is* a next time.

5. **The library is a growing organism**. There is always time to make a change when it comes to soft censorship and self-censorship. When developing your collection or making display decision, you must ask yourself, "Who needs this book?" Focusing only on whether or not a book will garner a challenge is not, usually, a collection development criteria. A library is a community institution and it should always keep growing, ever changing, to best serve its community.

Using Ranganathan's Library Laws to reframe our thinking about censorship has helped me tremendously in the last year. I see so many librarians put popular titles "on vacation" because they think those books are somehow less worthy than award-winning classics, but if those popular titles amplify and grow a reader's confidence, are they really less worthy? Are our personal biases for authors and topics preventing our books from finding their readers? Is the *threat* of a book challenge enough for us to set aside a book that would be life-affirming for someone?

The mission and vision of the library varies by the institution and community served. There is no librarian's Hippocratic Oath. The closest we come is the ALA Library Bill of Rights, which outlines our duties as librarians: to provide access to our communities, to challenge censorship, to protect an individual's right to privacy in their library use. There are thousands of memoirs and personal accounts of how access to information, to the right book, changed a person's entire life. We must fight to protect the intellectual freedoms of our communities through our actions as librarians, collection developers, book recommenders, and advocates.

Eliots Abound

Lorie Wackwitz

It all started back in the days when being a kid was as big a hassle as any other occupation. I've heard the talk:

"What a terrible shame";

"Such an awful waste";

or "Tisk, tisk, tisk—my, my."

Yes, I've heard them talking; don't be thinking that I haven't. They look at me with sad faces and those wide know-most-of-it-eyes, and I can hear them. I can hear them, and it makes me want to crawl into my track shoes and come out standing on one eyebrow. If only I hadn't discovered the relationship between teaching and censorship.

I was sitting in class one day, minding the teacher's business, listening to her describe Hemingway's writing style, when it suddenly dawned on me that instead of studying about how other people view Hemingway, I could be reading Hemingway.

I sat straight up in my chair, coughed several times, and began to recite T. S. Eliot's "Love Song of J. Alfred Prufrock."

"Let us go then, you and I,

When the evening is spread out against the sky

Like a patient etherized upon a table;

Let us go, through certain half-deserted streets,

The muttering retreats

Of restless nights in one-night cheap hotels

And sawdust restaurants with oyster-shells…"

What this had to do with Hemingway, I don't know. But it was literature, poetry, rhythm, and breath. And somehow it was… me.

So surprised was my teacher to hear Eliot's words against a sea of tired faces that she paused to listen. To me. To Eliot. In an instant we were one and the same, merged. Author and student. Deceased and daring.

In the next instant, my teacher deducted twenty points from my grade for behavior that was "disruptive to the learning process." I must never be moved to speak about anything other than approved material, and even then, not without permission.

Her reaction inspired me. I began carting extra books to and from class. I stuffed my locker with them. I left them for people as gifts. At first, I carried them simply to establish that my silence was not without protest. But then I began to read. The books that I carried replaced the friends that I lost, friends who didn't care to be associated with one who wrote poetry unbidden on classroom walls. My commitment became my passion. My passion became my life. At last, I was free!

So upset was the principal to learn of my newly found freedom that he decided to have me evaluated. During my lunch period, when I was totally immersed in *Their Eyes Were Watching God* by Zora Neale Hurston, the man grabbed and roughly escorted me to the school's library of approved books. Upon my arrival, the good librarian took one look at me and whispered, "Such actions! They could only be those of a philosopher's child!" Right then and there I knew that Socrates-the-Censor was running my school. I was his antithesis personality, the other Socrates. The Socrates executed for his questions more than the corruption of youth. But this was not that day. I had no interest in death, only words.

Moments later, the principal-turned-censor suspended me. I had one final chance to redeem myself. One week and nearly 20 books later, I returned to class determined to fit in. I would begin by explaining myself. The class had resumed discussing narrative structure as exemplified by the short stories of Hemingway. The term was nearly over. This was review. Perspicuity dawned. The path to constructive normalcy was clear.

On the day of my initial recitation, I had been out of context. I had, in fact, been reciting the wrong Wasteland! After all, we were discussing short stories, not poems. Ernest Miller, not Thomas Stearns. My comeback had to be within limits. The realization was harsh, but I knew this time I would have to conform. No, it had not been the wrong Wasteland that I had recited, but rather the wrong Eliot! My saga would end as it began, with the short stories of Hemingway. I rose from my seat. If silence could kill, we'd have all died in that moment. And then Hemingway spoke through me, a bit more whimsically than intended perhaps, but nevertheless he spoke.

"Mr. and Mrs. Elliot tried very hard to have a baby. They tried in Boston after they were married and they tried coming over on the boat. They did not try very hard on the boat because Mrs. Elliot was quite sick—"

There I interrupted Hemingway to ask a quick but important question.

"Excuse me," I said. "But what of the climax?" I sat back down. "I mean, it's all about a couple's frequent attempts to have a baby. Granted it is interesting that they do so everywhere. However, I can't see the rising action, let alone the climax. Where exactly is it?"

A loud chorus of laughter burst forth from the back of the class. I turned and with utmost sincerity replied to the chorus. "No, really. I don't see it in the story arc."

The laughter stopped. Behind her desk, the teacher turned blue.

"Silence!" She rose, her voice ascending with her. "I have had enough of your books and ideas, your sick questions and intentionally disruptive statements. I will not have you openly, or otherwise, discussing sex in my classroom. This is a serious literature class. In it we will not discuss Mr. and Mrs. Elliot nor the means through which they attempt to conceive. We will not discuss Ginsberg, Morrison, Salinger, Vonnegut, or Cisneros. We will not discuss *Ulysses*. Vulgar ideas create vulgar people.

You have become one of those people. So, get. Get out. Get out now. Grace not my door again."

And so, it was ended.

I sadly took my leave of Hemingway—the one book that belonged to the school—gathered up Black Elk and Angie Thomas and made my way down the aisle. Changed. Was it the literature, the ideas that changed me? I supposed only time would tell, though idealist writers might disagree. As I reached the door, I turned and addressed my desk with its lone book lying there, repeating words John Kennedy had said so many years before: "Liberty without learning is always in peril, and learning without liberty is always in vain." I hoped someone might hear me, hear him. Kennedy, at least, hadn't been banned. Not yet. But the me-Kennedy who left that day could never return. The me-Kennedy knew what so many others can never hope to learn: being a singular unique independent person is the hardest and most rewarding occupation of them all.

Note: The quoted works by Eliot, Hemingway, and Kennedy are in the public domain.

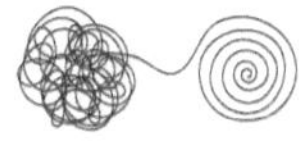

Forever Ago Now

Jane A. Hartsock, J.D., M.A.

When I was maybe four years old, I made the mistake of asking my father what diphtheria was. Born in 1931, and a historian to boot, he'd told me stories of children in his community—Oak Park, Illinois, and then Paw-Paw—who'd died from such diseases, diseases that, even as a very young child, I understood were no longer a part of *my* world. He answered my questions by pulling out one of his volumes of *The Encyclopedia Britannica* and showing me the entry on diphtheria. I was also interested in polio; my grandmother had it as a child, which gave her a limp.

Both entries included photographs of the pink, purple, and blue-stained pathogens under a microscope, and that night, when my parents turned out the lights, and my bedroom fell into darkness, the colorful dots, the echoes of light that danced in front of my eyes looked a whole hell of a lot like those images of diphtheria in *The Encyclopedia Britannica*. I was terrified.

Comfort was provided by way of rational explanation: Germs are invisible to the naked eye; you can't see them (not quite the comfort my parents might have imagined).

In any case, all of this was consistent with the view both of my parents held that children's questions should be answered. Fully. Truthfully. With illustrations, if available. And books are a place one can get her questions answered. My brothers, my sister, and I were permitted to read anything we could get our hands on, and I cannot recall a single time in my life that any adult in my world pulled a book from my hands and forbade me to read it.

By eighth grade, I had discovered the young adult section of the Monroe County Public Library in Bloomington, Indiana where I grew up. I could get there with a single bus ride (no transfer necessary), or if I didn't want to spend money on fare, I could follow the train tracks from Pigeon Hill into downtown Bloomington and then to Kirkwood Ave. At that time, the young adult section of the library was one-half of a large room on the first floor of the library. Children's books were on one side, teen books on the other, and tables where kids played chess divided the room. I may not be remembering this completely accurately; it was a long time ago.

What I do remember is the first time I read Judy Blume's *Forever.* The cover was white and the title in a font I can only describe as "eighties-fancy." It was worn—many hands had held this book. The creases along the spine of the paperback suggested certain parts of the book might have been read more often than others. I read that book cover-to-cover. It was the first time I read the word "come" as a synonym for "orgasm," and I remember thinking to myself, *Come where?* Eventually, the context clarified my confusion.

Seeing that the book was once again raising people's hackles, I recently reread it, wondering what I would think of it as an adult. As a tween, it was just a romance novel with people closer in age to me than the romance novels at my BFF Sarah's house. By the standards of 2023, it's pretty tame. Incredibly heteronormative. But reading it as an adult and a mother was indeed different. I noticed things I did not notice the summer before eighth grade. Like that Kat's parents are really good parents. They love her and her sister, they are sources of accurate and thoughtful information. They are wise. And they love each other. They model a healthy marriage.

I noticed the frank, nearly clinical accuracy of the sexual acts depicted in the novel. The descriptions at times sound like they could come from a Sex Ed textbook—not one in Indiana; we don't teach Sex Ed here. Maybe *that's* what's got people so upset. The book also sets the intimacy between Michael and Kat within the context of an older adolescent relationship where the two protagonists love each other.

SPOILER: Their relationship isn't *forever*.

I also noticed that the writing is not as sophisticated as most adolescents today would expect. Though they probably have authors like Judy Blume to thank for that considering the dearth of realistic fiction available to adolescents in the mid-70ss when *Forever* was written. But I still love this book.

Michael and Kat are 67 years old now. I feel somehow they're doing okay. Maybe they're friends on Facebook.

There are a lot of books I love for a lot of different reasons. But this book. *THIS* book is on the cusp of adulthood. It is too cold air conditioning on scrawny summer legs. It is the texture of worn paper under my fingertips. It is conversations with Sarah and Kelly about experiences we were curious about but not yet ready to have. Its soundtrack is "CHECK! CHECK! CHECKMATE!" It is served with oatmeal raisin cookies from The Red Chair Bakery.

Most importantly, though, this book is the philosophy of my parents, and now my own, that there are enormous dangers that lurk in the fragile life of a child. But they probably don't lurk in a library.

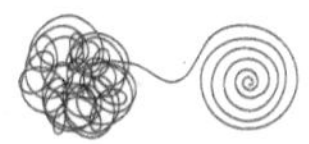

Mazi

Erica Duarte

Content Warning: References to self-harm.

Second-period English was a riot of activity when Mazi walked in. What the fuck was this? More of them were here today. The paunchy middle-aged man with sallow skin managed the computer, typing. The old female with the beaky nose and watery eyes managed a hand-held printer, and a new younger woman was sticking the printed stickers onto the back of each book they pulled from the shelf before replacing it. They were cataloging all the books.

Mazi, like everyone else, hadn't known anything about it, until the administrators started showing up in her classrooms. Her mom had no knowledge of it either, only gawked at the dinner table when Mazi asked why it was happening, then promised to ask around. A day later, her mother told her a recently passed law stated all public schools had to catalog all books for online public inspection.

Public inspection? What the hell did that mean? And why all the secrecy? But Mazi knew why. You didn't grow up in the bible belt without knowing how to play the zealot's game of chess that "Kept America's children safe."

Safe.

It was a loaded word. Mazi hadn't felt safe since she reached puberty at the age of twelve and knew without a shadow of a doubt that she could easily kiss, caress, admire, lust after, even love, both males and females equally and without shame. That was her secret. The game she never risked to play.

The young woman placing the stickers on the books turned and caught Mazi by surprise. Her stomach tightened as the bluest eyes she'd ever seen took her in, rested on her mouth. Mazi's cheeks heated, and she looked away.

"Don't mind them," Mr. Sherman, the youngish, bearded English teacher said in a tone that did nothing to hide his utter hatred of the spectacle taking place to his beloved books. "They'll get what they're after and be gone."

Mazi smiled inwardly, knowing exactly what Mr. Sherman meant. They could have the books on those shelves. But what they would never have, what they were actually wanting, were the books he had hidden in his desk. The books that he let Mazi read after he'd overheard a group of girls tormenting her over a stupid fucking glance she'd let linger too long on one of them.

That's right, Fuck you! She wanted to snarl. But she just put her head down. To endure this place was like being wrapped in barbed wire. Safe. Safe. Safe. Who exactly *were* they trying to keep safe? Certainly not kids like Mazi.

After school, as Mazi drove home in her gram's restored 69 Volkswagen Beetle, she took a route to avoid the intersection with the billboard that stated *There is only he and she, no they* like there was zero doubt, bought and paid for by the Dodson Branch Southern Baptist Church. To her surprised fury, she came across another. The bastards had extended their hate campaign to include *Holy matrimony is one man one woman.* Yet another reason why churches should be taxed. If they have money to blow on being so blatantly hateful, what were they doing in the shadows? The thought made her shudder.

One man, one woman...

She pictured the sapphire-eyed girl and wondered what her full lips would feel like pressed against her own. Like bliss. Like lust. Like love.

Love was not allowed in Mazi's life, not according to the Southern Baptist fools thumping their bibles, making these rules. Their reach invasive like kudzu, infiltrating the easily accessible minds of those who sought right-wing dominion. It made Mazi wonder if there would ever be a time when she could be openly loving? When she could touch the back of a hand, caress a neck, hold a heated glance?

It cut deep to be on the outside. They made it easy for Mazi to hate herself. To hate that part of herself she had no control over. To cut at the core of her or simply make it okay for her to cut the tender flesh of her inner thigh, that secret place no one would ever see. She did that more often than she'd ever admit, even though she knew it was wrong, wrong, wrong, so wrong. But what they did was worse.

At home, her mother hugged her. Then her father too, when he got home. They tried to understand. Tried to protect. But still, Mazi found it difficult to sleep.

The halls were eerily silent the next morning until the whispers started. Mazi slowed her steps to listen.

"Did you hear about Mr. Sherman?"

"He got caught giving an unauthorized book to a student."

"The parents were pissed."

"He's been put on administrative leave."

Mazi turned down the hall that held Mr. Sherman's classroom. It was a book no doubt the student needed but in this fucking place, *that* never played into it. Maybe nothing would come of it. Maybe it'd blow over. Maybe he'd be back in a week. But if Mazi knew anything, it was that this place always got their way. One man. One woman. One thin razor blade to sensitive flesh.

Sneaking into Mr. Sherman's room, she opened the bottom drawer of his desk and took out the books he stashed there. The earthy smell of worn pages filled her senses like the crocuses in early spring after a bitter winter.

"What is that? What are you doing?"

The girl's voice startled Mazi. She clutched the books to her chest. Blue eyes raked her from hip to neck, sending a flush of heat to her cheeks, exposing her in the best and most terrifying way. "Nothing. I'm not doing anything."

"What are those?"

"My books. I'm taking them home."

Blue eyes came closer, more than just beauty, more like magnificent. Tall with high cheekbones and a scatter of freckles across her perfect nose. Mazi's heart leaped to her throat, and she looked away hoping this girl was not like those other girls who taunted her for a slip of her gaze.

"It's okay. You can have your books," she said, inching forward, freezing Mazi.

This was the closest she had ever let herself be to a girl she found so utterly attractive. Close enough that Mazi could feel the heat of her breath as she spoke. Close enough that she could smell the coconut scent of her hair like sunshine, like sand, like she belonged to a place so much better than this cold, hateful town. She looked up into an ocean of blue, so clear and confident, a face so unafraid.

"I love this one." A gentle finger touched the back cover of a book poking out of Mazi's clenched fists. "It's one my book club is reading. Maybe you can join us to talk about it?"

Mazi got the sudden urge to cry. To run. To press her lips to that olive skin. But she just nodded as the lovely girl wrote a time, date, and place on a scrap of paper and handed it over, just as the final bell rang and Mazi walked out feeling blue eyes caress her stooped back as she left. Safety was a shadow. And Mazi had learned to live in shadow. Ironically, just like the church though in a vastly different game.

She took an even longer route home that afternoon. Roads that turned on themselves. Streets that took her out of her way and back again to avoid the screaming billboards.

In her room that night she cradled the books in her bed. The smooth spines, the thin pages, the words in black and white that told a story in colors of grey. A hand, a touch, lips to lips. Coiled fire. Lust turned quietly loving. Not one man. Not one woman. But human. Tears streaked her cheeks. Beautiful. No cold blade for Mazi that night. She rubbed old scars and raised silver lines. Too many of them. But no more. This night was one sweet reprieve found in shed tears, in words, in a story that was her. A story that spoke of a better place, a better life, even if it was imagined. A life she could maybe, someday have with a blue-eyed girl and her book club. If only, if only, if only she could play the game better. If only, if only, if only, she didn't have to play at all.

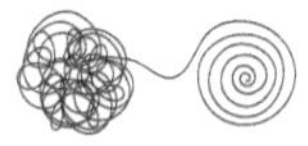

School of Athens at the Vatican

A.M. Hayden

FRESCOES, NOT PAINT AT all, not surface coated, instead colors mixed into wet plaster, *fresh* images birthing the wall itself, landscape, institution, Pope's library, and thin paper volumes, and the rope is pulled open and I walk into the slight room with theater screen sized paintings, a Vatican Grand Canyon I want to climb, backpack, donkey ride into, walk up to Plato and Aristotle center stage with their otherworldly and worldly yin and yang tomes, Heraclitus, his fire and flux and Buddhist-you-can't-step-in-the-same-river-twice impermanence, Pythagoras and his vegan harmony of spheres, immortal souls, women as equals, but only in his pocket, not in the astronomer's corner of Ptolemy and Zoroaster, where Raphael himself is antisocial artist, awkward in any setting, desperately looking for a dog to pet, exiled Diogenes laying on the steps below, barking with brutal honesty, *there's nothing shameful about being human!* Mojo Risin' of ancient philosophy in stank tatters instead of leathers, growling *you're blocking my light!* to Alexander the Great, agreeing with Socrates, happiness cannot be bought, speaking of there he is, gadfly taunting question after ironic question as truth's midwife, offense burning their faces, his sworn, cave-emerged duty to examine and escape, if only Nietzsche, Sartre, or Beauvoir were here, but not a cynical glimmer yet in 1511, maybe a 20th century Hopper version of *Nighthawks,* their arguments and *Je ne sais quoi* stirring in their cigarette smoke, and I can never teach

Kierkegaard without thinking of that one student who swore, *If I would have met Kierkegaard, I would have said, don't ever let go of what you love, you dumbass!* referring to Regina, but everything else too and Plato looks like Leonardo, pointing to metaphysical forms of *Good,* no one can teach us anything that is not already buried somewhere inside of us waiting to be unearthed, Gibran said this too, so there must be something to birth trauma shaking all knowledge to the ground, a loose sack of change turned upside down, spending our whole lives picking up the pieces, which is exactly where Aristotle points to truth, your feet in the dirt, don't miss the real forms by staring at Plato's Sun, and there is patient Hypatia, Neo-Platonic Smurfette of Athens, only one besides Raphael who looks directly at us, wonders where Clea, Thecla, Sosipatra, Diotima, Macrina, and the thousands of other unnamed brilliant word-filled women are at, Hypatia knows she would be blamed for a male ruler's actions, did she know she would be torn apart, literally dismembered piece by piece by an angry Christian mob in the street, and I think it was Socrates who said an educated person is defined by their ability to entertain an idea *without agreeing to it* and 2500 years later, we still look at those who climb out of the cave, dirt still under their nails, in fearful disgust, offense burning our faces

Important Note: This poem is included in the manuscript, *Old World Wings*, set for publication by Wild Ink Publishing in October 2025. The poem was *first* featured in *Flights Literary Magazine*, October 2023.

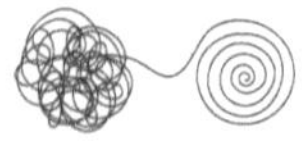

Stranger in the Archives

Vi Putrament

I EYED THE INTRUDER as they slid one of the more battered tomes into the volcanic depths of a handbag that hung off their shoulder like a single black wing. For a moment, it seemed as though a hooded demon had insinuated themselves into the dusty ranks of the archives to play havoc with my mind and senses.

The shock of it made me freeze up into an awkward slouch. Even though my feet were planted solidly into the concrete floor, my knees had buckled, and it took all the strength I had in my thighs to keep myself upright.

I wished I hadn't seen it. In all my years working in the archives, I'd never once had to confront a thief. I willed the intruder to look up and notice me, even consider putting the book back where it belonged, but no such luck. The hooded figure swished down the aisle, seemingly without a care or qualm in the world.

It was a rare sight to see a visitor crack one of these books open, let alone swipe one. I had no idea about the protocol or whether there even was any. I glanced around the main hall to see if anyone else had noticed the thief among the stacks, but the guards were still staring down at their devices, oblivious. Nothing ever happened here in the Archives of Earthly Literacy (AEL) in the city of K-South on KOI-7316.02 because not a single soul was interested in any of these dusty old books. Anything you ever needed to know could be downloaded from the cosmic cloud in nanoseconds. Frankly, the need for any sort of hardware had been obliterated.

I wasn't especially interested in books myself and most likely I would've chosen another line of work if the HR Ministry hadn't assigned to the archives. Like most people in the Cosmos, we don't decide what we want to do with our lives in K-South. A few bytes of data processed by the all-knowing algorithm always tells the committee everything they need to know about you. Within seconds, you get a message on your device telling you to show up at 6:00 am sharp at your designated place of employment. Apparently, I was qualified to be an archives administrator, but let's not be fooled. It was just a fancy title for someone who roamed around a dismal library awaiting the non-existent hordes of visitors to file in. Much of the job involved staring up at the ceiling and wondering what the point was to keep all these fading piles of paper lying around. What purpose did they serve in our brand-new fully automated, perfectly digitized world? No matter how hard I thought about it, the pieces just didn't fit together.

Most of the books that had arrived from Earth had been confiscated from the luggage of the first batch of settlers and burned. Until some gangs got wind of it and stoked a hugely profitable smuggling ring on the dark market. Mr. Banks, our founder and chairman, put his elite brain to use and quickly realized that it might be a better idea to salvage a few and showcase them in the most uninteresting and unglamorous space possible. He founded the archives as a warning to the public at large about the unappealing aspects of unbridled artistic license, not unlike the curatorial mission at the Torture Museum on the other side of town.

"This is the only way to temper this frankly unreasonable interest in literary contraband," he'd bellowed at the start of the opening ceremony.

Mr. Banks truly believed that if you made things accessible in the most boring sort of way, they'd swiftly lose their allure. You couldn't argue with a man with six degrees from three interplanetary universities, so I always assumed he was right. And sure enough, the architecture of the building was so impossibly drab that it was no wonder that for most people, it was nothing more than a glorified public toilet. And when a poor meandering soul did end up entering its walls in pursuit of a functional pissoir, they usually shuffled back out pretty quickly after their business was done.

As visitors were so rare, it was impossible not to notice when someone ended up lingering for longer than the typical 30 seconds before ducking out. I kept eyeing the stranger as they crept through the bookcases on the south side of the hall. The book they swiped had been collecting dust on a shelf that us adminis-trators referred to as the "illicit collection." Namely, books that the League of Literary Security (LLS) had definitively deemed unfit for human (and even alien, for that matter) consumption. The LLS had successfully tackled the threat of unruly fiction and prevailed, so that not a single shred of it could make its way into the fragile human subconscious. Still, despite the general lack of interest in our stacks, I could swear I'd just spotted a burglary in progress.

My thief was dressed in the typical galactic uniform of most people out here, that is, a snug-fitting jumpsuit in a sparkling shade of hematite paired with heavy boots. There was nothing out of the ordinary about their appearance and I might not have noticed them at all if it wasn't for the fact I'd almost certainly witnessed them steal something. They continued strolling the aisles like they didn't have a care in the world, a black hood with a holographic gleam hiding most of their face from sight.

Still, I could spy a hint of smugness, which was enough to stoke a flame of rage in my heart. Rage mixed with a twinge of awe, perhaps. I stood there, my chest quaking, while they meandered slowly between the aisles. I couldn't help noticing their slender hands taking on a translucent sheen in the frigid climate-controlled air as they perused the row of even rarer books at the top of the shelf, standing on their tippy toes.

I cleared my throat as a warning, but it came out as a hoarse crack. I supposed it was high time for me to approach the thief, before they slipped another book into their bag. There was nothing I craved less than to have to confront someone stealing something so worthless. With the black market shut down, none of these books would fetch more than the price of a packet of rehydratable spicy peas, maybe two with a discount. And yet, here we were.

I slid through the hall, slumping down, until I was right behind them. "Excuse me," I whispered. They didn't turn around, but they didn't flee either. Eventually, they raised their head, as if surveying a flock of birds soaring across the sky. But there was no skylight cutting through the roof, and no birds on this planet either, no creatures at all, in fact. I could only assume the point was to snub me.

"Excuse me," I echoed, the hiss of the first syllable heavy in my mouth. They raised their arms to adjust their hood, tucking a lock of silver hair back under its shining depths. All plans of sliding my hand back into the bag and confiscating the item dissipated. My arms were immobile at my sides, there was no way I could ever take anything from them. My heart fell into my stomach and flopped around. I recoiled at the possibility they might have a weapon, but just as I stepped back, they took a step forward.

"Don't go," they whispered into the air between us. I was sure I had imagined it, until I noticed their head turning slightly, almost imperceptibly.

"Listen, you and I both know that nobody cares about this place or any of this rubbish. So why don't you get along with your day and allow me to wrap up my visit in peace?"

I froze, struggling to keep from sinking into the velvet softness of their whisper.

Their voice rose to a booming pitch as they doubled down. "No, thank you, I don't need any help. I'm on my way out, there's nothing of interest here, just as I thought."

My panic redoubled and my heart sank again as the guards perked up and stared our way. It took the best of me to nod my head politely, turn around and make a gesture toward the exit.

"Just this way. I'm sorry you wasted your time in coming here. It happens to all of us. I would never have set foot in here if it wasn't my job, I can assure you," I said, mustering up a chatty tone to camouflage my panic.

They laughed at my pathetic joke, too loudly for sure, because the guards began to stare at us again. One thing everyone agreed on around here was that you just didn't call attention to yourself. You kept your head down, at home, in the street, at work, and everywhere else. There was just no point in getting yourself (or anyone else for that matter) excited. Excitement was what had led to the downfall of humans back on Earth. The goal was to act right and avoid falling into the same traps our primitive ancestors had succumbed to.

"Would you mind walking me to the exit?" they asked. "My eyes aren't what they used to be."

Now this I found surprising. The thief gave off a boundless sort of energy, like those immortal gods that humans used to believe in back on Earth. Then again in K-South, you could never tell how old someone was, with all the bionic treatments available. Only the privileged could afford a fresh pair of peepers every year, a new heart or liver, even. Nothing I could afford on an administrator's salary, but that was beside the point.

Judging by the quality of their attire, this thief had luxury status. And yet, from the way they leaned on me, they were probably compensating for a slight limp, which made them all the more intriguing. Something about this stranger made me feel I could trust them. Or perhaps I was merely prisoner to their charms, fealty to yet another powerful grip and authoritative air. Whatever it was, I had already succumbed, I could feel it in the depths of my belly.

Instead of releasing my arm the moment we approached the exit, they pulled me along, through the oversized doors and into the dusty streets of the city. That light in my heart propelled me forward without a thought to where I was going. We slid through the closing doors of the tram connecting the northern boroughs to the south. I struggled to calm my pounding heart as they grinned at me in that unspeakable way. My brain was too muddled to even care that I'd probably just lost my job.

Five stops on and we dashed through murky puddles into a grim apartment block, flying all the way up to the thirtieth floor, floating through the door, where it seemed we could finally speak freely.

"So, why'd you take it?" I demanded as soon as the locks on the door slid closed with an automatic and highly satisfying click.

I couldn't wait another second to find out the answer to the question that had been thundering in my head since I saw them secret that book away.

Their silver eyes glittered with a mischievous look from the rich darkness of their hood, just before pulling it down to reveal a face that was etched with a beauty I had not seen before in all my time on this silly planet.

"So that you might read it to me," they replied simply.

"Me?"

"You. Are you saying you've never noticed me before?" Their eyes were bright with feigned indignation.

I stared into the magnetic depths of their irises, incapable of admitting that I could have missed meeting them before.

"Well?"

"Well, no," I relented. "I haven't seen you before. I would have remembered."

"I've been to the archives every Wednesday of every week for the past six months and I've read nearly every book in the illicit collection. And one day I just decided that I had to keep this one forever." They stroked the fading book cover as though it were a kitten, as if it were the most precious thing in the Universe.

I gasped, half in horror and half in sheer admiration. Those books weren't meant to be read. They were meant to serve as a warning, a lesson that even the most despicable stories fade to dust, replaced by the righteousness and optimism of the New Galactic Vision, which was infinitely superior. I had never met anyone who actually wanted to read any of these books, especially as their language and forms were archaic, unfit for the new age of the Uber-human.

"Haven't you read them?" they exclaimed, their lovely face scrunching up in a wave of disgust. I supposed they regretted having brought me here, seeing how wrong they'd been in assuming I could be trusted. Their brow began to furrow with worry, maybe even fear.

I was ashamed to admit it. "No, I never even considered it. I was assigned this job by the HRM. I've never read a single one. Why would I?"

They stared at me, outrage looming in their gaze.

"Get out!" they shouted at last, leaping to their feet, clearly disgusted they'd been so wrong about whatever version of me they'd conjured up, watching me skulk about the archives for weeks, spying on me from the shadows of books.

"No, no. Let me explain," I protested, but the words got caught in my throat again. My face turned hot at the desperation leaking through my voice. "I'm not saying there's no good in reading, I just never had the chance."

It was their turn to gasp. After a moment, their shoulders dropped, their fury rising off their body in invisible waves.

"I will read it to you then." Their voice was kind and resolute. And I leaned back against the softness of their body as they began to recite a heady blend to syllables that my mind my spin and my heart soar. Words that were not meant to exist, which had been marked for destruction, the last of their sort, fated to oblivion once the air whittled the pages down to nothing. The melody of that voice, the song of these syllables, filled my head. It was the sudden intoxication that only poetry can bring. Nothing else in this world had ever made me feel this much, this deeply.

Hours passed in this state of half-delirium. Maybe a day. This must be the story of us, a tale of two souls that had been brought together in the emptiness of space, connected by the inexplicable, tied together with an invisible string of magic, our imperfect human bodies fitting together like poetry.

They kissed me so deeply, it felt as though I were drowning. They rocked me as I sobbed at all that I had lost through the ages, all the stories hidden from my heart.

Tome by tome, we brought home the most ancient tales of earthly lore, filling this one-bedroom apartment, floor to ceiling, with books. On weekends, we'd recopy the words of these tomes, bringing forth a new era of illuminated manuscripts for the digital age. Looking back, it was a dangerous enterprise, but we couldn't imagine giving up. We set up a radio channel informally known as "The Banned Width," where we read these stories out loud and transmitted them to our beloved readers throughout Cygnus. It wasn't until three years later that the LLS managed to intercept our scrambled signal and find us. I suppose we'd gotten too comfortable with our freedoms.

And even after we had been taken into custody, we held onto our stories, whispering them to one another through the airwaves that passed between our jail cells, our hearts and minds connected through the ether for all time.

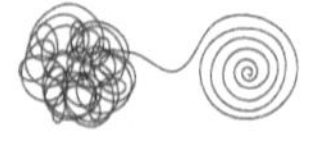

They Took Her Away

Melissa R. Mendelson

Lorna James lit up a room when she walked in, and her brilliant smile would calm even the slightest nerve. Her hair was always pulled into a tight ponytail, and her shoulders were set back, and high. She made eye contact with everyone. She made eye contact with me, and she would give me a secret, little smile. We barely exchanged words except recently, and we had a brief phone conversation or two. But that was as far as things would go because we had to be careful.

Today, Lorna James's hair hung low, her brown locks a mess, some curled, some not. Her shoulders were slumped. She avoided everyone's gaze, mine especially. She slid into her seat, mud clinging to one back heel. The Lorna James that I know would never have mud on her shoe.

White chalk screeched against the blackboard. Mr. Roberts. The teacher's hand shook over the S. He erased the S and wrote it again, but still, his hand trembled. Something wrong with his programming?

I returned my attention to Lorna James. We locked eyes. There was no anger. No fear. Nothing. Her gaze was empty, her light gone. She turned back toward Mr. Roberts and some kids nearby looked at me as if her change were my fault. Did they know about our conversations? Did they know what she had given to me?

My bookbag slumped against my leg. I should have left it in the locker. Maybe, I shouldn't have even put it in the bookbag, but my mother checked my room daily. She would deny it, but she didn't know about the small camera I had on my dresser. It was a suggestion Lorna James had given me.

"They're watching," Lorna James whispered to me the day before yesterday. "They don't want us to know, but we must. If we don't, we'll repeat history, and we have already repeated history."

That was the first time she spoke to me and in hushed tones because she was right. "They're watching."

I shook my head. Nobody knew what was in the book bag. I was safe, and I brought it here today to slip to Lorna James. Is that what happened? Did her parents know that she had it? Were they looking for it? Did they turn her in? Parents are supposed to protect, but I know mine won't. Will they come for me next?

"Ms. Burgess." Mr. Roberts announced my name as if I were already on trial. "Are you paying attention?" His sigh whipped across the room. "Open your textbook to page 54."

My hand trembled as I reached for my bookbag. One girl seemed to notice, but I opened the bag, knowing that it was small. Nobody was going to see it, and I pulled out the heavy textbook. The paperback almost came out with it.

"What's that?" Some boy two seats to my left leaned over. "What's in your bookbag?"

"A sandwich," I snapped at him and closed the bookbag, dropping the textbook onto my desk. "Do you mind?" I waited for him to turn away, but he stared at me.

"Page 54," Mr. Roberts repeated.

"Yes, sir." I complied.

The page blinded me with its little, black words. Their words. Only their words and the page felt as fake as its text.

"Mr. Roberts?" The girl from before raised her hand into the air. "I think she has something in her bag."

"I said it was a sandwich." Rage filled my voice, nearly rattling my body. "A peanut butter and jelly sandwich on white bread." I reached back into the bookbag and pulled it out. "Do you want it?" I asked.

Mr. Roberts was about to respond when he twitched. He reached for the back of his neck and looked at his hand. His hand was coated in blood. Yes, something was wrong with his programming. "Nobody move," he said stoically but only stared at me. "I'll be right back." He hurried out of the room.

Lorna James locked eyes with me again. Her pink lips were flat, no smile, no frown. Just an empty gaze. She reached up, her hand disappearing beneath all that brown hair, and rubbed her neck.

"No," I whispered.

"What's in the bag?" It was that boy again.

That's it. I threw the sandwich at the boy's face. It landed on his desk. *Can't either of you mind your own damn business?*

The boy rubbed his neck.

The other girl hissed and twitched. She also rubbed the back of her neck. "She has a book in her bag," she said.

We are being programmed. "No, there's no book in my bag," I said.

"Liar." That other girl pointed at Lorna James. "Look at what you did to her. I hope you're happy with yourself."

"I didn't do that," I said.

In the past, Lorna James would have jumped to her feet and defended anyone in trouble. She would have defended me. Today, she just sat there.

"I didn't do that," I repeated. But my voice shook.

"What are you reading?" That boy asked.

No, they can't leave me alone, and nice try. You almost had me.

"Doesn't matter." That other girl twirled her hair around her finger. "They already know. Right, Lorna?"

"Right," Lorna whispered. Her word was a sharp dagger lingering on her lips.

I turned cold. My heart slammed against my chest. Sweat raced down my back. *It was just a book. Just a damn book. So, what if they didn't want me to read it?* I looked at Lorna James. *She is what happens to you when you read something declared, Illegal.*

Lorna James's stare reminded me of a dead deer I saw once. Eyes wide open. No one was home, and I watched her push her long, brown hair aside, revealing irritated, red skin beneath. *Now, you're one of them. How could they do such a thing and especially to someone like Lorna James? All this because of a book?*

"Ms. Burgess."

It wasn't Mr. Roberts. He never returned to the room. My name was repeated from the loudspeaker nearby. "Ms. Burgess. Report to the Principal's Office."

My body was still cold, sweat ran down my back. My heart stopped racing. Maybe, it already surrendered. and I knew security was coming. They didn't follow the programming. They enforced it, and two large shadows fell over the classroom door.

"Go with them." Lorna James sounded like an automated operator. "Don't fight. You'll lose." A faint, faint trace of the girl that she used to be flickered. "I lost." She faded away.

Tears streamed down my face as I picked up my bookbag. I didn't bother with the open textbook left on the desk. They would make sure that I got that back or another one just like it because it was from them and only them.

I paused by Lorna James, surprising her by touching her hand. "It's not your fault," I whispered.

Lorna James looked at me with one tear sliding down her cheek.

"It's their fault, and we, we suffer from them."

I moved away toward the now-open classroom door. The security guards grabbed the bookbag out of my hands and gestured for me to walk toward the Principal's Office. I was on

Death's Row, heading for the electric chair, but no, I wasn't going to die. At least, not all of me.

-200-

Religion

Amen!

Ester M. Marquez & Lester N. Linsangan

Amen! As it notes,
Rise up, all righteous goats,
Who knows they are no white lamb,
Yet, they beat black sheep with a slam

Those mouths is chewing poisons.
With cruelty and senseless opinions,
Which can wreck someone's soul,
Was that their mission and goal?

What kind of food do they have?
Do they choose only their want and love?
And not those which reprimands;
Anger, lust, greed, body, and hands?

Have they all become dumb?

With too much in mind, they've been numb?
They think they are permitted
To make discernment on what they twisted.

We're all sinners at the end of the day,
We have no right to criticize without love and say;
"I love you, Lord, forgive the other."
When you push someone else to suffer

Fitting In

Kim Plasket

Content Warning: Religious abuse, mention of suicide.

As usual I had the same dream before going to a new church. I was back at my mom's Church. Her Pastor was telling me how everyone at the Church was going to go to hell because what they believed was wrong.

He was banging on the pulpit, his face contorted as if he were some kind of monster. "Sinners, all of them, including you, will be sent to hell for eternal damnation."

The entire Church congregation seemed to take this all in stride as if this was something they expected. When I tried to tell him that he was wrong, he lifted his hands to the sky and started to call out to the Holy Spirit to take my soul and send it to hell.

I could feel the hands of people pushing me closer to the Pastor. He was screaming how he had to lay hands on me to shove me into the depths of hell. So, there would be a chance God would save me if I asked Him with all my heart.

"I'm already saved by God," I said as I felt myself being pushed. I never let the dream stop me before so why was it making me dread this time? I took a few deep breaths and began to get dressed.

Scars shone like silver threads down my arms from failed suicide attempts. I wanted to fit in at this Church. I pushed my sleeves down and stayed at the back of the Sanctuary, hoping nobody would see me.

So far, the last Churches I had been to didn't feel right. I had no real reason for why that was. They were decent places that seemed to welcome me fine, but I couldn't feel comfortable. I was on edge the entire time I was there.

When I was growing up, the Pastor at my mother's Church would say. "Depression was Satan's way of showing you that you weren't concentrating enough on God."

I tried to tell my mom how I felt, and she told me to "Stop trying to get attention." She was the one who had to be at the front of everything that went on at the Church. No matter what was happening, my mom was there; she even taught Sunday school for many years.

My mother insisted depression was my fault. Apparently, the preacher told her, "If you paid more attention in Church, God would love you more."

I don't know about God, but I never had any close relationships with people because of my depression. I had my own apartment. I had a job where my boss was willing to understand those days that I had to call out due to my depression. I didn't know what it was until I left my house. I still knew that my trying to kill myself and still wanting to kill myself was a sin, so I never told anyone about it.

I had been looking at Churches for a while. I wasn't against churches; I just needed to find one comfortable in. Some would look at the overcast sky above this one, and feel a sense of hesitancy, but I decided to give it a chance.

I was sitting there wondering why it was still quiet when I noticed something.

A guy sat a few pews before me with a green mohawk for a hairdo. An older lady dressed like a Romani. So this place differed from other places I had visited.

I wondered what sermon the Pastor was going to preach. It seemed whenever I showed up at a new Church. The Pastor began to talk about depression being a sin as if he knew I was there. It began to make me think God would let these guys know.

I smiled when that thought crossed my mind. Since I was alone, I tried hiding the smile. It would look silly.

"She can smile," I heard a guy say.

I looked up into a pair of kind brown eyes. They didn't seem to judge me, but this guy didn't know who I was.

I thought I would be polite. "Can you leave me alone, please?"

"I could, but then again, Pastor Dave told us to greet our neighbors." He had his hand out, which I failed to see.

"Sorry, I didn't hear him." I shook his hand, hoping that would be the end.

"It's okay. Most people ignore Pastor Dave at first. It's only after the sermon that they start to listen." He said it as if there was some big secret. I had to admit I felt intrigued, plus the mirth I saw in his eyes was fascinating. "Okay, why do they listen after the sermon?"

He chuckled. "That's when he asks if we are having coffee after service."

"I'm sure." It was all alien to me, like people wanting to spend time with each other after Church.

"I'm Malachi. Yes, that is my real name." He chuckled as if someone had asked him the same question before.

"I'm Emmaline,"

"I'll call you Em," He said and turned back toward the front of the Church as the Pastor began to speak again.

The Pastor talked about how we are to love our neighbors. It didn't matter what our neighbor looked like or who our neighbor chose to be with.

"Does anyone have any questions?" He asked.

"Why do you always have a question time?" An older man asked.

"Because there is always someone who has a question," The Pastor said. He shrugged. "Even me, sometimes."

Malachi raised his hand. "What about someone who is very depressed?"

"Malachi, I told you before that God loves you no matter what. You know this. Everyone here knows what a dark place you were in." The Pastor said it with such emotion that I expected him to burst into tears.

"I hope nobody else feels this way," He took a slow, deep breath. I thought he knew I was there, and he was looking for me, ready to throw me to the wolves. He was going to tell me about my feelings of depression. My wanting to die was me allowing the Devil inside of me by not concentrating on God enough.

Just as the Pastor said that the overcast sky decided to become a full-fledged storm. It gave me even more pause to think he was talking about me. After all, I was the supreme sinner, so why else wouldn't the sky begin to rain down upon the ground?

"Pastor Dave, if someone was feeling that way. Does that mean they were going to hell?" A young teen asked. Her blonde hair lay on her shoulders as if she tried to style it but it just refused. I could see the sadness in her eyes even from where I was sitting. She was hugging herself for comfort as if she just needed something more.

"No, Molly. Are you feeling that way?" He asked as he moved closer to the girl.

"Yes, Pastor Dave." She hung her head in shame.

"Molly, my dear girl. You aren't in trouble. Why don't you and your parents stay after Church? We can all talk." he nodded at her parents, and the young girl started to cry, apologizing for being such a bother. Some older women gathered around her and held her tight as she cried.

It was a shock to me that people in a church were accepting of someone depressed.

All too soon, the service was over. The Pastor announced that there was a small luncheon and coffee afterward. As everyone got up to leave, I noticed a couple of young men holding hands as they walked out of the Sanctuary. They stopped before they entered the meeting room and shared a kiss. "Will you stop it and get in here?" someone asked, and everyone laughed, even the couple.

"You see, we accept pretty much everyone." As if I thought him up, Malachi was beside me. "This Church seems to draw in the black sheep. We play rock and roll during some of our services, frightening some people."

He paused and pointed at a man walking past with a crate of grape juice. "Our wine is grape juice because we have alcoholics who want to have Communion."

"This place was not what I thought it would be. From the outside, it looks like any other place. Ice cold brick that someone might find warmth in if lucky, but so far today." Then I thought about it. There had to be something going on since there was no way in the world this was a regular thing. They had to be putting on some act.

"Listen, I have to go. I'll be back next week." I told Malachi.

I was going to come in late to see how people were acting.

The following week, I came in a little too late. People were already milling around in the luncheon room. As I headed to join them, I glanced in the Sanctuary and stopped when I saw a man sitting towards the back in the shadows. But he wasn't far enough, so I could still see his face if I squinted.

It was... Pastor Dave. I wasn't a part of the Church, but my heart told me to contact him. I slowly walked in and put my hand on his shoulder, "Pastor Dave, are you okay?"

He was looking down at his clasped hands.

"Young Molly was found unresponsive in her bed by her parents this morning. They called me after they called the ambulance. How can I tell the Church?" He asked me as if I knew the answer.

"Will they get mad at her?" I figured they would because she said she was depressed. So, it was her fault.

"No, they are more mad at themselves." He sounded as if he wanted to cry.

"Why are they mad at themselves?" It doesn't make sense. This girl tried to kill herself, which was a sin, but her parents and Pastor Dave were sad.

"Because they think they should have known what she was thinking. If she was that depressed, she could have gone to them." He looked me in the eyes. "Why didn't she tell them?"

"She was afraid?" I said, thinking about how I always felt. "I know when I cut my wrists, my parents got furious with me and told me that I was a sinner, how I would never be right for God. Could she have felt the same way? No matter what she did, it would never be enough." I couldn't believe the words coming out of my mouth. It was as if all my doubts about the Church were pouring out.

"My girl, I don't claim to be knowledgeable about Religion. I know that God loves everyone no matter what, which is one thing I try to tell everyone here. I don't care who comes through those doors. Malachi is my nephew, and he went through some dark times. He was addicted to alcohol and drugs. He tried several times to kill himself; when he first came to the Church, it was his last chance before going to jail." He sighed.

"He spent weeks at the Church getting the drugs and alcohol out of his system. The entire congregation stood beside him; this isn't a Church, it's a family." He looked across the hall at everyone talking in the luncheon. The tears were rolling down his face.

I was a little taken aback that a man would cry in front of a woman. He wasn't ashamed to cry in front of me.

"Then don't you think they would want to know? I mean, my family sucks, but if they cared, then they would want to be there for her. I guess they would like to pray for her and her parents." Saying the word 'pray' made it hard for me because I didn't believe in the power of it.

"Malachi called you Emmaline, right?" He wiped his tears away.

"Yes, sir," His hands were clasped in front of him as if he was praying without even thinking about it and it had to be something he did out of habit.

"Emmaline, no matter where you find it, family will always be there for you. Ours happens to be in the Church. We found our family through Religion. Some churches expect you to show up dressed in pearls. We have had people come in dressed in sweats, but we don't care."

"Your Church isn't like any I've ever attended. At first, even though it made no sense, I thought it was an act." Surely it wasn't possible for people to like each other as much as everyone here seemed to enjoy one another.

"Everyone here does like each other. We have our arguments, but we still care about each other."

"Out there, religion is based on rules. It's supposed to be how everyone fears God. He will send everyone to hell if they don't do as He says," I told him, wondering if I was trying to convince myself or him.

"I don't believe that. Some things can be misunderstood about Religion. Man was the one who read the Bible, and Man was the one who decided what it meant. For us, love is what God wants. So, saying that, I guess I better tell everyone what happened. Youth Pastor Benson gave the sermon this morning while I was at home trying to figure out what to say." He sighed as if it was breaking his heart.

"Do you want me to stay here?"

"Do you mind? My wife is at the hospital with her parents. " He seemed sad, so I knew there was no way I would be able to leave. I followed him to the luncheon room, as he stood up, and took a deep breath before he stuck his head in.

"Good Morning." He cleared his throat, and I saw he was still fighting back tears. "Benson, thanks for filling in today's sermon. Molly's parents called me early this morning. They found her in her bed. They rushed her to the hospital." He paused, as people filled in their gasps and whispers. "Agnes is at the hospital with her parents, waiting for her to regain consciousness." He glanced at the Bible sitting on the pulpit.

"I had a sermon today that would blow your socks off. All I've been able to do is cry about that poor girl and her parents."

"Pastor Dave, do they think she will be okay?" Malachi asked.

"They don't know," Pastor Dave began to pace back and forth. "We can pray for her recovery." His voice sounded less forceful than I expected.

"Pastor Dave, are you okay?" Malachi asked. Pastor Dave hung his head. "No, son, as if I wasn't good enough. I'm also feeling guilty."

"Pastor Dave. Stop. You told me that to get help, I had to ask for it. This is her way of asking for it." Malachi stated as if he knew.

"Pastor, don't blame yourself. Her parents found her in time. All we can do now is join hands and pray," An older woman said as she grabbed the hand of the man next to her.

Everyone moved closer so they would be able to hold hands. It was unlike anything I'd seen. They were all crying and holding hands because they cared about one girl. Religion wasn't about hate, judging, and eternal damnation. It was quite the opposite here; this Church was all about love and giving.

After they got done praying, I was going to head out. Pastor Dave asked me if I would stay at the Church until they heard about Molly. He had both his cell phone and the phone for the Church there in the Sanctuary. I hadn't noticed it when I first approached him.

"Please, Emmaline, you are now part of our family." Pastor Dave told me. Several people agreed with him, even going as far as hugging me.

"I showed up here last week. How am I part of your family?" I had no idea how these people would think this.

"You were the one who helped me to see past my own grief. So, I was able to help the congregation and Molly's parents."

"Pastor Dave it wasn't that hard. You are a good man and while you felt the grief you knew that you had to overcome it to be able to help your family. I guess I had to stop and look around, I had to see how everyone here really seemed to enjoy being together. It made me see religion in a different manner." I had no idea if my words were making any sense at all but when he started to cry a little I knew he understood.

He thanked me again and again.

After I left the Church, I wanted to call my mom and tell her about everything, but I knew she would never understand. She was the one person in my life who would never understand anything related to anyone caring.

To her, Religion was supposed to be cold and uncaring. Anyone different. They had to be forced into some shell until they matched everyone else.

All voices had to match in unison; if someone couldn't sing, it was suggested they mouth the words. If they didn't know the prayers by heart, they got extra classes to learn them. This was something the Church said was mandatory. I had gone through plenty of those different classes growing up.

I sat in the living room battling the urge to call my mom. I knew it would be a battle of frustration, but I felt as if I were being led to call her so finally with my hands shaking, I dialed her number. Part of me prayed she was at some Church function and wouldn't be home, but she answered, and I could feel the poor phone in my hand freezing up as she spoke.

"Emmaline, have you finally given up your foolish notion that you can live without me?" Her first words to me in years. "The Church is ready to forgive you. All you need to do is admit you were wrong" She sounded so sure of herself.

"Mother, I only called to see how you were doing. I'm not calling to fight religion with you simply to check in on you" I was firm with my words.

"You have to see how wrong you are with this path, daughter." Her words got louder like she was the pastor of her Church, but this time was different.

"Mother, I'm not trying to be disrespectful of your beliefs, but they just aren't mine. While you might not accept it, I have found a Church that accepts me." I closed my eyes waiting for her to dump her usual vitriol on me.

"Emmaline, you won't be saved properly unless it is by my Church." She screamed at me but I wasn't listening.

"Mother, one more thing before we end this phone call and we are ending it. I forgive you for all the years of abuse. You call it parenting but I know it was abuse." I hung up before she could say anything else.

After the phone call, I was exhausted, so I laid down on the couch. My phone rang a few minutes later, startling me so much that I fell off the couch.

"She woke up about 10 minutes ago. The doctors say she will be fine." An unknown male voice said to me.

"Who's this?" I had a feeling it was Malachi.

"It's Malachi. You gave Pastor Dave your number so he could tell you when she woke up. He asked me to call you. I'm sorry I didn't tell you who I was immediately." He sounded sad.

"It's okay. Listen, would you like to meet for coffee one day? I'd like to get to know you more. I know this is a bad time with Molly waking up, but this feels as if this is right." I felt like I was being forward, but something about him drew me to him. I waited for him to tell me that I was insane and that there was no way he would want to be seen with me.

I knew from experience most guys. Even most people hated to be around depressed people because they didn't know what to do or say to make it better.

"I would like that. Pastor Dave told me you were exceptional." He sounded sincere, and I believed him.

I guess I had to go through the hell of my mom's Church before I found a church that could feel as if I belonged.

How Another Mourning
Becomes Electra

Maribeth Parot-Juraska

Let us go then, you and I,

just let us go,

before this evening spreads out its darkest sky,
like a habit wrapping around a nun.
Refusing to slice even a section of sun,
setting again as the whole damn pie.

While I, while we, implore a red, red sea—

All of us watching like starfish in our symmetry, stuck to rocks, pushed out by a tidal spree. Holding breath on shorelines, occasional samaritans flinging us too late in shallow waves. During the months, weeks, days, hours, before

their ruling. Nine people speaking for 330 million. Acting as if women are manufacturer warranty machines, waiting for others to reconfigure our fastenings with only little round washers, gaskets. Removing any rivets, brads, screws, bolts...

> *still rescuing bones of ancient sailors and destiny.*
> *Their fiery fists, now just fragments of fingers and knuckles*
> *across an aphotic floor with barges, half buckled.*
> *Boats busted and rusted. Slave ships with their chattel*
> *that rattled and battled, stunk and then sunk. All this debris;*
> *like thousands and thousands of petrified piano keys—*

Still lurking somewhere inside my stream of consciousness: Sepia photos, voices, legal filings; audio clips, testimonies, continuances; gavels, rakes, hallucinations, nightmares. Still using my comfort zones—prolonged isolation, spontaneous disassociation, momentary verse—to shield me. While waiting outside my state's courthouse with countless others, with dim hope, for the announcement of this landmark ruling;

> *Let us row. Let us row*
> *after all this wading, our labor,*
> *any sudden submersion of our*

hourglass—its every minute carrying decisions or revisions that a single sand grain can reverse—

All of this, leading to the same persistent, overwhelming question:

All of these human voices suddenly waking upon the outcome; some, their victory cry resounding like chainsaws gutting giant sequoias, redwood forests. Their sly smirks, wide grins, applause—all raw reminders of how any promise, any of our hopes here; now, only a flicker—a lit match tossed into viscous, murky liquor. Thousands upon thousands

of other women clustered, protesting: *Our Decision, Not Your Decision! Regulate Weapons, Not Women's Bodies! I Am Not a Womb!* Posters upon posters: Photos of male Supreme Court justices, photoshopped with faces of random women. Drawings of AR-15s shaped like female stick figures. Fallopian tubes springing from a uterus, shaped as antennas atop an old tv set, men in recliners holding remote controls. So many women singing or chanting, *Roe, Roe, Roe your vote,* hoisting posters of rowboats, oars—these, especially, triggering me most...

How dare they—again—
to disturb this universe?

Cameras outside courthouses suddenly zooming away, their built-in studio monitors now showing some U-shaped table, flanked by a group of news anchors, each talking one over the other. Some sweaty, corpulent guest alongside them, booming loudly over any opponents to today's landmark ruling. His voice beefy, bulging like his belly: While dismantling women into parts, like working radiators that still keep everything warm, and alive, but detract from a church's altar space. Or leak occasional drops of rusty red, staining their landlord's white oak floor—

(Their arousal of some impulse,
as a needle sliding from a pincushion.
Their breath, sometimes, of repulse,
as a stenchy belch waxed around their tongues—)

Obscure floor of crimson sea,
suddenly flipping itself on top of all of us,
on top of me; our boats overturning,
any oars captured by nightfall.

A single beak descending, without the eagle, without a seagull,

penetrating everyone deeply, completely—guts, mouth, bone
and all.

A flaccid crystal ball soon discharging its volumes into us, into
me,

of old, pulpous, grainy red sea.

Now on camera monitors: A scarlet red chyron, white capital letters, scrolling beneath images of the Supreme Court, announcing more breaking news. Of us, our protests, nationwide. The older studio guest, now replaced by different, deeper voices, delivering verbose accounting of how each Justice voted. Thousands upon thousands of even more protesters, supporting or opposing this ruling, shown marching, howling at our opponents, bystanders. Howling on sidewalks, in streets, more rudimentarily crafted picket signs affixed to hockey sticks, kayak paddles, rowboat oars. All beneath a looming fog; its viscous vapor spreading below night's sky, as white snakeroot secreting its milk. Seemingly innocuous—just some patches, just some white flowers—while edging closer. Closer. Closer still. Someone. Then someone else. Slipping...soon vanishing beneath their sounds: Cacophonous cries, thumping of running boots, bare feet; shrieks of something like tempered glass breaking, upon some overpowering thrust or fall. Until...

Some moment of motionlessness, posing itself as finished, at peace,

    as a bird after flying into the window.

    Until more relentless waves rise, each like giant wings, cresting, before their crash. Submerging everyone, before penetrating some of us once, or more than once, or even again, again, again, like me: Here. Here. And...

    There.

    Severing us. Dividing us all.

Until we stiffen, lose any remaining strength, begin this fall.
As we continue to spread, as we continue to sprawl.
Plunging together in our fragments—

like debris beneath a demolition ball:

Until,
I am a tooth, throbbing inside a severed, sinking skull.
I am a tooth, throbbing inside a severed, sinking skull.

———

At least a man was right about this: How human voices wake us. Voices of men with white hair holding white waves as those on their shining seas. Miles away, on their farms with red barns, red doors with white shackles, casting shadows of flags with their red stripes dividing white. Proclamation of their freedoms aligned in perfectly straight rows of white stars, popping out from contrasting blue, like asterisks.

Human voices that wake us, even when I no longer see their fruited fields, amber waves of crops and grain. When I am a stranger for hire, following gravel trails; a white man helping me over barbed wires. Some high white fencing, flocked by clusters upon clusters of white snakeroot, their toxic blooms posing as daisies. *Here, we go now...*

Just a little detour. Won't take long.

Human voices that wake us, racked with righteousness, as bread pudding packed inside a throat: *Fields as these—from sea to shining sea!* Schooling me on how faith explains this all—these plains carved by floods and Noah's boat heaving with spared life. How the Good Lord put trust in men, who worship God, to seed this blessed earth again. Conflating belief with virtue, privilege: *All this, made by me, 'cept on Sundays—is that today? Shame on me...This day, Sunday, for bending knees. Thanking Him for these bootstraps.* Chuckling: *Oh, pardon my manure.* Looking peculiarly at me, my expression: *When you live out here, little lady, in God's country, it coats your boots.*

Human voices tugging an arm, taking us near rows of prickly green corn stalks. *Life's greatest truths,* he says, placing one leg next to a stalk. *Just like that, every single one. Designed by God, my most favorite guy. As you will see—same as Him, same as me. Beneath His sacred sun, this bless-ed sky:*□
   Knee high by the Fourth of July.

Those human voices that wake us—and keep us awake: Measuring life by placing a body part next to produce, stalks of dent corn; not too long before boiling, mashing, their entire harvest into bourbon.

In the hospital room,
the women come and go,
asking for Michael. Where did he go?

And even now, I still remember that morning in Texas, all its shards of stained church glass fracturing my howling body. Delivering a baby, bearing brown: Into a fraction of world. Earth's ivory-white plates rattling beneath my latte hips. Some repressing voice from the adoption agency, saying: *Remember, after, how you'll need to labor more. The placenta. The cord*

to your body. Someone, snatch the scissors. While I wait to hear or see something, anything, of her: Hazel eyes, vibrant as Malachite butterflies, cocoa hair coiled like bean spirals. Veins, the color of blue gentian on tall mountains; strength in her hands of ivory piano keys, to mold herself and any dreams. If she is free of Tulia birthmarks. Not how they see brush wriggling in some forest, that they have their buckshot. As she is sliding out from me, a Tahitian Pearl, separating from a bulging brooch. Or

what they see: How I brace myself, a rodeo horse, bucking off its rider.

———

This is not what I am here to do at all.
This is not it at all!

———

Months before, their pictures. Squirting cold gel all over my belly. Muttering, like some gas pump clerk: *Let's see what you have to pay for there. Premium octane, gum, or girl. Speaking of...oh.... Oh....*Before teams of curious doctors overfill this small room, my panties revealing wet patches of sweat, the wand's jelly. Someone's index finger on the monitor, tracing space around a shadow, quietly mumbling. Her voice anxious, like a bank teller explaining to an armed robber: *Oh, I see...but...I can't even...Oh, unless if... Unless...no, wait...Ummmm...Ohhhhh....*

Under their new oath; they tell me, using big words I barely understand. Until this: How I must bear this state's new licit laws. *No choice now, but to take this to term.* Endure its labor, tidal forces—churning, charging, cresting—upon the waves of whitewater eventually breaking.

Alone.

———

As I become a bloated urchin rising in an uncompromising sea, crawling without knees in every uncontrollable wave. An IV bag, with its drug: *Something stronger, to speed the dilating.* Bringing her with me, to the nakedness swaying atop this ocean. Foreboding: How a laboring uterus is a splitting seashell in roiling sea, nearing shore, impinging upon uneven stretches of unequal land. Forewarning: *How, here is the hardest part—full dilation before crowning—The*

Undertow. Its unexpected pivots resembling inhalation under water, each challenging survival—like a tooth, still throbbing inside a severed, sinking skull. Pausing before the next wave—next, next—submerging, surfacing. While waiting. For when our separation transects these final gasps. (*Oh, Mr., please. Please...!*) This feeling within each contraction, every wave, of drowning,

like crawling across short wire space, bordered by two sharp barbs. Each wave waiting, furtively floating behind dark dawn. Its song of mourning doves; their plangent notes like flutes, lodged inside their throats. *Who WHO whoOOOooo whOOOooo whOOOooo.* How their woeful warbling now becomes

Me. As *Mourning Becomes Electra.*

No, not a character from *their Guy* or Bible; but instead, from yet another book they call to ban, with the same stories: Malignant lust, hypocrisy, murder, revenge; adultery, illegitimacy, rape, incest. The same ultimate aftermath for its victims: Subsequent loss, sorrow, despondency, anguish. A gaping void or tunnel, now called *the rabbit hole*, for relentless human suffering, for escaping human judgment. For overwhelming grief that hibernates inside us,

as the wavy quiver of cymbals after they strike, after any of their sound.

How grief—*Electra's*, mine—becomes the electricity for unyielding mourning. Penetrating like a current inside any connecting cables of contempt, shame, disgrace; remorse, regrets, violations—illuminating only more, the unexpected, unplanned, unwanted.

(Oh, but when that mother in *Electra* confesses: *I told myself it wasn't human not to love my own child.*)

Its aftermath, so oddly called *mourning*, wiring itself to sunless, dark space, rooting itself to humans, powerless, as insidiously as poison does to blooming ivy—

as insidiously as humans judge other humans.

Little or nothing about any Saturday night that He allegedly created. Rather, the vineyard escargot or canned snails it brings:

The A-list gallery, hosting black-tie-only guests all holding hand blown crystal glasses; meanwhile, the crude oil paintings hanging from spare nails and wire, tilting crooked on the wall.

Little or nothing about any ordinary dawn that He allegedly created. Instead, their conclusion of an overwhelming, wondrous joy to celebrate, to revere; that is, the most inherent part of being a woman:

For who becomes, in morning, a mother.

And, conversely, their judgment of any female's egregious grief, dismissively discarded as disdainfully disgusting; incomprehensibly inhumane:

For who becomes, in mourning, a mother.

(Oh, but when her daughter retorts: *I've always guessed that, ever since I was little, Mother.*)

How even more will need to speculate; how even fewer will understand; especially after others demand that books like *Mourning Becomes Electra* be outlawed, banned:

Now! Some deeper voice, speaking: *Push. Again. Again! With-*

out all the noise! One softer voice, truncating these commands. The deeper voice retorting, more harshly:

Now put your face in this towel. Do your moaning in that.

Others staying silent, while looking askance. *Hey! Hey! She,*

She made her choice! Just as a judge said, years ago! As I bite futilely into white cotton, chocolate-colored blood now spewing, heaving. *As soon as she becomes this way. A woman in this condition makes her choice. While We,*

WE think! And pray! For how this still happens! While singing of our sprawling purple mountains. In majesty!

Yet, still: Nothing about fathers who slip away, like their own human fluid, from their own transgressions or grave mistakes. Nor anything about how that pasty powder inside a flower might come from a wasp or stinging bee. How, in judgment,

one must live now, as this. While they wield their biblical scissors, and suddenly,

like fishhooks plucked from bloody cheeks; we sever.

———

While transitioning, what She has time to see:

Fog spiraling like curls of vinegar hair beneath ancient moun-
tains,□

beneath a mysterious Christ.
Groves of White Birch, forever forgiving its peeling bark for
warping.
A raw wound, searching for gauze.
Fear of holy water, trapped within an altar.
Bootprints melting away with rain outside some barn.
Fields ravaged by fierce crosswinds, stripping hope from buds,
*   green-tipped leaves.*
Nostrils of livestock exhaling exhaustion, steam, awaiting an-
other
*   grueling harvest.*
Flocks of honking white geese, flapping above a tall church
steeple.
A bird flying straight into the stained glass window.

My daughter, now cut away from every pulse of me. To them, our disconnect like one last drag of cigarette exhaled from swollen lips. As she comes out only.

Somewhat. Brown. (Somewhat! Brown!) Like the shade of standing water in a saucer, stained by tea leaves. And I breathe and breathe and breathe. Hoping with two upright knees. For these others. Who'll protect her now, in this fracture of world. Inside her tiny saucer. Soon leaving this place as rainwater on sills,

her memory of this all set to spill. While the placenta slides out from me as rusty egg yolk. Into the stainless steel bowl it goes. This afterbirth, its shades of resurrection lily pink, purple—losing all tint of my blood, as fiery lava turning to basalt, cooling into lumpy grey.

Nearby, their nostrils like impatient horses.

———————

(Mr...Mr...Please! Please!
This is not it at all!
This is not what I came here for, at all!)

Pushing my body harshly, again, again, into fiery layers of emerging, burning morning. Covering my face with rags soaked in ether. Eventually dragging me into darkness, like a bag of useless, extinguished stars.

Me. Holding the bloody, soiled sac.

Not he.

I scream just once into this void, so their version of God can know.

———————

How it finishes like this.

Some lordly man out there, one ring inside our nation's mighty oak. While I lie here, the poisoned ivy.

Sound of his heavy shoes kicking shut a red barn door; slices of dawn clinging to a rag he holds, soaked with ethers. Horses in stalls, their manure still exhaling its steam. *Who WHO whOOOooo whOOOooo whOOOooo:* The warning warble of mourning doves, like far away flutes—as something else flute-shaped rams deep, deeper—but only first—inside my throat. While he pulls my hair, kicks me so I crouch, kneel. Grips my skull, wrenches my neck; groans, chuckles:
  Knee high by the Fourth of July.

Those human voices that wake us—and keep us awake:

  Now put your fat face on the floor. Do your moaning in the hay.

His hips like a shovel tip: The blade pulling away darker layers of fertile soil, sacred earth. Digging, digging, digging for his earthquake. Deeply—deeper. Deeper. (*Pretty deep glass in this protester. Pretty deep. In her face. Not trampled, though, like that gal over there. Oh, geez. Hey. Hey, is that a...glass shard...in her eye? Hey, I need someone STAT! Over here! STAT!...Without all the noise! Hey! Face. Fat. Face. Towel! Do your moaning in...Purple mountains! Majesty! Fat face. Floor. Moaning. Hay! Hay! Hay!*) Digging more, more, for his earthquake. More and more....Deeper. Deeper still. Until...he's

right inside the hole. First, as white snakeroot leaking its milk. Before plunging. Plunging—plunging. His fingers clawing into my skin as metal tines on a rake. Again and again. Plunging. Plunging. His putrid purpleness. Profusely

exploding. Puss. Puss, puss—more puss. Imploding. Draining. Like a punctured pustule; a potbelly boil or carbuncle—

Soon followed by some moment of motionlessness, posing him as finished, at peace, as a bird after flying into the window. Before even more relentless waves inside him rise, each like giant flaps of wings, rising, cresting, before their crash, submerging anything I have left, submerging me, before penetrating: Here. Here. And...

There.
Until I stiffen, lose any remaining strength, begin this fall—

like debris beneath a demolition ball.

And what else, after that malignant Texas night; so much like my labor now, this morning:

A tablespoon of vomit hanging from my hair, like a cocklebur from damp forest. My hips drying like wet concrete. How I lie motionless, as if hanging from some tree.

Their checking a wristwatch, barking for coffee, scripting her vitals: *Not so black.* Discussing their ideas for completing some new form, documenting the date, time, of her entry into their version of life, of their world.

I don't dare to interrupt; though, if I did, what I'd say:

So patently, obviously not before today's morning or mourning. But definitely in enough time to reject any narrow notions of God's country, His purple mountains in majesty. And surely before her ever being inside a sanctuary with a priest, feeling their thick, leathery Bibles. Or perhaps upon her discovery of banned books, binding some of life's deepest truths. And long—long—after I awoke again, in mourning, far beyond dawn, that barn. After nearly drowning me. And never—(never!)—reaching that wire space, its two barbs, alongside me, for anyone here—or anyone, anywhere—to see.

No. No matter now. Not a single word that I could say. Because to them, I am that mother in *Electra: Just hush and go away.*

For only one of you must board the windows. Press into books all the flowers. Find a mourning dress. Learn to live by punishing herself. Forget the other.

And just as this, when all they do is done, without any further recognition, other voice or second thought; with her, any trace of me, already gone. They all rise. Turn.

And they leave.

———

While in the little chapel,
even more women come and go,
asking for Michael. Where in the hell did he go?

———

While far away, human voices wake me, singing in their eaves of how they see her now: *Riding seaward on some waves, combing the white hair of waves, when wind blows the water both white and black.* She lingers only somewhere they believe; and in my mindspace, I futilely try to conceal. Of how, why, she arrived so still—*"born sleeping,"*—

Her skin still translucent, stretching like melted glass, her tiny bones spilled inside a red-brown, rigor mortis vase. Her body, shaped like a balloon animal, as those the pediatric hospital clown had been creating down the hall: Kinks forming small bumps of arms and legs, her hands and feet still curled tightly, fingers and toes shaped like baby shrimps. A doctor somewhere in the building, allowed only to pen this little lamb; only for it to slide right down the steel chute.

Nothing for the agency which had been arranging: *Something that can happen. Uh, medical term. It's called....*their voices anxious, like a bank teller apologizing for some grave error to a customer. Nor anything for the hopeful parents—*You mean, some condition the birth mother has? Maybe?*—only wanting what they had been promised. Nothing, either, of my own promise—of what I might have become—before this place, that man: *The State of Texas vs Michael J. Alfred Prufrock.* Before he took me inside that barn. In God's country, his amber fields of dent corn; all of it thrashed after harvest. Then mashed, boiled, evaporated into bourbon, just as his sins.

While I am yet this tooth, still throbbing, inside a severed, sinking skull.

Til human voices wake us.

Of how their God, *He will provide.* Their Bible—where he

places his right hand to take an oath—with these stories of oars, here. For all my years upon years remaining, to sustain me. For me, for the requisite rowing.

Of all I am now, and ever will be—of all they only still see:

How, after all of him is done, I just let him push myself around, like a human mop, back and forth, across wet manure; back and forth, across that filthy ground. How I crawl away like a coach-whip snake, on my budding belly, never seeking holy ground. And how I so freely fall asleep, after saying I am drowned.

Swamp Religion

S.E. Reed

Content Warning: Child abuse.

Deep in the sultry Everglades, past the sawmill on Highway 29, there is a one-lane dirt road hidden behind a grove of blood orange trees. Every Saturday night it's crammed full of earnest folks lookin' for salvation.

You ain't nobody in the swamps if you ain't listening to Jessamine Lafleur and her midnight sermon. It's late, but I go when I can after Daddy passes out on the porch. I sneak the keys from his pocket.

A few years ago, after Jessamine's mama discovered she had the gift, her daddy and brothers built a giant canvas tent, with hand-hewn poles from ancient Cyprus dredged from the swamp. The tent fits perfectly in the clearing, swallowed up on either side by ratty palms and the blades of saw palmettos lookin' for tender meaty leg flesh to latch on to.

Fat armored cicadas climb outta the dirt hissing and writhing just to hear sweet Jessamine preach. Even the baby gators in the shallow murky water snap and growl along with the vibrations of stomping feet during her Evangelical prayers.

I hear her before I reach the entrance.

"You are here because you want to feel somethin' my friends!" Jessamine shouts from under the dome of the swamp tent. "I'm tellin' you, good Christian folks, that *HE* hears you!"

I lift back the flap and watch as Jessamine puts her hand to her ear and leans her head so the Lord can whisper those divine words into her mind. "He's tellin' me how much he hears you. When you're on your knees, in the light of the rising sun– he listens to your prayers!"

"AMEN!"

"Hallelujah!"

Jessamine's got the most precious face and red-painted lips. She stands proudly at the helm of her flock in a white gown. I heard her Mama washes her hair with willowroot in an old bucket behind the tent every Saturday afternoon. Then one of her sisters scrubs her feet with dried moss and honeysuckle. Sometimes when I'm lying awake in bed late at night, I imagine I'm there, watching Jessamine bathe for the sermon.

She's a swamp beauty if I ever saw one; tanned from sun-soaked days catching bullfrogs and butterflies—because during the week, she's just a fifteen-year-old girl playing in the Everglades.

"I know *HE* will heal you! Pray, my brothers and sisters," she bellows.

I find a place to stand in the back of the crowd. I'm tall for my age and can see over all the folks praying. Jessamine is mesmerizing. I can't take my eyes away. I am a moth to her flame.

"Who here needs help?" Jessamine asks. Hands shoot up and people shout names of loved ones in need of redemption.

"Take away my pain!" Cripple old Grann Thora cries out.

"God help me!" Mr. Lenny wails, with his one stumpy leg.

"Lord let me help these good folks!" Jessamine walks in a big circle and waves her hands up and down. Just her presence soothes the parishioners. Then she wanders down the center aisle, coming my way. Sweat beads across my forehead as she approaches.

"Nice to see you, Billy," she whispers. She smells like sweet ginger and licorice root. My cheeks flush. I nod and mumble something between a 'thanks' and 'you too'.

I would do anything for her.

"Let me hear you pray!" She cries out as she runs and twirls her way back to the front of the tent, where she raises her hands up to the sky.

We lift our dirty hands and lower our heads. I wiggle my fingers, just like Jessamine does, tryin' to grasp onto the magic of her religion. Then she leads everyone in the *Lord's Prayer*. It's a mighty powerful sound, a hundred of us swamp folk, all at once reciting the word of God. Then the band plays a song, led by her Mama and little sisters.

Jessamine sings at the top of her lungs about the forgiveness *He* alone gives in judgment for our sins. Her voice is a sound more pure than any angel sent from above.

"SING WITH ME!" She twirls and the white gossamer of her gown floats around her. She looks like a water lily at six in the morning when I go fishing.

The wicker basket gets passed around and we gladly put in any money we have left over from a week of working road crews on Alligator Alley or pulling up trees from the bottom of the murky swamp for the sawmill or canning in the factory outside of Everglades City.

Every dime we put in that basket means Jessamine Lafleur has another week of support. Another week to take our prayers to *Him on High*. And then, when I think the sermon is over and I turn to leave, Jessamine does something she ain't never done before. She calls her Daddy to join her on the stage.

"Daddy, you said you have something important you want to tell these good Christian folks before they leave," Jessamine waves for her old man to join her.

A hush falls over the crowd.

"Yes, yes, I have something I wanna preach tonight," he stands next to her. I'm not sure but I think I see Jessamine flinch when he puts his arm around her shoulder and squeezes.

But I must be mistaken because there ain't no way her daddy would hurt her or make her uncomfortable. Just look at what he's built for her out here in the swamp. Everything he's given up to make sure she can preach on Saturday nights.

He lifts up the edge of his shirt and pulls out a book he got stuffed into his waistband. He holds it high up in the air and the book shakes from the tremor in his hand. Everyone is mumbling, asking their neighbor, "What is it?"

It's a book; that much I can see with my own two eyes.

And the only book allowed in this tent is God's Book.

So, it must be a bible.

But the look on Jessamine's face is fear.

"SMUT!" He screams and waves the book. "DIRTY, FILTHY, TRASH!"

Grann Thora is in the front row, and she can see the book Mr. Lafleur is holding up. She screams, fainting dramatically.

"Whoever did this, whoever is peddling this SHIT around town, is gonna burn in hell!" He yells.

The crowd of reverent parishioners goes into a wild panic. I'm frightened, as all my friends and kin folk from the swamp erupt in chaos. They push and shove, shouting accusations, knocking over chairs, racing for the flap on the canvas tent.

That's when I see Jessamine struggling in her Daddy's strong grip near the back of the tent. I race around the edge of the crowd to get a closer look, bending down low real careful.

"You think I like doing that?"

I can see the spit flying from his mouth as he hisses at her in a blind rage. He's got a handful of her beautiful hair twisted up in his fist.

"No Daddy. Ouch, you're hurting me," Jessamine yelps and tries to get out of his grasp, but it only makes him pull tighter.

"What if someone here caught you reading that book? Ain't nobody comin' to listen to a trollop preach. That book is a gateway to hell."

"No Daddy, it ain't. It's just a beautiful book about people and I like it," Jessamine starts crying, cause after all, she's just a regular fifteen-year-old girl. And nobody likes it when their Daddy pulls their hair and yells at them.

Then without warning, he pops her in the mouth with the back of his hand.

Jessamine kicks him in the shin, and he looks like he might kill her.

"The Devil's in this tent!" Someone shouts.

Mrs. Lafleur hollers "The sermon is over!", trying to direct everyone outta the tent, away from Jessamine and her Daddy's fight. Her siblings too.

"Go on get! Go home!" Jessamine's brother barks.

I'm staying crouched low, keeping my eye on Jessamine, and that's when I spot the evil book in question. It's got a blue cover with a pair of golden eyes, the title says *The Great Gatsby*. It's on the ground, half covered in dirt. I sneak forward and scoop it up and tuck it in the back of my pants and pull my shirt over to hide it.

Whatever *The Great Gatsby* is can't be all that bad if Jessamine says she likes it.

"Billy, get the hell out of here, go home," my cousin John yells as he leaves. Where the devil did he spring from? Car doors slam and engines roar to life out in the humid, mosquito-filled night.

I don't want to be the last one here, plus I gotta get the truck home before my daddy notices its gone.

I look over my shoulder as I duck my head to leave.

Jessamine is gone.

My heart pounds. Did she get away from her Daddy? Why would he get so mad over a book anyhow? Jessamine preaches the word of the Lord and knows how to hear *his-voice-on-high*. Ain't never been a preacher in the swamps that got all the folks in town to come every week, like Jessamine.

And she's just a girl. The heat rises in my cheeks.

Just a pretty, sweet, smells like licorice, frog-catching, butterfly-taming, girl.

I gotta do something to save her. She's done so much good for all these folks, to give them peace and bring them to the light of the Lord.

Who cares what's in a stupid book anyhow? It don't mean Jessamine is the devil or that she's gonna do something wrong after reading a book, does it?

I run around the side of the tent, squeezing myself between the ratty palms hoping to find Jessamine out back. I'm prayin like I never prayed before that she's alright and all this is gonna blow over like a tropical storm on a hot summer afternoon.

That's when I hear—

"Daddy no!"

Jessamine's daddy's hitting her with the blunt end of a saw palmetto frond. The razor-sharp barbs on the end of it latch on to her flesh and rip the skin clean open. Her white gown turns blood red under the light of the full moon.

"You filthy little whore. You've ruined everything!" He brings the end of the frond down on her again.

Sobbing, Jessamine crumples to the ground and curls into a ball to protect herself from the abuse.

"Leave her alone!" The words escape my lips before I know I'm sayin them—like someone is speaking for me. "She ain't done nothin' wrong." I race over and pull the book from the back of my pants and wave it around like a white truce flag. "This is *my* book. Not hers, she was just protecting me like the good Christian girl she is."

"So, it was you? HA! I knew the devil scum who brought that filth into our town would reveal himself." Mr. Lafleur turned to face me. His eyes blazed with a fire I never seen in no man's eyes before. My knees tremble, my mouth dries up. Suddenly the words I thought were coming from the good Lord are gone.

"No, Billy, don't do this!" Jessamine uncurls herself and stands. "It wasn't him Daddy, he's just being nice. I bought it from some lady at the gas station. A city woman traveling through town selling books."

But her Daddy doesn't care.

He's ready to beat me with the barbed saw palmetto frond; a beating I'm willing to take if it means saving sweet Jessamine from any more lashings. But he drops it and reaches for something in his pocket. It makes a click.

I know that sound well, bein the son of a swamp fisherman.

A switchblade.

My daddy uses his to skin the muddy green flesh off catfish. He says the sooner the skin comes off, the better the meat tastes.

Catfish. Swampy, muddy, bottom fish. A funny thing to think about when a knife enters your gut. A night like tonight is a good night for catfishing. I suppose I should go home and get the fishing gear while daddy is sleeping and set up by the edge of the swamp, try and catch a few. My head feels light.

Jessamine's screams flood my ears, but my mind is pretty hazy, and I don't know if her Daddy is beating her again. I just keep thinking about my own daddy and the smell of freshly caught catfish, rolled in cracker crumbs and frying in the heavy, black, cast iron skillet.

The Great Gatsby. What sort of book it is?

That'd be a good name for a catfish– Gatsby. I must've pissed my pants because something hot and warm is running down my pant legs, and I can't hold myself up and fall to my knees. That's when I guess I know it. Mr. Lafleur really did shove his knife in my belly cause he thought I gave Jessamine some book. Some words on a page. Some words that don't mean nothing except what it is you wanna believe 'em to be. Kinda like the *good book*. I see it now, clear like that blood-red gown. Like that blade in moonlight.

It's only good cause someone says so.

And I don't know if *God Almighty* is watching me no more, but the moonlight sure does look pretty through the palm trees. I close my eyes and suck in the smell of citrus in the humid night breeze. The splashing of baby gators on the edge of the swamp makes me smile.

There really is no place like the Everglades on Saturday night.

THE LIBRARIANS

ERIC DIEKHANS

A NOVEL EXCERPT

Serah reached the second floor ofthe abandoned home and found a short, narrow hallway with two open doors. She leaned on the floor with one foot, ready to leap back if it gave, but it seemed sound. Leaving faint footprints in the thin layer of dust, she padded softly down the hall and entered the closest room. Cobwebs nestled in ceiling corners. The scraggly fingers of a tree branch crept through a shattered windowpane, pointing towards a rusted bed frame as if reaching for the room's former occupant. Otherwise, the room was bare.

She moved to the second room. Traces of pink and blue flow-ered wallpaper clung to plaster. A child's dresser stood against one wall, the two bottom drawers pulled halfway open. Her excitement grew as she took tentative steps across the floor, but her shoulders slumped when she reached the dresser. The drawers contained only straw and feathers from a bird that had nested there.

A jagged fissure ran across one drawer's bottom. A hint of bright green and yellow in the crack caught Serah's eye. She tugged on the handle, but the water-warped drawer was stuck.

Hinges squeaked downstairs. Serah squeezed her eyes shut and prayed it was the wind.

The floorboards downstairs groaned under steady footfalls. She stood motionless. Surely whatever was inside the house could hear her heart pounding.

"Serah, where are you?"

Imnah. A warm wave of gratitude washed over her. Papa always said her brother could find a weasel in a briar patch on a stormy night.

"I'm up here."

"Don't move," Imnah said. "I'll come up and get you."

"Be careful of the fourth step," Serah called.

"I see it."

The stairs creaked and a moment later, Imnah's large frame filled the doorway. Sweat dripped down his dirt-caked face but his eyes shone with relief. "Mama's gonna have a fit when she sees you."

"Come look at this." She turned and peered over the drawer's rim. "What do you suppose it is?" The hidden object's vibrant colors stood in sharp contrast to the barren room.

Imnah looked over her shoulder and stroked his chin. "Papa once told me a retired Gleaner moved out here with his young daughter. He returned from a gleaning acting strange and didn't want to be around other people anymore. But he died long before we was born."

"What about the girl?" Serah asked.

Imnah shrugged. "I don't know."

He grabbed the handles with big, rough hands and yanked hard. The whole dresser moved. He propped a heavy work boot against the bottom and pulled again. The drawer popped free with a screech of wood on wood.

Imnah flipped it over and set it on top of the chest. He carefully peeled the thin, rectangular object from the wood and brushed the dust away. Nothing in Serah's imagination could have prepared her for the strange, wondrous treasure he placed in her shaking hands.

A drawing on the front featured a window with a red and green striped curtain pulled back to reveal a full moon and stars shining outside. A fireplace blazed bright next to a window. A framed picture of a cow jumping over a second crescent moon hung above the mantel. She carefully turned through the sheets of paper that were like the ones in the Preacher's Bible. But these pages were a delight of color, nothing like the thick, leather-bound volume the Preacher kept locked in a cabinet.

This must be a book. She had never imagined another one existed in the world, outside of the Preacher's lectern. "Why do you suppose the girl hid this?" she whispered.

Imnah's eyes circled the room until his gaze fell on her again. "Maybe she was saving it for someone like you."

Serah visited her new treasure under the porch whenever she could sneak away from chores or farm work. Her brother gave her a small lantern and a scrap of canvas to sit on, and she found an old blanket in the closet to wrap around her shoulders. Imnah tacked up swaths of canvas to create a hidden room next to their house's stone foundation. He attached another piece to the floorboards above her to make sure no light leaked out.

In Sunday school, Serah learned about the one Good Book written in God's language that the Preacher read and translated for the congregation. She was taught that no other book existed. Now she knew that was a lie. If anyone found hers, they'd likely burn it and put her in the pillory.

Serah leaned against the cold, rough stones and admired the drawings under the dim glow of the lantern as she tried to decipher the story. She imagined every possible scenario for the little bunny, its serene mother (Or was it the grandmother?), the kittens, and the delightful little mouse. But she could never come up with a riveting tale like the ones her aunt told about ogres and witches. The two rabbits never left the cozy bedroom. No threat appeared. Their world appeared placid and comforting.

Sometimes Serah imagined she lived in her own snug home, where there were no dirty dishes, no washboard to rub her hands raw, no farm work, and no annoying boys like Reuben. Immersed in her make-believe world, she forgot the deep longing to escape the monotony of life that clung to her like dust from the fields.

The mysterious black symbols that accompanied the pictures appeared on most but not all of the pages. She examined every black line and tried to coax meaning from them until her eyes ached. The symbols were clustered together, sometimes in twos or threes, sometimes in longer strings. Some clusters repeated themselves. These must be important, and she drew them in the dirt using a stick.

THE

AN

THAT

FOR

She counted how many times each appeared and noticed where they were placed. Other strange, tiny marks also repeated:

.

,

The first mark reminded her of a stone in the sand, the second looked like a tadpole. What did the symbols mean? No matter how often she drew them and how hard she squinted, they refused to speak.

The following Sunday, Serah ran to catch up to her family as they mounted the steps of the big stone church. Reuben huddled with his friends Nebdiah and Pharez on the top step. When Serah reached them, Reuben's lips turned up in a salacious smirk. "Hear about Eve?"

Serah's insides twisted. She had forgotten all about Eve and her friend after she found her book.

"No," she snapped, stepping past the boys.

"She and Matthew ran away," Pharez said.

The knot in Serah's stomach grew tighter. They had escaped over the Wall. She should have told Imnah.

"He was already betrothed to Martha Ketchum," Nebdiah said.

"A man should have more sense," Reuben said. "If the bears or Heathens don't get 'em, the Gleaners will catch 'em quick."

Serah had never seen a bear. She imagined sharp teeth tearing into Reuben's smug face. "If you saw a bear, you'd run crying to your pa," she said.

The boys' laughter burned in Serah's ears as she entered the chilly, cavernous church. She made her way through the crowd to the pew where her family always sat. Everyone around them seemed to be talking about the escape.

"Are there really bears in the woods?" she whispered to Imnah as she sat down beside him.

He squeezed her hand. "Don't worry, Eve and Matthew will be gleaned before anything happens to them." Serah squeezed her eyes shut and shook away the image of the stark wooden pillory that blighted the town square. She had never been allowed to watch the Gleaners mete out God's punishment, but wasn't it better to be humiliated and spat upon by townspeople than to be eaten by a bear or murdered by Heathens? She scanned the sanctuary. Matthew's family attended another church, but Eve's parents and her two younger brothers were normally a fixture two pews over. If they were in worship today, they would already be exiled to the balcony.

The pews were full, just as they were every Sunday. Churches were almost as abundant as hogs in New Goshen, but most of the city's prominent citizens attended First Church of New Goshen. They dressed in black or dark blue suits and always took the front pews. Their wives paraded to their seats in elaborate hats decorated with lace and flowers, and gleaned dresses in radiant hues like wrens and warblers.

The Gleaners sat behind the town's elite, big men pressed shoulder to shoulder, backs ramrod straight, an intimidating line of black leather and shaved napes. Serah's family sat toward the back of the lower level. A balcony stretched above the sanctuary's rear, reserved by custom for families of the Shunned. Only someone foolish or unhinged would venture upstairs by choice.

The choir stood in tiered rows beneath the cross. Their angelic voices soared to the buttressed ceiling.

A mighty fortress is our God.
A bulwark never failing.
Our helper he amid the flood.
Of mortal ills prevailing.

Eve, with her auburn hair, always stood out amidst the sanctuary's muted tones. Her absence from the choir's front row weighed heavy on Serah's shoulders.

The hymn ended. The choir and congregation sat. A hacking cough started up somewhere in the back and the wind blustered outside the windows. Her brother Thad pressed his bony frame against Serah in the chilly room. Her sister Jael lay with her head in their father's lap. Their mother's dark hair was tucked under a scarf. Mama held Imnah's hand, an affection few other boys his age would tolerate.

The Preacher rose from his high-backed chair and stepped to the lectern. His inflexible, commanding frame contrasted sharply with a face like risen bread dough. He drew out a silver key attached to his waistband and unlocked a small cabinet at the lectern's base. A tingle shot through Serah as he pulled out the only other book she knew still existed, a massive black leather-bound Bible. The gold-edged paper glistened as he opened it to a page marked with a red ribbon.

The Preacher surveyed his flock with cold, unforgiving eyes that seemed to single out Serah. "Listen for the word of God," he boomed. If the choir's voices carried Serah closer to heaven, the Preacher's deep baritone pulled her firmly back to earth.

Lowering his eyes to the page, he read from the Holy Bible. "Whut mun you'd, havad hungrud shap, if loath un, do hot laft nin and nin witnus, na got aft thy loos, un fon it?"

As the Preacher rumbled on in God's inscrutable language, Serah's eyes drifted to the enormous gold cross. She said a silent prayer that Eve and Matthew would be safe from bears and Heathens. But she couldn't help adding a prayer born from her desire for adventure.

Please, God, let them escape the Gleaners, Serah added to her prayer.

The heavy thud of the Preacher closing the big book brought Serah back to the hard wooden pew. Bowing his head, he asked for understanding of His divine language. Only then did he translate.

"What man of you, with five sons, if he loses one, goes after what he lost until he finds him? And when he does, he layeth his rod heavily on the wayward son's shoulders, and casts him into a dark pit."

The Preacher's voice rumbled like thunder through the sanctuary. "For the man must set an example for the others, that they not be tempted, and fall into Heathen sin. It is good and right in God's eyes that the man lose one son rather than five. Amen."

The congregation and choir rose to sing another hymn. Like everyone in New Goshen, Serah knew the words by heart, but today they were water in a sieve. Her thoughts drifted to Eve and Matthew. Were they so wrong to want happiness? Serah would never say it out loud, but she didn't believe they deserved the punishment waiting for them.

Thunder rumbled outside the church's stained-glass windows. The Preacher read and translated the passage about Noah's ark, comparing it to New Goshen, and promised they too would weather any storm.

When the service ended, parishioners made their way to the exit as they talked of the rain and the misery it portended of flooded fields and ruined crops. The Preacher stepped down from the lectern and circled with the Gleaner Commander and sub-commanders at the sanctuary's rear. A heated discussion ensued.

Thad and Jael raced ahead of the departing parishioners to splash in the puddles outside. Mama and Papa were absorbed in a conversation with their neighbors and didn't notice Serah lingering behind. Was she the only one who realized the big Bible still sat on the lectern, out in the open for anyone to approach? For a long week, she had kept her vow not to visit her book. Now God tempted her with another sweet fruit.

A burning desire to compare God's book to her own compelled her to slip down the aisle. Her knees almost buckled as she mounted the steps to the dais. No one but the Preacher was allowed up here. If someone spotted her, she'd have no place to hide.

Her head rose barely a foot above the lectern's top. She had never seen the sanctuary from this perspective. The Preacher and Gleaners continued their discussion. Blood pounded in her ears and her hand shook as she touched the Bible's rough spine. The book smelled of mildew and stale leather. She opened it to where the red ribbon marked the day's reading. The paper was as thin as butterfly wings. The pages blurred as fear of ending up in the pillory overwhelmed her senses.

She forced herself to focus. A frame of swirling gold leaf bordered the text. The symbols were a fierce black against yellowed paper. Their bottoms were thick and flat, and the tops curved or receded to sharp points. Some were so large they leaped off the page. At first, she was sure they were nothing like the simple symbols in her book. These markings were holy, as different as heaven from earth.

The hum of conversation in the church faded, along with the sound of the rain, her fear, and the burdens of her life. She was back in her sanctuary under the porch, drawing the symbols in the dirt.

Her finger traced God's symbols. They were more opulent than the ones in her book, but she recognized the lines, the patterns, and the repetitions.

AND

THE

A

.

,

They were all here. God wasn't confined to a single, unfathomable volume. He was in her book too. Everything she had learned in Sunday school was thrown into doubt. Were Jesus, Moses, and Elijah no more real than the two rabbits and the little mouse, and a cow jumping over the moon?

Serah glanced up. The Preacher shook hands with the Commander. A hint of perplexity furled his forehead as if he were trying to remember an important task. Serah closed the book but was trapped like a rabbit in an open field while a hawk circled overhead.

A metallic clatter resonated through the room. Everyone looked to a back corner where Imnah stood next to an angry usher, the offering plate and weekly tithe scattered like pebbles at their feet. Imnah's eyes met Serah's before he knelt and helped the usher retrieve the coins.

Serah raced down the steps in three long strides, enfolded again in safe anonymity.

-300-

Social Sciences

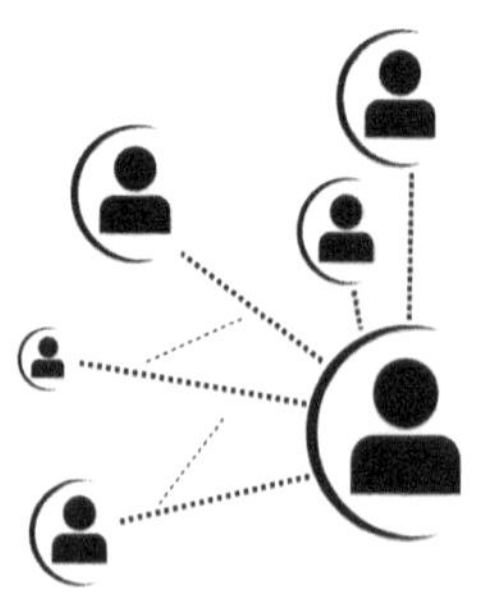

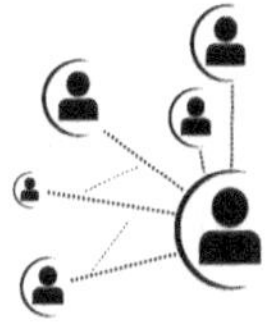

Alexandra Again

Kelly Webber

One common misconception about the Library of Alexandria is that a great fire engulfed one of the greatest collections of the ancient world. In reality, the library's destruction was more gradual. Across the history of the Library of Alexandria (nearly one thousand years), it suffered from multiple incinerations at the hands of leaders including Julius Caesar and Theophilus.[1] For those whose hearts ache for centuries of knowledge lost, Alexandria evokes an incurable nostalgia. Unfortunately, history is known to repeat itself. Nazis burned books deemed "un-German" in May 1933[2] and firefighters battled "the most challenging, frightening fire that they've ever confronted in their careers" at the Los Angeles Central Library in April 1986.[3] As the United States continues defunding public libraries and education, and the political right pushes an increase in book bans, we risk yet another Alexandria – if not by flames, then by culture wars and budget cuts. Right now, the

American people have the opportunity to extinguish this folly before it's too late.

In the summer of 2023, I found myself digging through the remnants of a middle school library untouched since the district lost its librarians to budget cuts over a decade ago. As I developed the library's online catalog (ironically, or perhaps serendipitously, via a software named Alexandria) I could not help but feel as if librarians are simultaneously straddling the dark and golden age of libraries. On one hand, we have a lack of funding for libraries while book bans explode in the news. Many question the value of libraries in the age of Google and Kindle. On the other hand, librarians are as innovative as ever, providing books and technology no matter the challenge. Librarians who responded to COVID-19 closures by providing students with mobile hotspots to access their virtual education[4] demonstrated that as the world becomes more dependent on technology, libraries will rise to the occasion with practical solutions.

My own high school attempted to ban a book that is still frequently banned a decade later: *The Absolutely True Diary of a Part-Time Indian* by Sherman Alexie.[4,5] While the school board debated a brief mention of masturbation, eighth-grade language arts classes watched *Romeo and Juliet* (1968), which includes a partially nude scene of a fifteen-year-old girl. I cannot help but suspect that the cries of profanity were—and still are—a cover-up for underlying bigotry. *The Absolutely True Diary of a Part-Time Indian* was my first exposure to Indigenous narratives about life on the Spokane reservation. In the words of Alexie himself, "[Those who oppose the book] are simply trying to protect their privileged notions of what literature is and should be. They are trying to protect privileged children. Or the seemingly privileged.[5]

Book bans disproportionately affect minority groups. Out of the top ten banned books of 2022, half were challenged for LGBTQ+ content; other grounds for removal included depictions of police brutality, abuse, and sexism.[4] By censoring the content of these books, we risk further marginalizing our students already at risk of discrimination and abuse. Accessing library books at all is a privilege. An estimated 30 percent of school districts in 2018-19 had "no librarians in any of their schools. Districts with more students experiencing poverty, higher levels of Black and brown students, and include more English language learners were less likely to have librarians."[6]

Fortunately, librarians are highly adaptive and consistently dedicated. Just as we delivered books on horseback to remote areas during the Great Depression[7] and via bookmobile during the height of the COVID-19 pandemic,[8] we are working every day to fight for intellectual freedom no matter what the obstacles. I am often asked why I chose to become a librarian during "these unprecedented times," and to me the answer is painfully simple: every community deserves access to information, technology, representation, and quality literature. It is not sufficient to regret history's lost libraries; we must look forward and build a future that lives up to its promises of equality and intellectual freedom.

<u>Sources</u>

[1]mymcpl.org/blogs/historical-libraries-library-alexandria

[2] encyclopedia.ushmm.org/content/en/article/book-burning

[3] npr.org/2018/10/13/656896695/mystery-of-a-massive-library-fire-remains-unsolved-after-more-than-30-years

[4] ala.org/news/sites/ala.org.news/files/content/state-of-americas-libraries-special-report-pandemic-year-two.pdf

[5] hiseye.org/1896/his-eye/staffer-responds-to-book-controversy/

[6] slj.com/story/SLIDE-study-fewer-school-librarians-in-districts-that-need-them-most

[7] smithsonianmag.com/history/horse-riding-librarians-were-great-depression-bookmobiles-180963786/

[8] nationalgeographic.com/travel/article/libraries-respond

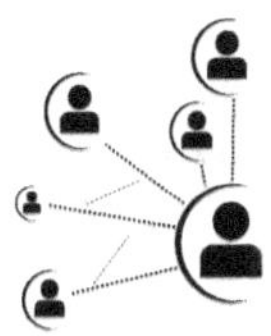

Being and All

Thom Hawkins

The officers stopped me
on the street and led me
into an alley for questioning.

"Who are you?" they asked.
I told them my name.
"No, no," their silhouetted
heads turned side to side.

Then the clubs came out: "Who
are you when you're by yourself?"
a voice hissed in my ear.

"Are you being or becoming?"

yelled the other. "Answer me,
boy! Are you mind, body, or both?"

They gave me no chance
to answer. I let them define me
into submission.

Beloved Crocodile

Ester M. Marquez & Lester N. Linsangan

Oh, the beloved crocodile
You have such a wonderful smile
Consisting of a regal profile
Living a tremendous lifestyle
But you are supposed to move
'Cause you have plenty to prove
There are tons of areas to improve
And not another scheme to approve
Why fix an eminent track that can't be shaken?
And chase someone else's golden?
Change an existence, cherished and hidden?
Demolish greatness for fame all of a sudden?
I really am clueless about what most see
Do they see you as something shiny?
I view you as something green and slimy,
And will gnaw any living thing, you're greedy
Have we really gone, imbecile?
Trusting a dangerous reptile

To lead, to decide while being hostile
In an era that will surely take a while

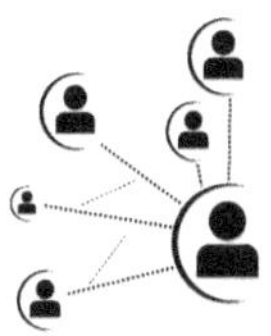

FRACTION OF THE WORLD

WRYANN TRISTHAN A. BENITEZ & LESTER N. LINSANGAN

Greed is something us humans are "programmed" to have
A fraction of the world would agree, maybe even more than one halve.
The power it holds against a person is massive
But having an abundance of everything makes them passive.
"Once granted everything, you can't do anything"
A quote that encompasses Greed in just a "ding!"
Having everything makes a person a useless tool
Like how a sheep is used for its wool.
But is greed really alive in a sense?
Greed is merely an idea, something inanimate, hence;
Us humans are the ones making it "alive"
WE are the ones that make greed thrive.
Our greed for love, money, and power
Is what made the world's relations sour

Greed starts with simple banters that end in war
Once we succumb to greed, 3-nil would be the score.

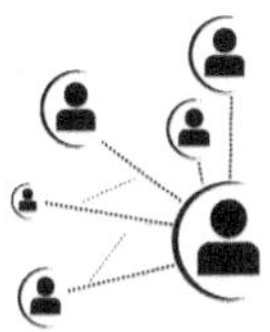

Frantic Illusions

Caleb William D. Catalan & Lester N. Linsangan

there was a misanthrope named Pardef

he despises people

he thinks humankind is irresponsible

every time he goes out, they produce a cacophony of sounds

his brain and his whole body can't function when they're

around

for him, they cause such tragedy in today's reality

they're making it strenuous to walk and talk properly

"those humans make it so complex"

"it's making me lose all my reflexes"

humans cause troubles, that cause excruciating pain

that has now made Pardef insane

but it turns out Pardef was not misanthropic

he was paralyzed, deaf, and psychotic

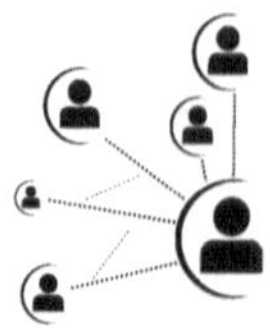

Magnum Opus

Caleb William D. Catalan & Lester N. Linsangan

a sensational piece that has been made

was once caged

got locked and trapped in one's power

a treasure of a masterpiece devoured

suppressing a glorious opus

is like denying the traditional and cultural focus repudiating a

remarkable custom

is like taking away the spark of freedom

when will we have the autonomy

when will we obtain multitudinous opportunities

how can we equip and achieve mastery

when can we produce phenomenal literary

when will they allow us to be legendary;

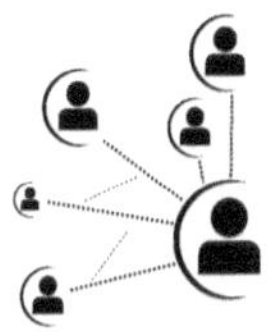

New Policies

Thom Hawkins

My first day as the head of HR,
I banned hugs because a co-worker
hugged me once and I did not like it.

On Tuesday, I banned all public
displays of affection. Neither my
ex-wife nor her new husband work
here, but word will get out
and they will know I disapprove.

Wednesday there were no more
handshakes—some people
have sweaty palms and no one
to look after them.

Thursday—eye contact,
a gateway touch.

By Friday, no one could speak
because there was no one left
to speak to. I announced
my retirement to an empty room.

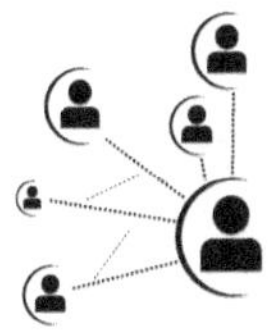

Reading With His Daughter

Amy Nielsen

I tucked the documents the attorney had given me into a folder. Documents that meant Dad was officially unable to make his own health and financial decisions—grateful he'd signed them before it was too late.

"Dad, it's time to go," I shouted into my former guest room.

My father sat in the worn recliner he insisted we bring from his former Sun City independent living facility.

Conspiracy theorists shouted book-banning rhetoric from the television. "I knew it," he barked. It's been books all along."

"Dad, books aren't taking over the government. Here let me help you get your shoes on."

"I can do it myself." He bent over and almost plummeted to the ground.

I grabbed one of his loafers. "Just slip your foot in. I got you."

He mumbled some swear words followed by, "Your old man can put his shoes on."

"I know you can. Just trying to help." With his last loafer in place, I pushed his wheeled walker in front of him. "Alrighty let's go. Attorney Foster can't wait to see you."

"I don't need that thing. I can walk without it." Dad pushed the walker out of the way.

"Remember what Dr. Harvey said. One fall and…"

"Fine, give me the damn thing." Dad took the walker and pushed himself toward the door.

I grabbed the folder, my purse, and keys. This would be the last visit there with Dad. The next time I'd see Attorney Foster, I'd be alone. It broke my heart.

On the drive, Dad complained about the Brandon traffic, which I agreed with. Then complained about the Florida heat, which I disagreed with. Growing up in the Sunshine State surrounded by patches of plump strawberries, I couldn't imagine living anywhere else.

"We're here." I pulled into Foster Elder Law Firm. The residential brick building turned commercial always reminded me of our old home back in downtown Plant City.

I shook the memory away, got Dad's walker out of the trunk, and opened the passenger door.

Dad didn't want my help any more than I wished he didn't need it. But I offered my hand.

He took it and up righted himself on the walker. "Take me to Foster the Great."

I rang the bell on the firm's front door. A tall dark blonde let us in.

"Hello. Rachelle is waiting for you both in the conference room. Follow me."

Dad struggled to push the walker over the worn Persian rugs in the lobby.

Dark blonde offered to help. "Sir, let me move these out of the way."

"Hon, back in the day I played college football at Florida State. Star running back. These rugs got nothing on me." He attempted to lift the walker over a rug seam and tumbled.

Dark blonde and I both grabbed him. "Dad, you're a few years out from star running back."

He shot me a glare but accepted my help.

The law clerk moved the rugs. Then she put a hand on my shoulder. "You're a good daughter."

Tears welled behind my blue eyes, the same bright blue as my father's. "Thank you.'

The clerk helped my father into a chair at a conference table. I sat next to him and patted his weathered hand. Years as a strawberry farmer had been lucrative, but tough on his body.

Attorney Foster sat amongst piles of folders and fancy pens. She stood and offered a handshake across the table. First to Dad. "Good to see you Mr. Parke." Then to me. "Ms. Parke."

Dad pointed to her wedding ring. "I thought you were waiting for me."

She chuckled. "Don't take this the wrong way, but my husband might be upset if I told him I was leaving him for a client. Not to mention it's highly unethical."

"Dad. Stop." It wasn't the worst thing he'd said lately. But he'd never said anything like this in front of his lawyer. The disease was really progressing.

The young attorney smiled. "Totally okay. My job is to make you both comfortable. Including your charming father."

The last thing I felt was comfort. Taking my demented father's rights away—from the man who'd help guide me through every major decision of my own life. It didn't seem right, but necessary.

Attorney Foster explained what we were signing and why. With each signature, Dad's shoulders slouched more. At one point I grabbed a tissue to blot a bit of wet mascara before it slid down my cheek.

"Well, that's all the medical documents. The last thing is asset disclosures. Before we sign these, Mr. Parke, do you have any other assets not reported?" She shuffled through the documents. "I have your banking and savings, and your financial planner sent over everything from his end. Anything like Savings Bonds or cash or anything else that is not in a financial institution."

After she asked the question, Dad's eyes focused on the wall behind her. Six framed book covers filled the space between overfilled bookcases—Pride and Prejudice, Anne of Green Gables, Huckleberry Finn, Little Women, The Hobbit, and To Kill a Mockingbird.

Dad pointed to the artwork. "I'm not telling you anything more until you turn those books off."

Mrs. Foster's eyebrows furrowed. "Excuse me?"

I glanced at the covers. "Dad, what're you talking about?" Many of those books he and I had read together when I was a child.

"Those books. I've heard it on the news. Sharing all our secrets with the government. I'm not falling for it."

"Mr. Parke, I can show you this artwork isn't electric or connected to WIFI or anything. Just book covers I framed of my favorite classics." The attorney lifted a frame from the wall to show my dad there were no hidden wires or infrared discs.

The irony that Dad wasn't the least bit concerned about her open laptop, cellphone, or smartwatch, all devices allegedly known for sneaky marketing—framed book covers were his concern.

"That's what you say, but you don't know. If you won't take them out, I'll only write it down." Dad scribbled some numbers and notes on a piece of paper and slid it over to the lawyer.

She picked it up. "Mr. Parke, we'll make sure your assets are properly protected."

Then to me, "Ms. Parke, I'll update your father's documents and since he's listed you as Guardian Ad-Litem, I'll have you come in next week to finalize." She held out a hand.

I shook it. "Thank you. And I'm sorry."

The law clerk helped Dad up and the attorney pulled me aside. "Ms. Parke. I'm sorry to tell you this. But what you've done today, it's in the best interest of your father. We don't want to get to the point where we must get physicians involved. It gets very complicated."

"I know. The book thing. Again, I'm sorry."

"Your father's one of my favorite clients. Always has been. But with the growing culture war on literature, I'd steer him clear of less news and more Price is Right. Keep him in a good mindset."

"Got it."

Then she jutted in front of me. "Mr. Parke, it was an absolute pleasure seeing you again. You take care."

The law clerk secured Dad in his front passenger seat and waved goodbye.

"Good visit," Dad said.

"Yes, it was, Dad, yes it was." As I pulled out of Foster Law, I decided I'd make a phone call to cut the cord when I got back home.

Despite the protests I'd expect from him, my father wouldn't spend his last days watching conspiracy theorists' cable news.

He'd spend his last days reading with his daughter.

Author's Note: Sometimes the truth is more unbelievable than fiction. Such is the case with this inspired-by real-life very recent story. Book-banning and anti-literature rhetoric push false narratives into vulnerable minds. Then they marinate, multiply, and morph into a much worse, more dangerous version. As citizens of intellectual freedom, it is our duty to prevent these false narratives from penetrating the minds of those we love.

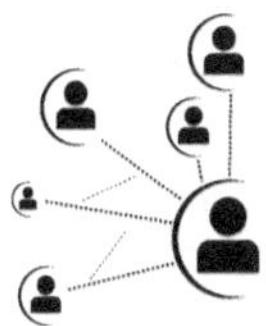

The One and Only Emma

Dana Hawkins

HER FINGERS TREMBLED AS she swept blush across her cheekbones. Back and forth, the soft bristles tickled her skin, and she took a moment to appreciate the sensation. The pencil dug deep into her skin as she arched a brow. She tilted her head and sucked in her cheek like the tutorial said and checked her reflection. *Not bad.*

The eyes were more difficult. She had studied—oh boy, had she studied. She'd stole glances at her mom's Cosmo magazines, poured over YouTube tutorials, stalked online beauty influencers. But today was her first time actually *doing* it.

The articles couldn't have predicted the involuntary flicker of her lids as she drew a pencil line. The videos couldn't have prepared her for the tears shed and how each swipe filled her soul. The research definitely never mentioned that make-up would make her feel complete. Beautiful. Validated. *Human.*

The eyebrow arch was too much. She was twelve, not twenty-five. She didn't want to look grown-up. She just wanted to look *herself.*

She wiped it off and started again. Starting with the eyebrows, then eyelids, then lips.

An hour later, she released her ponytail and shook her hair to her shoulders. She'd been growing it out for three years now. Maybe when she reached high school, she'd have hair to her waist.

She pulled out two butterfly clips, the ones her dad set out on the counter along with the make-up, and a handwritten note that said: "I love you. In any form." Her fingers grazed the glitter, and she clicked open the clasp. After tugging her delicate wisps to the side, she clamped it closed. Her mouth twisted. The clip was lopsided and heavy. But also, so pretty. She decided to leave it.

She patted the side of her hair and batted back a tear as she stared at herself—a mirage come to life, a dream turned reality. This is who she was, who she'd always been. She'd dreamt of this day, to meet herself in her wholeness, to hug herself and tell her she was free. Alive. Perfect.

She flicked the tears with her pink polished thumb and inhaled. Tonight, she could cry. Right now, she didn't want to ruin her make-up.

A knock rapped on the door. She dropped her brush, then froze. They knew what she was doing. They even bought the supplies. But she wasn't quite ready for them to know her the way she knew herself.

"Ethan?" Her dad's voice sounded behind the oak door.

She cleared her throat. "Dad, please. We talked about this."

A thunderous silence followed.

"I'm sorry, Bud. It's gonna take me some time. But that's on me, not you." Moments passed, then a cleared throat, then a sigh. "Can we try this again?"

She grinned. "Yes."

A knock on the door. "Emma?"

She smiled. The first time she heard her name—her *true* name, from her dad's mouth. She wanted to hear it a million times more. Her hands gripped the knob, her belly twisted, her mouth dry. She took a deep breath and opened the door.

Her father's scrunched eyebrows and pulled-in lips faced her. The silence swallowed her. The *click, click, click* of the clock screamed. Each second was a minute, and each minute was an hour. She patted down the side of her hair, her pulse thudding in her ears, bile creeping up her throat.

Her father took another deep breath. His face softened. His shoulders relaxed. "You look beautiful."

Author Note: Celebrate and affirm our trans kids—including letting them see themselves positively and authentically in books.

-400-

Language

The Tinker

Riley Kilmore

Moonshine handed me the jug he'd filled, but not before he took him a swig like it were some tax Pap owed. Moonshine had another name, but no one used it. Burl Matheson, I'm pert near sure Pap once said.

See, I'd worked out a trick for remembering names and such by seeing them in my mind like they was titles on the covers of books. I don't know why that worked so well, but I guessed it was just cause I had what Ma called an "uncanny fondness" for books. I'd gotten that from her. My earliest memories were of her reading to me. Half the time back then I didn't know what any of it meant, but I liked the way the words fluttered outa her mouth like moths and lit soft in my ear. They sounded the way lake ice does at first thaw, cracklin' and poppin' like it was whispering promises.

Moonshine looked me up and down with his one good eye. His other'n always looked left like it were stuck there, like it feared someone was sneakin' up on Moonshine and had to keep watch.

"You be growin' like a weed, boy," he said, then mussed my hair. "Now be sure that jug gits to your pap full as I done sent it. Hear?"

I tried to smile to be polite, but I don't think my mouth heard my brains tellin' it what to do. "Yes sir," I says. Then I handed over the sack of taters Pap sent for pay and headed down the holler, Moonshine laughing at my back.

The day had dawned fine and clear, the sun not yet climbed too high but already burning off the damp. It was only the cusp of spring on the mountain, but winter's grip was already a faded memory, as if it had always been early April and always would be. The crocuses were long done, and patches of jonquils dotted the woods, adding their sweet perfume to the mossy, musky smell of the awakening earth.

I reached the road and hadn't but walked around the elbow in the crick when I come acrost that wagon. I knowed right off it were a tinker's cart by all them pots and pans and whatnots strung off it. The tinker was hanging a feedbag off his horse's face when he heard me comin' and turned sharp like he'd been caught stealing eggs. His face relaxed some when he caught sight of me.

"Well, young man," he says, "aren't you the sight, coming down off the slope there. I thought you might've been a bear coming out of hibernation."

He looked a small man—maybe just underfed—a bit older than Pap, I'd say, but not near so long in the tooth as my Papaw.

He wore a suit like it were Sunday, but a Sunday ten or twenty year ago by the sight of it.

I walked up to his wagon to get a gander at all his goods, and he startled me a little by holding out his hand. At first, I thought he wanted a swig, then realized he was just wanting to shake my hand. It weren't too often someone offered to shake the hand of a young'un, so it made me feel a bit more growed than I'd felt half an hour ago up at Moonshine's place.

"Paul Harding," he said by way of introduction before dropping my hand.

"How do, sir?" I said, but I was distracted and forgot to give my name back.

He saw me eyeing his wares. "New pot for you Ma?" He took one down and let me hold it once I set down the jug. "Maybe a nice jackknife for you Papa?"

My eyes roamed over every manner of thing a body could think of. He had bolts of calicos and linens Ma would have swooned for. He had every sewing notion she could need. They was shiny new tools any man would covet but none I knew who'd be able to pay their price. I seen wooden toys and brass candlesticks, hardwares of every kind, and tin pails to tote them in. They was even some cured hams and ropes of sausage strung like garland on a Christmas tree. That whole wagon looked like Christmas morning and then some.

Then I seen it, something better'n all the Christmas put together, there, up on the worn seat at the head of his wagon.

"Fancy books, do you, son?" He handed me the book, and I held it like it were a hymnal. Then I read the title line by line, saying the words out loud. "The Grapes. Of Wrath. By John—" I tried that last word a few times but couldn't get past the first few letters.

"Steinbeck," the tinker said, studying on me as I ran my hand over the cover for the feel of it. "That's good you can read, son. Not a lot of folks around these parts do. How old are you?"

"Twelve. My Ma taught me, mostly. But we got ourselves a school, too, and I go 'cept for when it's plantin' and gatherin' times, or when we're too holed up for a heavy snow and the like."

He chewed on the inside of one cheek almost like he had a plug of chaw, but I knowed he din't.

"Tell you what. I'm finished reading that, so I'll trade it for whatever you have in that gunny sack slung on your back. And maybe I'll throw in a little something or two extra. The book and maybe something special for you ma and you papa, eh? But can't let anyone know you have it."

"Why not?"

"It's a book people aren't supposed to be reading."

"Why would someone write a book if it ain't supposed to be read?"

It seemed like he considered my question a long time and acted like he had to look hard, way in the back of his head, for the answer. Then he just said one word. "Ignorance."

"What's that?" I asks him.

"Willful stupidity."

Now it was my turn to reach deep inside my head, but I couldn't make hide nor tail of what he meant. It reminded me of what I'd been thinking of earlier, words striking my ears like melting lake ice. "Will I get in trouble for reading it?"

"Yes," he said, almost before I finished the question. "Good trouble."

I cocked my head like our coon when he don't know where a noise come from.

"Learning is always good. Reading is always good. Broadening your mind is always good. But learning and reading and broadening your mind makes trouble for those who profit from the ignorance of others."

His words went on cracklin' and poppin' in my mind all the way home.

That night I lay in the loft looking down on the firelit room below. Ma stood polishing her new pot with the tail of her apron, admiring it. Pap sat at the fire, the glow of the flames glinting off the blade of his new jackknife. His old one were so nicked and wobbly it wouldn't have seen another winter, so I were glad I chose it.

Ma says to Pap, "I can't get over him getting these fine items for what few things he had with him in his sack. What was it he said? He got 'em for an apple, a slab of sausage-baked pone, and some jerky?" She set her pot on the sideboard and made to take off her apron, saying, "Why, I'll be."

"He's a good boy, Bess. Another'n his age, come acrost a tinker in a trading mood that free, woulda chosen things for hisself."

I slid back, quiet like, so as not to disturb their illusion of privacy. They thought I was already asleep. I rolled onto my tick and tugged the quilt up some, then slipped my hand underneath the tick where I'd tucked the book against the floorboards. I just wanted to feel at it one more time.

I hadn't started in on reading yet because anticipation is part of the magic of most things. It's kinda like the sight of a perty gift under a Christmas tree that you can see but can't unwrap for days. After Sunday-go-to-Meeting the next day—after my chores were done and before Ma set supper—I planned to steal up to the mow an hour or so and tackle it. I planned to stash it up there, too, under a loose board I knew. Bit by bit, whenever I'd be able to snick out unnoticed, I planned to climb into the mow and read more—savor it slow like books are meant to be taken in, like the candy they was.

I never did see Mr. Paul Harding again. I guess he were just passin' through.

I showed the book to Ma and Pap eventually. It musta been about two years later. I'd waited till I was nigh on too big to take a switch to, but Pap din't know nothin' about it being a book no one was supposed to read, and he din't care one little smidge I had it. Ma asked if she could read it. It were a little worse for wear, having been kept in the mow, and me musta having read it half a dozen times through, but she done it. We never talked about it, though. The story, I mean. It were kept like a secret between us, something we'd shared but couldn't discuss.

I still think about that tinker's words now and again, but I haven't figured out what makes some folks think they can tell others that they gotta go on being ignorant like them. It seems a lot like sausage-baked pone to me. Some don't like it; they'll only eat plain pone with no sausage baked inside, and that's fine. But can you imagine them settin' there, telling other folks *no* one's allowed to eat sausage-baked pone either, since *they* don't like the taste of it?

Why, that's just plumb crazy.

The True Word

Thom Hawkins

Early cultures believed
if you knew the true
name of something
you could control it.

Waistline is wrong, then.
There's another, secret word.
Unknown also are the words
for hair loss, famine, war.

It turns out it was up to us
all along: the poets, the writers,
the English majors.

All we need is a safe word.

The Words of Others

Miranda Huba

THE DOCTOR KEPT ASKING her the same question. "Can you tell me your name? Can you tell me your name?"

Hadn't she answered this already? It was hard to hear amongst the hospital din. There was a constant white noise like an anxious radio picking up bits of other people's stories. Quiet little yelps amongst the dripping, sucking, and suctioning. If she could just turn the dial a little more to the right maybe she could find the right frequency again. This wasn't it.

The doctor leaned in closer, and then closer again. She was young, her hair in one of those messy buns, and her scrubs gray worn, and ragged. She would have blended into the depths of the wall and its horrid paint job if her eyebrows weren't so thick with concern. "What is your date of birth?"

Whatever this game was, she found it silly and unnecessary. But she wanted to cooperate. It was only polite. But where were the words? There were none coming. Cumming. She laughed.

The doctor caught the smile, and seized on the opportunity to start the game again, "Can you tell me where you were born?"

Well, she would if her tongue wasn't stuck in her throat. She could not seem to move it along with her lips and teeth to create the gorgeous diphthongs and consonants required to play this hospital game. Out of the corner of her eye she saw a body mummified in blankets being wheeled on a gurney, without any rush.

Why was there no rush? Maybe that was part of the game, is this person alive or dead? The doctor did not flinch at this rolling parade and kept her eyes steady on her. She wanted to tell her that she was a writer. That she had been working on a short story with her writing group. In a folder by the bedside table, that's where they could find it. About her childhood. It would answer a lot of the doctor's questions.

The doctor reached for her hand, and she quivered at the skin contact. Everything in here was so cold to the touch, the needles, the linens, the bedframes. She just wanted to be warm. Her idea of medicine as a child had been much cozier than this. Small-town doctors with leather satchels that contained herbal tinctures and plant poultices concocted by the oldest person in town. Instead, she was in a bleak ward named after the wealthiest person in town. The doctor pressed the coldness further into her, "Is there anyone at home we should contact?"

Didn't they have this on file? She had been led to believe they had large files for every person on earth. The doctor was saying something about resuscitation. Recitation. She grew up in a generation where they still did that. She had all sorts of poems in her head, tidbits, phrases, maxims.

"*Patience is a virtue....*" Something like that.

"Grace, can you tell me the name of your family doctor?"

So, they had known her name. Grace. Well, Grace's biggest concern was not that she had been found unresponsive, half naked, one hand holding onto the bed and shivering. Her biggest concern was that she was in the middle of a novel by one of her favorite authors. Page 144. A library book. She was never late.

The doctor pressed on determined to draw out some sort of utterance, "We understand you have two daughters?"

"Yes." Well, she could blurt that out. Yes and no, the simple pleasantries, but not the words that make language interesting. Words with movement and texture. They were not coming. She wished she could put the doctor at ease, she seemed stressed. She was not going to die. Too many books to be read, stories to be written, and articles that sounded interesting. She had not read anything by... the name of the author was escaping her. Many famous lines.

The doctor was explaining something about a stroke. It sounded complicated. Then she heard "left side." Left. The writing hand. Well, this WAS getting complicated.

She knew they were looking at her as old. But it felt like only yesterday she had graduated with her Bachelor in English. She had been in an all-girls dorm. She had been protected there. Then the world got her. Men. They always told her she could do whatever she wanted. They would support her. Let her write.

They lied.

So, it was soft lights at night reading the words of others. The words of others. That is exactly what she was trying to conjure up at the moment. She wanted to impress on the doctor her grasp of language. The words were still there, she knew they were. A care aide had come in and put the TV on one of those sensational news stations. It wasn't helping things. Someone was talking about somewhere in someplace a book was being taken from a shelf. Maybe it was the author she could not remember.

Many famous lines.

The doctor's tone changed slightly from gentle to gentle urgent. "The next 24 hours are going to be crucial; we will be monitoring you constantly and will be conducting another CT scan in the morning."

"Ok."

Ok? Was that all she could muster? She wanted to ask if the scan would show where the words went. Where the words went. They were stuck somewhere amongst the tissues, folds, and cartilage. The small-town doctor would surely have a tea for such an ailment. If she could not write them, she would have to speak them. Just a sentence. She could start there. A full sentence. But which sentence? So many to choose from.

This is what you get for following directions she thought. Directions had led her right to this very moment. She remembered a course she had wished she had taken in university. "The Bible in Literature." Some insecure professor had told her it might be too rigorous for her. She would look to see if they still offered it. The Bible, that is another one she hadn't read. Not at the top of her list though. She was regretting that she had recently indulged in a best-selling celebrity memoir. What a waste of her time. If she had known a medical emergency was about to befall her, she may have chosen something more robust. A classic. The memoir was entertaining, however.

The doctor was rubbing her concerned brow. "We're hoping the pressure slowly decreases."

The brain. Could she still read? She searched the room for words. She was hungry for words. This particular environment was devoid of them. Sterility had come for the words by way of bleach and bright lights. Not even a poster with some sort of public health message, just layer upon layer of muted colors. The brightest thing in the room was the TV, and she could make out the text at the bottom of the screen, barely.

Grace swiped at her face with her good hand, "Glasses."

The messy bun on the doctor's head perked up, "You usually wear glasses?"

Grace pressed hard where they should be, "Yes."

"I'll make a note."

How many pleasures can be lost in an instant she thought.

"Bear with me just a few more questions, then we'll do some bloodwork and let you rest."

The doctor began writing something on the whiteboard attached to the wall. Perhaps that counted as decor. The doctor's writing was all acronyms and codes. Not actual language. *What a piss off*, she thought. To be in a room absent of any words. There was a side table. She would get some books on there when she could. The doctor was now backing out of the room. She seemed nervous to leave.

Now the TV had a panel of people. A Chorus of "experts." She could not make out exactly what they were saying, something like, "Now remember we saw this before in the 80s" It was all rehearsed, Sophoclean in their words and gestures.

"We have to remember power of the courts."

"People want choice, so let them have choice."

"I mean they could go the way of parental advisories."

"You know, I actually see real opportunity here."

"There are some interesting startups addressing this very issue."

And round and round the circle it went. Nothing of note. Note. She needed a notecard. She had hundreds at home.

"Please," she implored to the doctor who was about to be sucked out of the room to deal with the others' pleading cries.

"Please what, Grace?"

"Please, I need to write something down." A sentence! Shocking how something so simple the day before was now so laborious.

"Oh, dear I don't want you to overexert yourself."

"Please, I have something to say, doctor."

"I promise after you get some rest, we can try to have you write something."

"I-I need to write down something before I forget."

"You need to rest; your brain has experienced significant trauma."

Grace closed her eyes. The convincing was exhausting.

"I'll see you first thing in the morning,"

And with that, the doctor was sucked back into the chaotic furor of the hospital halls, behind each door its own specific horror. Grace had just been one stop on the train of catastrophe. An aide entered hurriedly, "Now just let me close these blinds there is too much light, and who turned this TV on? We don't want too much stimulation."

She squinted, the same way she did as a child before they handed her glasses. The words on the screen came into focus.

"Counties rush to remove books from shelves to avoid felonies and fines."

Then the aide grabbed the remote. She heard the click. Then it was dark, and the room had no words. And she only had hers to speak, so she said silently.

"I will not regret the words I have spoken and the ones I never said."

Too Much is Not Too Much

Maria Juweyn Liwag & Lester N. Linsangan

Crumpled pages,
The pen ticks like a clock.
Ink has been imprinted,
With stories threatening to come out.
"It's too dark to be said",
Forbidden words are unacceptable.
The desire to speak to the bone,
But gaze and curses have been thrown.
Deafening silence,
With words that cannot be said.
Sliding it to the tip of the tongue,
But tears quickly run instead.
Don't wait for the crow to turn white,
Instead, be an eagle in the sky.
Side by side, we don't have to be the 'typical',
For the hands who keep us satirical.

-500-

Science

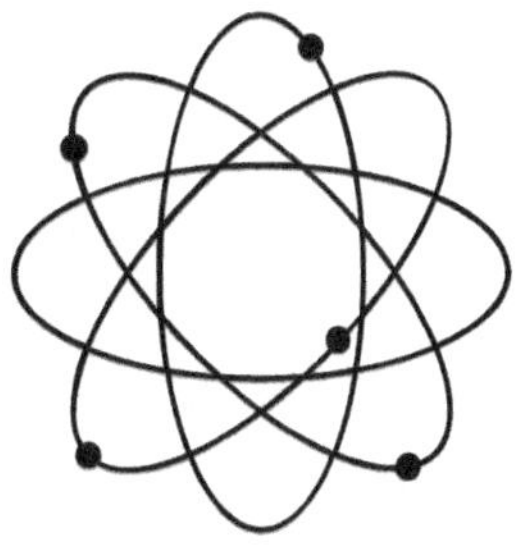

Becoming

Abigail F. Taylor

The science is this: Oscar Pistorius's carbon-fiber legs made him fifteen percent faster and twenty percent lighter than all the other athletes he competed against in the 2008 Olympics.

The fact is this: Last year, she competed in the Chicago Marathon and lost to Kelvin Kiptum by one minute. One measly, fucking minute. She knows she can be faster. She's done everything physically possible and is at peak performance level, right now, at this moment. She is superior in so many ways and could make the cut for the American Olympic Teams without so much as batting an eye.

Except, she knows she will always be fifteen percent slower and twenty percent heavier than she could be.

It takes a while, perhaps not as long as it should have, considering, but she finds a doctor, Christine Whitcomb, lauded for her achievements in biotechnology and kinesiology. She likes Dr. Whitcomb, bald and compact like a tiny, armored car, because Dr. Whitcomb cares more about the exploration of science than she does about her reputation. So far, it's paid off. The good doctor gets away with a lot of things that bend and slide around what is considered morally just. She's paid to do it. People want to know, *governments* want to know, how far the human body can go.

At first, she is offended that some nobody would find her and beg her for the necessary adjustments. She is not a back-alley Tijuana surgeon, after all, and does not appreciate the manila folder, stacked with proof of mental stability, that this young woman gives her. The runner refuses the diagnosis of body dysphoria. She loves her legs. She has amazing, sculpted calves and a freckle just above her right knee that looks like an arrowhead. But she loves being faster more. Besides, one day she will die and what good will her legs be then? She confesses that there were many considerations of jumping in front of trains or cars so that her legs might shatter. Dry Ice was, briefly, another option. The risk of an infection, depriving her of the full capacity of her lungs, stopped her. Some nights, the overwhelming need of an amputation makes her vomit.

So, the two women take a trip to an undisclosed location where an amputation can be performed without (much) scrutiny.

She thinks at some point she might be awake during the operation. She does her best not to move, or to moan with too much vigor. She can feel tears tugging at the tape around her eyes, the tube pressing down on her tongue, compressing yesterday's final meal of orange juice and saltine crackers. Between the whining of machinery is the harsh snicker-snack of a blade. A bone saw. Through the tape and her stubby lashes, she thinks she might see the dome light Dr. Whitcomb works under, a radiant sunshine.

I've lost myself, she says to herself, imagining the tendrils of sinew and veins sliding out of her like old laces pulled and snapped from the eyelets of her running shoes. She forces herself to rest, to resist the swell of panic that is choking her with fat hands.

Dr. Whitcomb left her, unnamed and charted, in a sunny hospital bed with a window that faced the ocean. She is nowhere to be found, no note or letter of recommended care. No evidence that she was ever in the country to begin with. At least her sutures are clean and in neat little rows, placed in such a way that the scarring won't hurt as much when they rub against the silicone socks and the funnel where she now must slide in her stumped calves. She's been left with a waddle of excess skin, too. Some cushion for the newly blunted bone. Eventually, she will not only be fitted with carbon fiber but with a series of pads and threads that connect to the neurotransmitters of her brain, and she will be able to move the false, hollow shapes of her as though she'd been born this way, fully formed from her father's thigh. Because of this particular implant, there will be debates on what part of her is qualified as human and if she is trans-mechanical, will she be allowed to compete with others who have functioning, fleshy and fallible body parts?

The law will always point to Oscar Pistorius.

Years from now, she is asked about the procedure by the media, the pop magazines who are interested in scandal and shock rather than the scientific community, those very people who love to study her in private but shun her when there are no shadowy places to whisper in.

She's broken all the records. She's won awards, proved herself worthy to stand among giants. She did exactly what she needed to.

But why? Why give up a part of yourself for such a vocation?

Because each person must choose her boundary. She must know that to achieve greatness to move the goalpost of acceptable enhancements.

The facts remain: The body is a machine that produces hormones to feed the muscle. It is a tool of survival and skill. The soul is the amalgamation of genotypes and phenotypes. A woman is the expression of her endurance and how far she must push herself. She must inhabit all factors of what makes her; the beautiful bits of her she needs to destroy for a glorious purpose that is suddenly as much outside of herself as it is within.

One day a Dartmouth professor of psychology will invite her to be a guest lecturer for his introductory class and she will be asked again and again: but why?

Because she could.

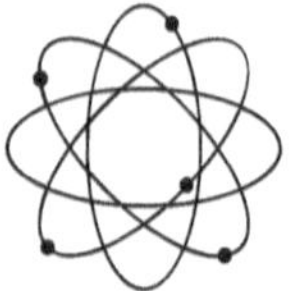

HUSHED WHISPERS

J.K. RAYMOND

CONTENT WARNING: TRAUMATIC ENCOUNTER with incompetent medical personnel during a pregnancy check.

This is a memoir of just your run of the mill middle class white woman and just how little she was aware of how powerful and delicate her body truly was. And, just how dangerous an attempt to bring life into this world can be. I'm talking about real life drama, just like the ones on television where a pregnant person screams and someone comes out to tell their significant other they are going to lose them, or the pregnancy or both. We haven't come so far away from that for it to be just a staticky black and white memory on television. These dramas are lived out every second a woman or person with a uterus draws breath in this country and the outcome for their survival is getting dimmer and dimmer by the second.

Most things like that are still kept hush-hush until it's an emergency, down to the second decision and that is the saddest part. With more information at our fingertips than ever before, people with a uterus in the United States are still no wiser on just how quickly their life can be taken while attempting to carry a pregnancy to term or in just how many ways life can change if they are lucky enough to walk away.

I was thirty-one the first time I realized how powerless and purposely unaware I was about the body I possess. From my first period to menopause and everything in between, all conversations were hushed whispers at worst or quiet giggles at best, but always dirty little secrets from the giggle to the grave. I'm the first generation and only generation to grow up complete with the safety net of Roe vs.Wade at my back and without it, I would be dead already.

Do I have your attention? Good. Because banning books is the same as digging graves. Let's start with mine.

My nightmare happened about thirty-one years after The Supreme Court passed Roe V. Wade into law. Barbaric in that they laid no formal foundation to help people understand why law was necessary for the betterment of humanity. The law was simply laid, and we the people were left with our opinions and choices and that was that. A win in that we were one step closer to better lives for every American, but that is where it stopped. Left with no way to move forward from opinions, we would always be a nation divided on a fact. That fact being abortions are necessary health care. Without required education on the subject and inalienable rights to it, we have become stuck in the inertia of talking point mire. One group always knowing the verdict could be swayed if opinions were swayed.

But here is the thing. Health and bodies are not opinion, they are medical facts. We the people must be formally educated on all the reasons a person who becomes pregnant is in fact risking their life and what that looks like scientifically. Not just when an emergency has deemed the information necessary, but long before the need may ever arise. Education on these risks will not only educate women, but it will also educate men, the entire populace of adults. Shining a light on the science will leave no room for ignorance. This foundation will remove the need to balance how people *feel* about these lifesaving procedures, reducing psychological trauma, making recovery and quality of life attainable. The way things stand now, bodies containing uteruses will never be seen as anything more than the opinions others have about it and because of that those very real bodies will just keep piling up.

I'd had ultrasounds before, for gallbladder issues, stuff like that, but this ultrasound was going to be different. This time I was pregnant. This particular ultrasound was what they call an in vitro ultrasound, which they told me on the phone, but never explained what that meant. I had never had an ultrasound while pregnant and thought it was just standard terminology. You can imagine my surprise at the twelve-inch wand my twenty-year old ultrasound technician pulled out along with a stark white condom. "No." I thought as Becky rolled the saddest looking condom of all time over the twelve-inch rod and all of this just before covering the whole thing down in ultrasound goop. Becky was busy explaining to me that the fetus wouldn't show up on a regular ultrasound and I was busy trying to act like the whole ordeal was completely normal for me on a Tuesday at 1:15 as Becky made herself comfortable by pressing her armpit firmly over my right knee, pushing my socked heel further into the ice-cold stirrups.

I was already on the edge of a trauma induced panic attack when the knee hugger asked me to help guide the camera into my vaginal opening. "No." My internal monologue whispered again, long, and slow. I damn near died of embarrassment as I reached between my paper covered legs to help Becky do her job.

"You can let go now Mrs. Houser; I've got it from here."

Back to the business at hand and that hand was digging for gold somewhere near my left ovary.

"Mrs. Houser."

"That wasn't my fucking name," my inner monologue screamed, testier and testier.

Mrs. Houser had never been my name, never would be. But some jackass somewhere at United Health Care decided to put my husband's name behind mine and now I would forever be known as Mrs. Houser at any physician's office I went to. I tried switching it back, but they wanted proof from the state that I had changed my name back to Raymond. No, I'm not shitting you.

"Yes, Becky," All smiles I was; I swear.

"Are you sure you didn't stop to pee before coming into the office today? "

"No, Becky, I didn't stop to urinate before coming in, just like it said on the sheet."

"That's odd, things aren't looking right, but your numbers are reading o.k.."

"Becky," I clear my throat, to gather my shit, "Ma'am, I'm in here because I'm spotting at seven weeks pregnant which I am still a bit shocked you haven't noticed."

Becky just looked at me vacuously.

"Listen, Becky. If the numbers on your chart don't jive, I suggest you go grab my Dr. and let her have a go at solving this puzzle. Eight years in medical school should have her sorting this whole thing out in a jiffy, don't you think?"

Becky just stood there.

"You're making this super weird Becky. Who runs this show? Is it a dude? I bet it's a dude isn't it?"

She could fear the Neanderthal in charge, you could see it.

"Becky grab yourself a Kleenex and I'd love some of those paper towels to clean up. Then go out there and tell them all what a bitch I'm being and that I actually insist on seeing my physician on bleed-out day."

Becky awkwardly handed me a crinkled handful of thirty-grit paper towels so I could clean up and then got the hell outta there. Not that I blame her, knowing what I know now of my chart and condition, I never should have been that low on the totem pole to start with. And Becky who was about two weeks out of night school definitely should not have been anywhere near my situation, period.

The mishandling itself was a trauma. They don't tell you that, but it is. It's so clinical you feel like you're one of a gazillion petri dishes that have been stirred up by that wand, at your very own hand no less, but no worries it has a fresh condom on it. And let's not forget how low those lights were. Ambience is everything. Skeevey.

Now, down to brass tacks.

A double knock at the door, an introduction, and a clear conversation about my concerns today and we were back in vitro without my help and to top it off, the screen was turned round so that I too could see references. Things were looking up.

I lay there in the dark and there was the woosh, woosh, woosh sound, which by all accounts of years of t.v. watching meant "good" but not knowing what your eyes were seeing leaves you with only your ears to trust.

And then there it was, that specific sound of the "heart-beat." Which we now know as neurons firing, followed by quiet clicking in the dark, no words, just clicking. When the tenured clinician got up to excuse themselves from the room, I wasn't yet familiar with the half smile protocol while they cradled my bad news in their latex gloved hand, as they said, make yourself comfortable, the doctor will be with you in a minute.

Sucker punch.

You didn't tell me to put my legs down, to get dressed or give me a thirty-grit paper towel to wipe away the ultrasound lubricant. Comfortable was about the last thing I was or could be in this liminal place.

One minute later, the doctor had the in vitro tube shoved up to my tonsils as she explained I was pregnant with fraternal twins, each having their own sac. Fetus A was just where they needed to be, Fetus B was stuck in my fallopian tube and I was beginning to bleed out.

In under two hours I was prepped and ready for a surgery whose name and definition I never knew existed. My formal education for all intents and purposes was complete through a collegiate level and I didn't even know what my body was doing, or even capable of doing, when attempting to carry a pregnancy to term. A second wave of trauma came over me as tubes were placed here and I.V. lines placed there.

"Would you like to speak to clergy or have clergy present?" I was asked as the potential fatality of my condition became clearer with every opened sterile wrapper that fell to the floor, sending a very clear message, there is no time to be tidy about things. With a one-two punch I took traumas three and four like a champ.

I closed my eyes as the anesthesia began its work, my reality getting darker still as the doctor explained I may not have both fallopian tubes when I woke.

But I did wake, thank the goddess I woke. Trauma punch five hit when it was explained to me that we lost both fetuses. Upon the shock on my face, the Dr. took my hand and explained that no matter what had been done that would always have been the case where fraternal ectopic pregnancies were involved.

Well, that may have been information readily available to her, but it had never been available to me.

My only chance at a win was coming out of that room alive with the possibility of trying to conceive naturally again. And

I'll be damned if that isn't something every person with a uterus should have the right to know.

The sacred halls of medicine were built in the backwoods on the backs of women sorting out what did and didn't work for women by women and at some point it was snatched out from under them.

And so, take this as an educational reckoning if you will. If you forbid us the education you "inherited" from us, while denying choices that do not belong to you, we will remove you from the equation of the office of Senator or Governor as a whole. In case you forgot, we still have the right to vote, for now.

If that doesn't work, we will figure out how to treat ourselves again and skip the middleman. After all, necessity is the mother of invention.

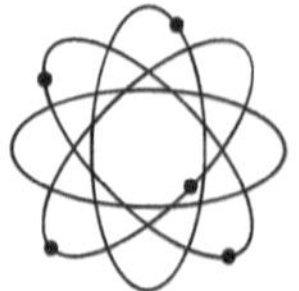

The Doctor of Bear Creek

Bruce Buchanan

Genevieve Burleson placed a final armload of firewood on the stack beside her pine-plank cabin. *There,* she thought. *That should feed the cookstove for at least two weeks.*

Satisfied, she slurped a dipper of cool water from a wooden bucket. Summers were mild in Bear Creek, North Carolina—a remote mountain community in the shadow of Mount Mitchell, the highest point east of the Rockies. But even an active 23-year-old could get hot and tired chopping wood all afternoon.

She brushed sawdust off her denim pants, washed her hands in a tin basin on the front porch, then stepped inside of the one-room cabin. *I suppose I should think about cooking something for supper before long. But first... I intend to relax a spell.* Her bookshelf entirely filled one of the cabin's four walls. From it, she selected Charlotte Brontë's *Villette,* a new release Genevieve had picked up on a recent trip to Asheville. Having enjoyed

Jane Eyre enough to reread it three times, she looked forward to diving into this tale.

But she had no sooner propped her brown brogans on the handmade porch rail and cracked the cover when she heard an awful cry from down the mountain.

"Miss Genevieve! Miss Genevieve! You must come quickly. It's Clarence—he's taken ill."

An out-of-breath Athalia Hamrick huffed her way into Genevieve's view. The Hamricks were Genevieve's closest neighbors—if a half-day trek on a curvy mountain mule path could be described as "close." Genevieve didn't get much company, and her geographic isolation had little to do with it. Her neighbors didn't trust her because they suspected she might be a witch (laughably false, although spellcraft would probably make her chores much easier), a lesbian (true, but that was no one's business but her own), and a supporter of abolition and women's suffrage (also true and non-negotiable).

But such rumors made it hard for a woman to make friends in 1853. Still, her neighbors also knew she was the most educated person in Bear Creek. Most had little, if any, formal education. However, Genevieve's Pa—rest his soul—sacrificed to pay her way to boarding school, then college. She had excelled in science, which she continued to study on her own. Plus, Athalia was one of the few people to treat Genevieve with kindness rather than suspicion. So she put her book aside.

"Slow down, Athalia!" she said, giving up her seat and offering the woman a dipper of water. "You say Clarence is sick? What's wrong with him? Be as specific as you can."

"He–he's a-burnin' with fever," Athalia wrung her hands. "He liked to never wake up this mornin', and he's so weak... I'm afeared he may die!"

Clarence was Athalia and Clyde's seven-year-old boy. A shy, sweet child—and way too young to die. "Did you fetch Mr. Smith?" Genevieve asked, secretly hoping the answer would be "No."

A miller by trade, Ananias Smith had no more medical training than any of his neighbors. But what he lacked in knowledge, he made up for in haughtiness. He had declared himself to be Bear Creek's unofficial doctor decades earlier, and his neighbors had meekly accepted him in that role for so long that the title "Doc Smith" had stuck. With everyone other than Genevieve, that is.

"Yup. Doc Smith come out yesterday, but Clarence keeps gettin' sicker... I just don't know what else to do."

That's what I was afraid of. Smith's bogus remedies are doing more harm than good-—he may even be inadvertently killing the child!

"Come on, mother. Beulah will take you down the mountain," she said, fetching her trusted mule's saddle. "I'll hold the reins and walk alongside."

"You mean... you're comin' to help?" Athalia asked.

"I'm coming," Genevieve said, taking the woman's trembling hand. "Lord willing, I'll be able to help."

The trip down the mountain went much more quickly than Athalia's trip up, particularly with Beulah's aid. The Hamricks lived in a simple cabin similar to Genevieve's. A dirt path took them to the back of the house, and Athalia's husband Clyde ran out to meet them. Athalia gasped, "Oh, Lord—Clarence! Is he…?"

"No, he's holdin' on, but barely," Clyde said.

Genevieve ran into the cabin, where she found the boy, pale and barely conscious, on a straw-stuffed cot. Perspiration matted Clarence Hamrick's dark hair to his face, and even now, he was still sweating. When Genevieve approached his bedside, she noticed red splotches on the child's neck.

She pulled the thin patchwork quilt off his shoulders. Sure enough, she found a fragment of burlap rag wrapped around Clarence's elbow as a makeshift bandage. An alarming amount of blood stained the cloth dark red.

Bloodletting—that fool Smith and his superstitions! One more bloodletting may kill the child.

"Clarence?" she said, gently waking the boy. "Clarence, I'm going to need you to open your mouth. Can you do that?"

The boy didn't open his eyes, but he complied. Just as Genevieve expected, the child's tongue was red, swollen, and covered with tiny white bumps—almost like a strawberry. She held a lit candle near the child's face and saw his tonsils were similarly infected.

"Miss Genevieve?" Clarence said in a scratchy, barely audible voice. "I… I'm so scared…."

"Well, that's why I'm here—to help you get better!" Genevieve filled a tin cup with water. "Here, drink this—all of it. But not too fast."

She wet a clean cloth and put it across the boy's febrile forehead. *Poor child. He's so dehydrated his mouth is dry as sand. I'm sure Smith told them to deny the boy water to drive out the "humors" causing his fever. The fool!*

"Leave the front and back doors open, please," she instructed the parents. "Keep the shutters open, too."

Athalia did as Genevieve asked, but said, "How will that help my boy?"

"It won't—but the cross-ventilation will help keep the rest of us hale while he recovers." Genevieve washed her hands with a cake of lye soap. "Also, be sure to clean your hands thoroughly and often, especially after touching Clarence or his bedding."

The boy's father stared blankly. "Open the shutters? Wash my... I don't understand."

"Germ theory, Mr. Hamrick," Genevieve explained. "The brightest minds in science and medicine now accept it as the truth. Your son has scarlet fever—an infection caused by germs, a name for microscopic organisms far too small to be seen with the naked eye."

She pulled a clean handkerchief from her front pants pocket and dried her hands. "One day, we will have medicines to treat such infections, but for now, he needs lots of rest and plenty of water. Oh, and fix him soft foods—gruel, broth, creamed potatoes, that sort of thing. He won't wish to eat because his throat is raw, but he needs nourishment to keep up his strength."

"Germs? But Doc Smith said the humors was what was ailin' him!" Athalia exclaimed. For centuries, Westerners commonly believed that four basic "humors"—blood, yellow bile, black bile, and phlegm—controlled the body's health. People became sick because one of these humors had become unbalanced, according to this theory.

Genevieve sighed. "Many people share those inaccurate and unscientific beliefs. But it doesn't make them any truer. 'Unbalanced humors' have long been debunked as a cause of illness. And many of the treatments to balance these so-called 'humors'—such as draining blood from the patient, starving them, or forcing them to regurgitate their food—" she waved to the prone boy. "—actually make the patient weaker. I'm afraid that is what has happened to Clarence."

The Hamricks looked at each other, apparently not knowing what to think. At least they were trying to take in her words. She smiled as she grabbed each by the forearm and said, "But your boy is young and healthy. And God willing, he should recover—as long as Smith doesn't try to kill him again."

Clyde put his arm around his wife's shoulder, and she leaned into his chest. Genevieve didn't need to be a witch to know her words "He should recover" had been a tonic to these terrified parents.

"Oh, and if he can't sleep, give him a spoon of corn liquor mixed with honey," Genevieve said, "I normally wouldn't recommend giving whisky to children, but a small dose will help him rest."

"But we don't have any corn—" Athalia noticed her husband trying to hide his grin, "Clyde! You sneaky devil!"

Genevieve had just delivered her instructions when they all heard the clomping of a second mule's hooves on the dirt trail behind the house.

Ananias Smith was a dour little man with a balding head, gray beard, and stern blue eyes. When those eyes spotted Genevieve standing in the cabin, his frown drooped even lower than usual.

"Miss Burleson," he sniffed. "I did not expect you to be here." He carried a small wooden box into the cabin and set it on the family's table.

"And I did expect you, Mr. Smith," Genevieve replied. "I came here in part to appeal to your sense of reason."

"What are you talking about, woman?" Smith opened the box and produced the tools of a gruesome trade: a scarificator, a small brass instrument containing multiple blades; a glass cup; and a syringe. A Nineteenth Century doctor used the scarificator to cut open blood vessels, usually in the patient's arm. The syringe then would draw blood from the patient's body into the cup.

"Please, Mr. Smith—I have information you must hear first. Just hear me out." Genevieve placed herself between the bedridden boy and his potential executioner.

But Smith continued to prepare his tools, not even looking in her direction. "No. Now step aside and let me attend to the boy," he said.

"I will not!" Genevieve declared. "Not until we discuss this case and how your bloodletting is doing more harm than care."

"Miss Genevieve says that germs, not humors, are to blame for our boy's ailment," Athalia explained.

"Nonsense!" the short, stocky man sputtered. "Bloodletting is the only remedy for fevers. I would not expect... one such as you to understand such things. But you?" He pointed a stubby finger at Athalia and Clyde. "You are a Godly family! Don't tell me you are entertaining her evil and unholy ideas?"

Genevieve shook her head and took a breath before speaking. Logic, not anger, was her only path forward. She also knew convincing Smith was a lost cause; although she continued to address him, she intended her message for the others in the room.

"Mr. Smith, where does Scripture describe science and reason as 'evil,' to use your term?" Genevieve said. "I can point you to a stack of scientific literature supporting my position that germs, not 'an imbalance of humors,' caused this child's illness. Can you prove that your methods work?"

She knew he couldn't, and he just glared at her, his face reddening by the second. But before Smith could launch another baseless attack, she turned to the Hamricks. "But you are the boy's parents, and the decision on how to proceed must be yours. I can only plead with you to listen to your minds as well as your hearts."

Athalia and Clyde said nothing but looked in each other's eyes again. After a minute, she whispered something and he gave a quick nod.

"Mr. Smith, we appreciate you a-comin' up here. We really do," Athalia said. "And we appreciate you tryin' to help our young'un. But...we're gonna try things Miss Genevieve's way."

Smith slammed the lid on his wooden case, his face now nearly purple. "You side with this sinful, sapphic woman over me? Very well. You and your child deserve whatever ills befall you!"

Genevieve folded her arms, glaring down at Smith. "That is the difference between you and me, Mr. Smith. I couldn't care a whit about being right. My sole concern is with this child's recovery."

Athalia and Clyde Hamrick stepped up to stand at Genevieve's side, and with finality, she said, "I think the Hamrick family would appreciate you leaving." With a "Humph!", Smith did just that. Genevieve, who had been holding her breath, waited until he was outside the cabin to exhale.

Clarence's fever broke the next day and within three days, he felt well enough to eat normal meals again. By the following week, he was up and playing with his siblings. So nine days after her initial visit, Athalia returned up the mountain to Genevieve's cabin, this time to deliver a homemade apple tart—along with her eternal gratitude.

"That is too kind of you, Athalia—and far more than I could eat by myself," Genevieve said. "But I have an extra plate if you would join me...."

The two women spent the next two hours telling stories, eating apple tart, and sharing laughter. When it was time for Athalia to go, she said, "Thank you again, and please don't be a stranger, Miss Genevieve... or maybe I should call you Doctor Burleson!"

Genevieve settled into her front porch rocking chair and picked up *Villette*. But her mind kept returning to Athalia's parting words. She knew she had many long nights of additional study ahead of her, but she couldn't wait to get started.

Doctor Genevieve Burleson. Yes, I think I could like that.

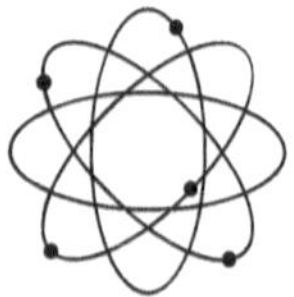

Your Last Shot

Melissa R. Mendelson

Rain pounded against the window, smashed into the door, but it wasn't just the rain. It was them. They had found me out, and my fear flashed in me like lightning across the sky. Their chaos thundered in my ears. The needle almost failed to find its vein.

They kicked in the door, obliterating most of it, and splinters flew toward me like little spears. The glass needle slipped through my fingers and shattered against the floor. They stormed past the debris and seized me with wet, cold hands. I struggled but it was useless. They dragged me from my chair and hurled me outside, their stares burning into me like the serum now running through my veins.

"No! Don't burn them," I screamed but some people kicked me in the side and in the legs, knocking the wind out of me.

"Burn! Burn! Burn," they chanted.

All the books, all those texts that I managed to save, they threw into a pile on the ground like it was nothing but garbage. They set it all ablaze, all those pages that could never be rewritten, and they cheered like they had won some big victory. They had no idea what they just did.

I felt sick from the injection and soon slipped into unconsciousness. They probably hoped that I was dead. I was not. Instead, I was put on trial shortly after.

Those like me had been executed. Some had even been put to death for a lesser offense. I was spared, which surprised me, but I was condemned to life imprisonment. I was placed in solitary confinement, a small cell with cold, brick walls and a few rats as company. They didn't care if I talked to the rats, and my one guard ignored any mention of Science.

I don't know how much time passed. I don't know what became of my family or my friends, or friends I thought had. I don't know anything but this lone guard. He sat still, solid in his chair, facing me, no emotion except for the hate in his eyes.

One day, the guard walked to his chair. His gait was shaky, his skin pale. He coughed. It wasn't the kind of cough to clear your throat. It was the kind that was chased by sandpaper in your lungs. He coughed again.

I moved closer to the bars, watching him. He couldn't sit rigid like he did before. His eyes flickered, so many emotions, but the hate was still there.

"Are you sick?" I asked.

The guard approached the cell and gestured for me to come closer. He coughed in my face.

"Now, you can die like the rest of us." He smiled and took his place on the chair, facing me, but he shuddered almost as if death had laid a hand on his shoulder.

"Die like the rest of us," I repeated, wiping the spit from my face. "Another virus?"

He didn't answer me.

"If only you people believed in Science, then maybe, maybe there would have been a vaccine."

"Hogwash." The guard tried to summon up more hate but he didn't even have the strength anymore. He smacked at his shoulder, but that would not chase death away. "There's no such thing as Science." He spat on the floor beside the chair. "Science." His sickly pale skin stretched into a grin. "You'll be feeling it too. Real soon."

"There could have been a vaccine, if you didn't destroy the texts, the books, especially the ones that I had. That was your last shot."

No answer.

"At least, I'll live," I said.

"Bullshit." His laughter was like two sticks being rubbed together, but there was no fire left inside him. "Takes two weeks to kill you. I hope I live long enough to see you dead."

"We'll see. You're in what? Week one?"

He didn't answer me, closing his eyes, and he never closed his eyes. He was close to his end, and death was ready for him.

A few days passed, I think. I gave up trying to tell time. There were no windows in my cell, no way to tell day from night, just a dim light over my cot and over the guard's chair, and he staggered to his chair. He had his key chain out in the open, which he had never done before. He looked at me. His fear soaked into his gaze.

"You're not sick." He wobbled on his feet. "Why are you not sick?"

"Because I administered the cure right before I was caught," I answered.

"Bullshit." He doubled over, caught in a painful coughing spasm. "Lies," and blood-tinged phlegm flew across the floor. "There's no cure," he growled. "They wouldn't have stopped you if there was."

"The people that came for me never asked. They just ignored the broken syringe on the ground. What do you think was in there?"

The guard shook his head. "You couldn't have known that this was coming. There was no way to predict this."

"I knew from the reoccurring viruses that a bigger one was coming. I was right."

"Oh, you're proud of yourself, ain't you? Well, I got a surprise for you."

I looked for the gun, but there was none.

"I have a knife in my pocket, but I won't waste that on you." He dangled his key chain at me. "I got something better than that."

"What?" I asked.

He waved one small, silver key at me. "Your freedom."

I held my hand out for the key.

Grinning that sickly grin, he popped the key off the key chain and into his mouth. He swallowed the key. "Now, you might not be sick." He gagged, then coughed. "But you can die a slow, painful death anyway. Solitude and Starvation."

He fell to his knees, all his strength gone, wasted to get one more good kick in, or so he thought. He laughed horridly once more as he laid down on the floor. After one last ugly rasp, there was nothing. But his eyes still looked at me.

I reached for him, my fingers just brushing his foot. He was once a large, solid man, now reduced to half his size, but it would still take a lot to drag him over to the cell. I tried again, but my shoulder cracked. Ah, crap!

I fell back and rubbed my shoulder. Pain seared across my arm, but no broken bone was felt. Just a badly pulled muscle, and I would be feeling that for quite some time.

I looked over at the body. It would take time, maybe a long time, but I would pull that shell of a human being over to me, cut him open with his knife, and find the key. Then, I would be free.

"The best-laid plans of mice and men...and Henry Bemis." I lay down on my cot and rubbed my shoulder, flinching at the pain. "The small man in the glasses who wanted nothing but time. It might not have been a nuclear bomb that ended this world, Henry, just a viral one."

-600-

Technology

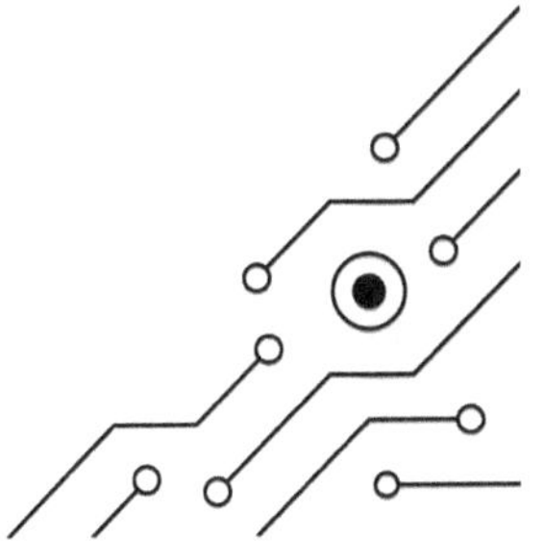

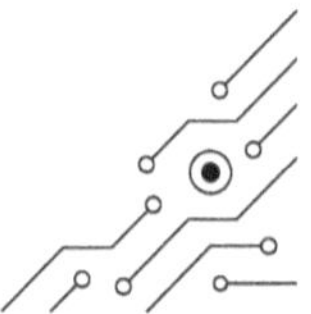

Age of the Vocaprompter – Year 5012

Demi Michelle Schwartz

Content Warning: Death of a Parent and Censorship via Electrocution

I pull my fleece blanket over my head before clicking on my flashlight. The golden beam dances over the worn cover of the stolen book: *Age of the Vocaprompter: The Most Innovative Technological Advancement in American History.*

I strain my ears. No creaks. No footsteps. Only the low hum of the air conditioner.

I set the flashlight beside me, aiming its beam toward Mom's copy of the only book that exists in the United States. After wiping my clammy palms on my pajama pants, I flip through the book to reach the folder tucked between two yellowing pages toward the middle. As the chapters flash by, I get snippets of the horrendous truth I've read multiple times now—the fires set to books across the country centuries ago, the banning of all writing utensils, and of course, the invention of the speech serum and Bluetooth technology that controls all verbal communication. I grit my teeth. The Vocaprompter isn't innovative. It's despicable.

And it killed Dad.

My chest squeezes. Tears prick my eyes. No, I will not fall apart now. Alexa turns six tomorrow, and I refuse to let my little sister be injected with the poison that has tainted my blood for over seven years.

I open the folder and sift through the classified documents Mom keeps hidden, since she's the Secretary of Communication. When I reach the one called, *Bluetooth System Self-Destruct Procedure*, I scan the paper for the thirteen-digit sequence that has haunted me for days.

6, 1, 8, 5, 5, 1, 9, 1, 6, 5, 5, 3?

I chew the inside of my cheek, staring at the question mark.

CREAK!

I jump, making the documents crinkle.

CREAK!

Someone is definitely outside my bedroom door. I've learned to step over the groaning wooden floorboard while stealing the book and returning it to Mom's closet shelf every night for the past four months.

Hardly daring to breathe, I click off the flashlight before returning the folder to its proper place and closing the book with a soft thud. After slipping the leather-bound abomination under my pillow, I crawl out of bed and stand barefoot on my plush carpet. Silvery light filters through the window from the full moon. I take a cleansing breath, catching a whiff of the vanilla-scented candle I lit earlier in the evening.

Reflexively, I grab my Vocaprompter from my nightstand, somehow resisting the urge to smash it against the wall. Breaking the cursed tablet didn't work in my favor the first time. I only got a new one paired to the liquid transmitter the speech serum carries through my veins.

I cross to the door and crack it open. Faint sobs break the silence.

Alexa.

My throat constricts. Alexa is too young to be living such a nightmare. If I had lost Dad at five years old, I don't know what I would have done. Thirteen isn't much better, but at least I'm old enough to fight back. I've always loathed the Vocaprompter, but Dad's death by the hands of the government's wicked invention was the last straw for me. I'm either going to put a stop to the damaging censorship in my country or sacrifice myself trying.

I step into the shadows and follow the sound of Alexa's cries to the living room. The lamp casts a glow over my sister. She's curled up on the black-suede couch beside the stone fireplace, clutching Dad's urn to her chest. Her aqua eyes are puffy, strands of caramel hair clinging to her wet cheeks.

My knees weaken, and I grip the doorframe with my free hand. For four months now, Dad has been nothing more than ashes in an ornamental box. Through watering eyes, I glance at my tablet, where words flash onto the rectangular screen.

"Alexa, it's okay," I read aloud as I approach her. The words being put into my mouth are a lie. Nothing will be okay until I destroy the Bluetooth system and restore intellectual freedom to this messed-up nation.

My sister sobs harder, tears splashing onto the urn. I sit beside her and wrap an arm around her tiny shoulders.

"I miss Daddy," Alexa gasps through cries that twist a knife in my stomach.

"So do I," I read, my voice wobbling.

"I'm scared," she whimpers.

I swallow hard, tightening my grip on my tablet. "Why?"

"I don't want to get a Vocaprompter tomorrow," she says, sniffling. "I don't want to say the wrong thing and die like Daddy."

The pain in my chest becomes so great, I won't be surprised if my heart ceases to beat the speech serum through my bloodstream. If I don't act tonight, Alexa will lose control of her voice.

"You're not going to die," I say, ignoring the stream of fake reassurance on my tablet. "And you're not going to get a Vocaprompter, either."

An electrical surge zaps through my veins. I double over, panting. My pulse skidders.

"Lotus!" Alexa grabs my arm and shakes. "Lotus!"

The agony subsides. I blink black spots from my vision and look at my tablet.

10 zaps remaining.

I gulp. Using up ninety of my one-hundred zaps in only seven years must have me on some kind of watch list. Ten more, and I'll end up just like Dad and thousands of others.

The most recent rebellion occurred last autumn. Protestors gathered in the streets and shouted their hate for the Vocaprompter, until night fell, and bodies littered the ground—teachers, small business owners, construction workers, citizens of all different ethnicities, religions, races, and genders. The politicians and their wealthy supporters collected the bodies like they were trash and moved on with their lives as though nothing had happened.

I shudder. This oppression has to stop.

And it's stopping tonight.

"I love you, Alexa," I whisper. "Whatever happens, never forget that."

The second zap strikes. Alexa cries something, but I can't make out her words through the searing pain. I put my head between my knees, drawing in shallow breaths. My sister can't experience this, ever.

I stand on quivering legs, not bothering to read my tablet. I know full well I only have nine zaps left.

I hurry into the hall. Footsteps thump after me, and I spin around to find Alexa, her face shrouded in shadows.

I can't afford another shock. Keeping my jaw clamped shut, I take Alexa's sweaty hand and lead her to her room.

"Lotus, what are you going to do?" she asks in a small voice.

I only shake my head and hug her. The scent of her cherry shampoo tickles my nose. I squeeze her small form, wishing I could stay.

But I can't.

I have to go.

After releasing my sister, I nudge her gently. An anguished cry rips from her throat, but she doesn't fight my nonverbal plea for her to go back to sleep.

I rush to change into sweatpants and a short-sleeved shirt before retrieving the book from under my pillow. As quietly as possible, I tiptoe into Mom's room and take soundless steps to her closet, returning the book to the top shelf. I fight the urge to look at Mom lying in bed as I move to the nightstand. My stomach drops. If I don't survive my mission, Mom will have to bear the weight of another loss.

Before I can psych myself out, I grab Mom's key to the Pool lying beside a glass of water and slip it into my pocket. For the first time, I'm grateful Mom works for the worst government department. Breaking into the building will be easy. After tonight, maybe the United States will revert back to a time when books were part of life, and Americans could speak their minds without getting electrocuted.

I love you, Mom, I mouth. Then I run from the room, slide on flip flops, and leave the house.

Almost two thousand years ago, Loquiton replaced Washington D.C. as the capitol—or so I've read in the book. The moon offers enough light to see by as I follow sidewalks lining paved streets into the heart of the city. The warm July breeze tangles in my light-brown curls, but shivers trace down my spine. As residential homes blend into steel government buildings, I toss the self-destruct sequence through my mind for what feels like the millionth time.

6, 1, 8, 5, 5, 1, 9, 1, 6, 5, 5, 3?

Maybe the numbers stand for a word and figuring it out will reveal what the question mark represents.

Cars zoom by, but luckily, no one stops to see what a kid is doing wandering the city at this hour. Skyscrapers stretch into the darkness above, the velvety-black night sprinkled with stars. My throat swells. Dad is watching over me now, and all the others who died for simply yearning to embrace the free speech promised to Americans once upon a time.

6, 1, 8, 5, 5, 1, 9, 1, 6, 5, 5, 3?

The two sets of fives nag at my brain. What if they stand for a letter? I pause at a crosswalk and gnaw on my bottom lip. The fifth letter of the alphabet is E.

My nose burns from the speeding cars' exhaust and sewage wafting from the metal grate beneath my feet. When the coast is clear, I bolt across the street and weave my way to the domed building with the Pool, the moonlight bouncing off circular windows. Unlike the towering structures clustered together in downtown Loquiton, the one housing the Pool is only two stories tall. Somehow, that makes it more sinister.

I gulp as I run through the sequence again. If 5 is E, 6 might be F, but if 1 is A and 8 is H, that doesn't make sense. F, A, H, E, E can't be the start of a word.

Maybe I should turn back. If I can't crack the code, what's the point? I banish the idea from my mind. I'm out of time. Alexa is out of time. I must do this tonight.

I sigh as I approach the building, my flip flops slapping on the concrete. My heartbeat accelerates. I scan the area, but I'm alone. It makes sense there are no security guards nearby, since the only people who have access to this place are those who work for the Department of Communication, like Mom.

"Here goes nothing," I mutter under my breath as I approach the steel door.

A fierce zap sparks through me. Gasping, I trip on a crack in the sidewalk. I fling my hands out to break my fall, sending my Vocaprompter flying. My breaths come sharp and fast. I roll onto my side, wincing from the scrapes on my palms.

Once the fresh wave of agony passes, I glare at my Vocaprompter. That wasn't the first time I had spoken without thinking.

Groaning, I scramble to my feet and pick up the tablet. I turn it upside down, so I don't have to stare at the warning. Yeah, yeah, only eight zaps left before my heart stops. I don't need the stupid device to tell me so. If my plan works, I'll no longer be punished for speaking freely.

My teeth chatter as I climb the concrete steps to the steel door and pull Mom's key from my pocket. Hand trembling, I slide the key into the gleaming lock and turn. The click makes me jump. Planning my mission for months was one thing, but I'm so close now, I can taste the sweet freedom on my tongue. Still, I can't believe I'm about to break into a government building, dive into a pool of poison, and try to destroy the system that has been censoring communication for centuries.

The door screeches as I push it open, and the hair on my arms stands on end. Once I cross the threshold and let the door snap shut behind me, I'm plunged into total darkness. I lean against the door, the steel cool through my thin shirt.

While I wait for my pulse to slow, I return my focus to the sequence. If the numbers stand for letters, they have to count to twenty-six.

My breath catches. Maybe the 1 and 8 should be combined for 18. If so, the letter is R.

F, R, E, E.

"Free," I gasp.

My fourth shock of the night sends me sagging against the door. Electricity attacks my nerves. Sweat drips down my neck. At this rate, I'm going to zap myself to death.

As fast as possible, I pair letters with the rest of the sequence and come up with S, P, E, E, C.

My fingers shake around my tablet as the final letter falls into place.

H.

I bite my tongue to resist blurting out the sequence is code for free speech.

The question mark should be the number 8, since H is the eighth letter of the alphabet.

I push away from the door, adrenaline coursing through me. I've finally figured out the missing number. Not a single sleepless night I had spent staring at the sequence was wasted.

I smile to myself. The path ahead is clear now—enter the code and bring down the system for good.

After returning Mom's key to my pocket, I feel my way along the wall with my free hand. Instead of finding a light switch, my fingers brush a metal banister. My stomach swoops when I take another step and meet a flight of stairs.

Really? Stairs? Everyone knows climbing steps in the dark never ends well, but let's see... I read an off-limits book and classified documents for months, stole Mom's key, and snuck into a government building in the dead of night. What's one more risky venture to add to the list?

Heart pounding, I ascend the stairs. My footsteps echo around the hollow space. When I reach a landing, I pause, the darkness pressing into me.

I take tentative steps forward with my hand outstretched and come in contact with two circular holes in what appears to be another steel door.

A retina scan.

My mouth grows dry. I step to the door and position my eyes in front of the scanner, staring into tiny red lights. Mechanical scrapes break the silence, and I shiver.

"Lotus Quinn," a robotic female voice says as the lights flash green.

I remove my face from the scanner. Before I can decide what to do next, the door slides to the side.

For a moment, I only stand there, gaping. The Pool emits light-green light from bulbs dotting the bottom, illuminating the lumpy, slime-like serum filling it to the brim. It appears to be about fifty feet in diameter and at least ten feet deep. Though I can't see it from here, I know the number pad for the Bluetooth system is in the exact center, where a drain would be in a normal pool.

My nose stings from the pungent, acidic odor drifting from the poison. Windows are spaced out along the curved wall of the chamber. Off to the right, a rack displays a row of hazmat suits made from red rubber. Of course, the high concentration of the serum would definitely burn away flesh. My stomach grows queasy. I'll have to wear one of those suits.

The steel door starts to glide shut. My muscles tense as I rush into the chamber just in time to get sealed inside.

"Welcome, intruder," a computerized male voice booms, making me yelp. "Death mist activated."

"Death mist!" I cry. "What?"

The electric surge brings me to my knees on the tile floor. I really have to stop blurting things out without thinking first, but death mist? My body shakes. Not a single one of Mom's documents mentioned death mist.

A sickeningly-sweet scent fills my nose. Eyes wide, I scan the shadowy chamber, lit only by the bulbs in the Pool. The vapor must be colorless. I swallow hard, my tongue practically turning to sandpaper.

I set my Vocaprompter on the ground before shoving myself to my feet. As I run toward the hazmat suits, I glare at the Pool. So much for only having to protect myself from liquid poison. Now, I have to deal with an airborne one, too.

The sweet mist thickens. A headache builds between my eyes. Holding my breath would be pointless now that the fatal gas has already flooded my respiratory system. Reaching the rack, I kick off my flip flops and grab the smallest suit I can find, though it's still two sizes too big for me.

Hands quivering, I step into the suit's boots and pull the rest over my clothes. I stick my arms through the sleeves and wiggle my fingers into the gloves, the rubber clinging to my sweaty skin. My vision becomes fuzzier by the second. Looking at the pad on the bottom of the Pool through the disgusting serum will be hard enough without the death mist affecting my sight, too.

Coughing, I tug the suit's hood over my head and position the mask over my face. Even though the suit has its own built-in oxygen source, I know full well I'm about to trap the death mist inside with me.

My head feels as though it's inflating like a balloon as I zip the suit shut. I take a step and stumble. Clenching my teeth, I fight to regain my balance, but my feet slide around in the boots as I inch toward the Pool's edge.

This is for you, Alexa, I think before diving into the serum.

My body hits the poison with a splash. I kick my feet, swimming toward the lights below. I inhale through my nose and wheeze from the sugary vapor circulating through the suit.

A ring of bulbs comes closer. I peer through the greenish glow and barely make out a gray square inside the bright circle.

The number pad.

I swim faster, my strokes sluggish from the oversized suit, the lumpy serum, and my fading consciousness.

My heart skips. I can't die. Not yet. Not until I destroy the system.

I reach the bottom and float a few inches above the pad. After adjusting my left hand in the glove, I push the green button on the top of the pad to turn it on.

"Enter the desired sequence now," a mechanical voice prompts.

My mind has grown hazy, but I remember the sequence and its secret code.

Free speech.

No more censorship. No more zaps.

I punch the number 6, followed by 1, 8, 5, 5, 1, 9, 1, 6...

I convulse. The green haze before my eyes dims.

No, I will not die. Not yet.

My lungs seize. Squinting through the murky veil draping my eyes, I press 5, 5, 3.

One more number. Just one more.

With my heart pounding out of control, I jab my finger into the last number.

8.

"Self-destruct activation request," the voice says. "Press 1 to proceed or 2 to cancel."

My eyelids flutter. Every breath is a dagger to my ribs. With the energy I have left, I stab my finger into the number 1.

"Self-destruction in 60, 59, 58..."

I gasp. No... I need more time...

"57, 56, 55..."

I should've expected this. My throat swells closed as I place my boots on the bottom of the Pool.

"54, 53, 52…"

I kick off the bottom as hard as my weak muscles allow and propel myself toward the surface. The translucent, vomit-colored serum sloshing around me churns my stomach.

"51, 50…"

My ragged breaths fill my ears. My arms and legs feel as though they have turned to rubber, but I swim, and swim, and swim…

"49, 48, 47, 46, 45…"

Swimming through the speech serum is like forcing my way through chocolate syrup. My muscles strain. I have to escape before the whole chamber blows.

"44, 43, 42, 41, 40…"

I slice my arms through the poison. When my head breaks the surface, I inhale sharply, only filling my lungs with the death mist in the suit once more.

"39, 38, 37, 36, 35…"

The countdown blares from all directions. Tremors seize my body, but I manage to grip the Pool's edge and haul myself out.

"34, 33, 32, 31, 30…"

I grip the suit's zipper and yank it down. Tugging and twisting, I free myself. As soon as I inhale the chamber's noxious air, I gag. I can't die here. Mom and Alexa can't wake up to another family member gone. That won't happen. I won't let it. Mom needs me. My little sister needs me.

"29, 28, 27, 26, 25…"

When my blurry gaze lands on the door, my weak heart falters. Somehow, I know the intruder alert has locked me in here.

"24, 23, 22, 21, 20..."

I stagger to my feet and dart toward the nearest window. My bare feet thunder on the tiles. The room sways, but I keep running.

"19, 18, 17, 16, 15..."

Reaching the window, I double over, clutching my stomach. The death mist clogs my lungs.

"14, 13, 12, 11..."

I grip the window's latch with clammy fingers and unlock it. Am I really going to jump out of a building? It's either that or get blown up. I bite my cheek so hard, I taste blood.

"10, 9, 8..."

I shove the window open. The fresh breeze blasts me in the face, and I gulp it down.

Air. Clean air.

"7, 6, 5, 4..."

Trembling all over, I climb onto the ledge and dangle my feet over the drop. Bushes line the side of the building, dusted silver from the moonlight.

It's now or never.

I can't hear the end of the countdown over the blood roaring in my ears. Squeezing my eyes shut, I throw myself off the ledge.

I scream. Wind rushes around me. My body collides with the prickly needles of a bush just as an explosion rocks the earth. I fly through the air and slam into the concrete feet away. My bones ache from the impact.

I don't know how long I lie there. Eventually, I sit up, moaning.

Fire blazes in the building, yellow-orange light illuminating the night. Smoke pours from the shattered windows. An alarm wails, no doubt waking everyone in the capitol.

After inhaling a deep breath of freedom, I push myself to my feet and run—well, hobble. The death mist and blast from the self-destruct procedure have really messed with my coordination, not to mention my throbbing bones from the blunt-force impact.

Hooded figures swarm the area. I stumble but don't fall. Even though my body feels like one, big bruise, I push forward, my bare feet hardly grazing the concrete as I race toward the shadows of the nearby skyscrapers. After surviving my dangerous mission, there's no way I'm letting the government catch me.

"I did it," I pant as I bolt farther from the flaming building and gathering guards.

It takes a moment for me to register the absence of the zap that should have knocked me to the ground. I smile weakly as the summer breeze replaces the death mist in my lungs.

I have control of my voice. Alexa will never get zapped for speaking her mind. No one's words will be censored ever again.

We're free.

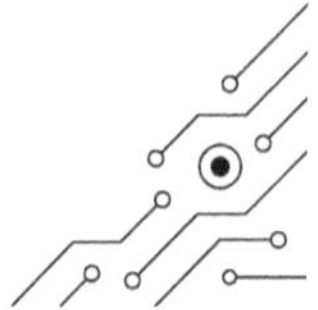

Burn

Helen Z. Dong

Maia had been smiling for so long her cheeks had begun to hurt. Still, when her assistant suggested she rest before her next engagement, she declined. She stood, face tingling, shaking hands with every climate scientist, professor, or journalist that came to greet her at the foot of the stage.

This was Maia's first year attending the Festival for the Advancement of Humanity as a speaker, not just as a bright-eyed little girl clinging to her father's jacket or an aspiring young scientist hoping to make her mark on the world.

"Congratulations, Dr. Han!"

"What a wonderful speech. You should be so proud."

She had dreamed about this day for decades. If enough people congratulated her on her work, if enough people beheld her with admiration and respect shining in their eyes, then Maia might start to believe them.

"An immense accomplishment!"

"I'm looking forward to your future work."

Outside of the festival's venue, the sun was beating down relentlessly, making the ground so hot that it sizzled at a touch. But the air inside the carbon fiber dome was chilled to a comfortable temperature. Once upon a time, people made these dome structures out of steel. These days, a steel building would quickly turn into an oven.

"Thank you." Even with the low temperatures, Maia's palm was beginning to sweat with how many hands she was shaking.

If she thanked enough people for their compliments, then all her work might actually *mean* something, and maybe...

"Dr. Han, is your device really going to save us?"

The last person in line to speak with her did not reach out to shake her hand. Her chest tightened.

"Dr. Alpin," she said. The smile fell off her lips.

For a moment, they regarded each other in silence. In the months since she'd last seen him, Dr. Alpin seemed to have become more youthful. There were laugh lines now around his mouth and the dark circles under his eyes had disappeared. She wondered if he was happier now that he had resigned from the labs, and if he could see what she had been through since.

"You've changed," he said, finally.

"So have you," the muscles in Maia's face twitched. "Time away from the lab seems to have treated you well."

Dr. Alpin's lips curved upwards. The way he looked at her, the pity in his eyes, made her skin crawl.

She felt compelled to say something. "You never even said goodbye,"

That booming confidence she'd had onstage was gone. Maia felt small, now. Bitterness reared its head for the first time in weeks.

Dr. Alpin opened his arms, as though welcoming her for a hug. Maia turned her gaze away.

"Dr. Han...Maia..." Her former mentor's voice was heavy and full of with emotions that she couldn't be bothered to identify. "I had no choice. You should know—"

"There is *always* a choice!" Startled, several people turned to look at her as they passed. Maia cleared her throat. "There is always a choice." The bitterness flowed from her throat to her tongue and out from her lips. "Just not everyone is in a position to make one."

"Maia..."

"I know you were able to make the perfect choice, Dr. Alpin," she hissed, careful to keep her voice level. "But *I* wasn't in a position to do the same."

Unlike him, Maia had a sick mother and a mountain of debt.

Dr. Alpin pressed his lips together. "I know that, Maia."

"Do you?"

Her heart pounded in her chest.

"I don't have what you have. You...you have *everything*!" Maia gestured around them, pointing at the looming walls of the giant festival dome, at the hundreds of people milling back and forth between exhibitions and speeches that all promised too much hope.

When Dr. Alpin didn't respond, Maia felt compelled to dig deeper.

She pointed towards the back of the stage, where the holographic images from her presentation still hovered. "It works!"

Dr. Alpin's eyes followed her finger. A black box with a rotating propeller hovered several feet above the ground. Above it, the words 'Airborne Carbon Energy Capture Device' glittered under artificial lighting.

"I figured it out the night before you resigned," Maia said. "I was coming to the labs to tell you, but only Cael was there, and they told me you were already gone."

There was an unreadable expression on her former mentor's face.

"It works," she exclaimed, again. In case he didn't hear her the first time.

"I have no doubt it works. You're a brilliant scientist."

Maia let her arm drop. She swallowed, but her mouth was dry.

Having joined Dr. Alpin on his research just months after graduating from her climate education program, Maia had always felt that she had a lot to prove. She had been a dreamer and she had been naive. But she had worked hard over her two years under Dr. Alpin's tutelage, she had worked her body to its limit for the hope that their work would transform countless lives.

For so long, Maia had been waiting to hear him affirm her abilities. Now, he'd finally done so.

Her head spun, but her chest still felt empty.

She wondered if he was only saying those things to placate her.

"What else happened that day, Maia?"

Maia's lips curved upwards of their own accord. Laughter threatened to bubble up from her chest. The question was so benign, as if Dr. Alpin wasn't aware that he was asking Maia to tear open old wounds.

She shouldn't laugh. But to laugh would be better than to cry.

"Are you alright?"

"Hmm?" Maia swallowed her smile and the lump in her throat. "Yes. Yes...just remembering what happened after I found out you were gone."

She had been upset. And then angry.

"You weren't there, so I told Cael about my breakthrough. We started working, just like we would on any other day. Then, I was told that Dr. Yarrow wanted to meet with me.

"But when I got to her office, it wasn't just Dr. Yarrow there. It was her, and some man I had never met before. You know who it was, don't you? Because he must have said the same damn things to you that he said to me."

She'd recognized from his name that he was the father of one of her former classmates. That classmate had had no issues landing a job after graduation—having a parent on the board of one of the best laboratories in the country came with its perks. Maia remembered every single word that man had spoken to her.

We won't move forward with the testing for your carbon capture device.

She remembered how her brows furrowed in confusion, how her heart had sunk into her stomach.

We need you to present it at the festival, tell the people what they want to hear about "progress" and the "future of humanity." But we can't use it.

Maia had asked so many questions, and all the answers he'd given had pointed towards one single, undeniable truth.

You understand, don't you, Dr. Han? This lab can only run because of our generous sponsors.

The powerful wanted the weak to have hope, but never salvation.

"You know what that man told me—" Maia took care not to let her voice shake. "—when I asked what I was supposed to do if people started picking my farce of a speech apart?

"He laughed. *Laughed.* And he said most of my audience won't be smart enough to ask questions as long as my words bring them hope."

Let me make this easier, Dr. Han. She'd watched the man tap a number into a tablet, then display it. *I'll show you a number, and you tell me what you think.*

"He must have offered you the same things he offered to me."

Dr. Alpin pressed his lips together into a thin line.

He was disappointed in her. Maia *knew* that he was disappointed. But it wasn't fair for him to be. It wasn't *fair.*

"I couldn't walk away, Dr. Alpin. What was I supposed to do? I couldn't walk away."

The amount of money offered was more than she had ever seen in her life.

"My mother is sick." She hated using her mother as an excuse, but she also *needed* Dr. Alpin to understand. "I *needed* it. I *still* need it!"

When Dr. Alpin still said nothing, she held her hands up in front of her chest, palms facing the dome ceiling, fingers grasping at the cold air. She breathed the chill into her lungs and remembered that outside, the air was so blistering hot that it could melt a person's insides. The horrifying image of her mother in the hospital after noontime heat exposure, delirious and barely alive, was plastered to the back of Maia's eyelids.

"You have everything!" She said it again because it was true. "Money, family, your reputation." A legacy. A promise of being remembered. "You could walk away because you have *everything*."

At that, Dr. Alpin drew in a deep breath. Maia prepared for him to admonish her, to lecture her, to tell her that she had crossed some invisible line. But instead, he gestured towards the steps leading off the stage.

"Shall we walk together?" His tone was even and gentle. "I noticed on the schedule that you have a demonstration soon. I wouldn't want you to miss it."

Along the dark walls of the festival dome, the date, time, and temperatures of the inside and outside were displayed in bright lettering. It was already well past noon. Her demonstration was scheduled to begin in less than ten minutes.

"Right," she mumbled, feeling empty. "My assistant must be wondering where I am."

They walked together wordlessly for a few minutes, side by side, passing by countless tables set up with holographs, physical prototypes, and tablets to monitor interest.

With the din of thousands of footsteps and endless chatter crashing like ocean waves around them, Maia could pretend that the two of them were still coworkers. Last year, she had been here to assist Dr. Alpin with his own presentation and demonstrations. Between engagements, they had walked together around the festival dome, discussing the work that was being done by other labs and other scientists, thinking about how they could apply new learnings to their own research.

So much had changed in just a year.

Dr. Alpin was the one to break their silence. "It's not your fault, you know?"

"Isn't it, though?" Guilt had been eating away at her for months. "I'm perfecting the ACEC because I want to. But it won't change a thing. Like you said, the world is on fire. It's burning. And because of me..." *It will continue to burn.*

"Not you." Dr. Alpin shook his head. "The world was already on fire when you were born."

Maia had been born into a world where the natural air was too hot to breathe and the atmosphere too thin to protect Earth's surface from going up in flames. All Maia had ever wanted was to secure a safer way of life for future generations. And she had gotten so close. She *was* so close.

But close was as far as she was allowed to get, and it would have to be enough.

"It's not your fault."

It certainly felt like it was her fault.

They walked silently towards the edge of the dome, where demonstrations were held in private rooms all day long. Entry was granted first to invited journalists, then to scientists and professors of related studies, and then finally to any laypeople who were interested. Maia remembered standing in line for demonstrations when she was younger, hoping and praying that she would be able to get inside. Most of the time, she had been denied.

Maia felt like a fraud on her way to demonstrate a device that would never see the light of day.

She cleared her throat. "How many of the prototypes being presented today are actually going to be released one day?" Even as the question left her lips, Maia wasn't sure if she wanted to hear an answer.

"I'm not sure," Dr. Alpin said. "We've all had to sign those nasty contracts, but even if we didn't... I doubt many would be willing to admit that their work is ultimately meaningless."

It was an objective statement, but Maia still hurt hearing it.

No matter how many times she went over her reasoning for staying at the lab, Maia couldn't get rid of the sinking feeling that she was doing something terribly wrong. When she looked at Dr. Alpin, all she saw was the image of what she wished she could be.

Righteous. Moral. *Good*.

That was how history would remember him.

How would it remember her?

Is it better to be remembered as a villain, or to not be remembered at all?

There was no right answer to that question.

Dr. Alpin's lips were moving, saying something, but all Maia could hear was a ringing in her ears.

If *he* had been in her position, her *exact* position, would he have made the same choice?

The heavy pit in Maia's stomach said no.

Dr. Alpin stopped walking. In front of them was a door labeled S938. Her demonstration room.

"Maia," Dr. Alpin sounded like a parent trying to calm a particularly anxious child. "You are a great scientist, and you are still a good person."

Maia frowned.

"One day, you will do good," her former mentor continued. "Maybe not today, or tomorrow, but one day."

"How?" Everything Dr. Alpin was saying sounded like empty platitudes. If there was one thing Maia had learned over the past few months, it was that there would always be someone with more authority dictating her every step.

Dr. Alpin shrugged easily. "You know, I haven't figured it out yet."

Maia scoffed.

If *he* couldn't figure it out, how was she meant to? They were all just tiny cogs in a machine working desperately to keep it from breaking down. From the outside, the broken machine must look like some tortured artist's magnum opus – something to be fascinated by, horrified by, but not something to be fixed.

"Dr. Han?" A short girl with a shrill voice hurried out from the demonstration room door, interrupting Maia's thoughts. "Oh, thank goodness! I was worried you wouldn't arrive on time."

"Come in, quickly!" Her assistant squeaked, reaching for her arm. "Everyone is already inside!"

There was no line waiting outside the door. Maia supposed the room had already been filled. Either that, or nobody was interested in her work. Which would be just as well.

Maia turned towards Dr. Alpin and tried to think of something to say, but her chest was full of feelings that she couldn't find the words to convey.

"Go," her former mentor said, smiling. Maia couldn't tell if he was feeling sorry for her. "And good luck."

Before she could respond, Maia's assistant was already ushering her through the door. Dr. Alpin stood where she'd left him until he was out of sight.

The room for her demonstration was small, crowded, and loud. Her assistant cleared a path for her to get up to the table, where her working prototype of the ACEC lay on its side. She placed her hands on its smooth surface. People quieted, watching her.

Maia looked at the gathered faces. She saw her late father in the wrinkled complexion of a middle-aged man. The images of Dr. Yarrow and the lab's executives were superimposed on the bodies of professors and journalists. And at the very front of the crowd, a young girl peered up at her with wide, bright eyes.

Seeing her, Maia felt her throat close up.

"Dr. Han?" Her assistant called to her from a few feet away. "You can begin now."

"Right."

Maia Han wet her lips, picked up the little black device, and began.

The ACEC's propeller whirred. The crowd gasped as Maia went through the motions of showing how the tiny device could take in excess greenhouse gas from the air and convert it into fuel. But outside the room and the carefully constructed walls of the festival dome, the world continued to burn.

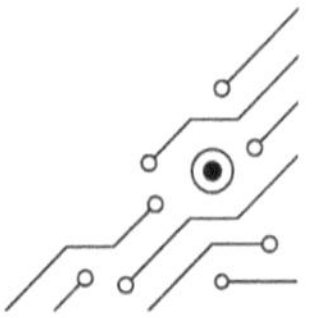

(De)generative Chats

Katie Mahood

A civilization — developing tools.

Evolving, creating societal rules.

Breakthrough achievements in science and math.

Advancing our industries, shaping our path.

Easier transport and cures for disease.

Emergence of limitless ICTs

Infinite answers, 'intelligent' chat.

A sentence from this source, a fragment from that.

Facts with a dash of political seasoning.

Data that's inbred with circular reasoning.

Nuggets of knowledge unearthed without light.

Silent canaries are brushed out-of-sight.

Our primary resource for (mis)information.

Are we on the brink of de-civilization.

-700-

Arts

A Sonnet of Stone-Cold Stupidity

D.S. Lerew

'Twas Michal who first turned contempt-filled eyes
On David dancing unabashéd there
As he raised joyful hands up to the skies
Half-naked in his ephod underwear.
But Michelangelo went further still;
From chiseled marble, he showcased the man
In naked glory, and 'twas fine until
Self-righteous, triggered prudes imposed a ban.
And now, a hedge in old St. Augustine
Conceals a statue that for centuries
Has been admired and never thought obscene.
Yet now, this David is called porn—oh, please!
If Michelangelo'd foreseen this shit,
Would he've still carved, or said, "To hell with it"?

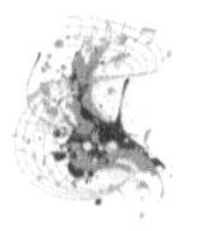

Banished Books Centre Stage

Jacque Vickers

Searing untarnished pages betwixt a theatre stage
At a quaint street library for all to engage,
On tiny shelves, books in their original form furled
In an arising emergence around the world
Banished books, symbolism, stealth
Pinnacles restoring emotional health
Humanity in all its forms, a representation,
All book genres respected, no condemnation
Unblemished pages on the street
Nourishment, a soul's retreat,
Follow a time conscious white rabbit
Journey on wistful, a wondrous habit
Unfolding as the author intended
On a journey engaged, criticism is fended

Books by hand of the author retain
Exploration, for the mind to gain
Momentum in flight with a quill
Flourishing, performed instil
Untarnished pages, a light in the dark
Journeying, enlighten a spark.

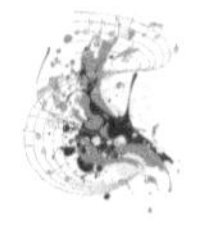

Art Saved My Soul & Sanity

Victoria Holland

Let me introduce myself.

I am Victoria.

I am neurodiverse, plus-sized, female, queer, mentally ill, pagan, and I have a career in the arts. I have to introduce myself like this to you because I need you to understand my experience is not, and has never been, "normal." My entire life has been a process of defining and redefining myself because the system in which I grew up could not properly meet my needs. I was a believer in magic, raised Catholic. I was neurodiverse living in a neurotypical environment. I was queer with expectations of heteronormativity upon my shoulders. I was queer with expectations of heteronormativity upon my shoulders.

I grew up in a world where other people reminded me in one way or another I do not belong. You know what helped me understand myself, instead?

Art.

Books helped define my morality and gave me purpose. Television gave me empathy and an expanded love of storytelling. Music gave my soul language and connection. Theater gave me community. Photography gave me freedom. Gaming gave me adventure. Film gave me critical thinking. Visual art gave me expression.

I cannot be without art. It is what saved me.

People support censorship with the claim of protecting their children. Their perspective is *censorship for safety*. But the problem is whether supporters of censorship intend this or not, what they are actually supporting is *generality for safety*.

Assimilation for safety.

Oppression for safety.

There are billions of people on this planet with unlimited variations in personality, psyche, ethnicity, creed, origin, and belief systems.

That diversity is part of the beauty of art.

To supporters of censorship: There are just some things that we, as human beings, all know. Children are precious and must be protected, love is as important to us as water and oxygen, and every single person on this planet is a rich, complex individual with their own beliefs, goals, tastes, and past. YOU know that. *I* know that.

Don't you think diversity is beautiful?

We, as human beings, *create*. We create communities and rockets and gardens and skyscrapers. It is as much a part of our nature as loving and breathing and fighting. Our souls are beautiful and infinite, and they need to be able *to breathe*. Art is just *such a natural way* for us to express that awesome energy within us because sometimes mere words are not enough. Instead, we need to create heartbreaking music and soul-shaking films and whole, living, breathing worlds. The vast depth and space within each of us weaves *so much beauty.*

That is what the arts are.

They are a direct reflection of the human heart.

You will remember I said earlier that *other people* always feel the need to remind me I don't belong. However, that statement is not completely true because it was other people who created all the art that I love. It was other people that created all the art that helped me understand myself. That helped me define myself and save myself. The human heart must, and will always need to, *express*. From that magnum opus film franchise to that short poem written on a Tuesday to express one's frustration.

It all counts.

Which is why to censor the arts is to censor people. Art is imagination and expression and creation. Art is communication. Art is connection. Art inspires, educates, and expands. Art touches and changes every one of us. Art blesses us with *compassion*.

To censor the arts is to censor *my* ability to understand *you*.

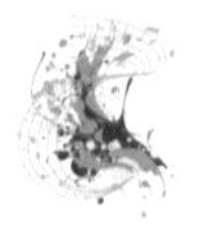

No Light Without Shadows

Shaelynn Long

In the name of love
you would
limit human understanding
gained from artistry
ensuring that only your truths
are told--
but nothing good ever comes
from a singular perspective
but those warnings, too,
will be lost to the fires
you light around these stories
that stand to protect us from our own corruption,
greed, hatred, and maleficence
scattered throughout our history.
In the name of protection
You would

Belittle the understanding

Gained from artistry

Ensuring that future generations

Will hate and fear and enslave

Others to this singular perspective

Because the warnings—

The art—

Have been lost to the fires

Lit around our stories,

That existed to mark history's truths:

the beautiful, the ugly, the mundane, the extraordinary.

In the name of love

You would

Make sure no one else ever understood it.

She Kept Her Words
Without a Pillow

Melissa R. Mendelson

Content Warning: School & home bullying (verbal)

Her arm was draped across her chest, her hand on her shoulder. Her short hair graced the back of her neck. Her dark chocolate skin danced between light and shadow. Her stare focused on the full-length mirror against the wall. Was she admiring her perfection, or was she searching for her flaws?

With this image inside my head, I wrote, "I want to kiss your back." I did not need the kids on the bus to try and grab the journal out of my hands, but I wanted to add one more line. "I want to taste your skin."

A boy nearby tried to reach over and snatch the journal, but I wrapped my arms around the journal, pressing it to my chest. I heard the bus driver yell for the boy to sit down. He did but not without giving me a dirty look first.

I put the journal inside my bookbag as the school bus screeched to a halt. The girl always got off one stop before me, even if we lived right near each other. I didn't look at her. I didn't even know her name, but I felt her eyes brush over me. I heard her say something the other day about turning fourteen. My birthday was coming up soon, and I would be the same age. I could tell her that, but not with the other kids around. They would tear me down in front of her, and I didn't want her to see that.

My stop. "You're fat," the boy barked as I got up. "You're ugly. Fugly." He laughed, and so did the other kids.

It wasn't enough for that boy, who tried to trip me but failed. "See you tomorrow." He flashed a dangerous grin.

I hurried off the bus and toward my house. Some other kids yelled something out the window, but I ignored them. The girl was up ahead walking to her house, and she glanced at me. But I looked away. I always did.

Once safely inside my bedroom, I tore the pages out from my journal. I pulled a pair of scissors out of my desk and cut up my words. I piled them on the desk and was about to sweep them into my hands when I stopped. "One more," I whispered.

"I would love to know you, the you inside, not the you searched for in the mirror," I wrote.

I pulled that page out of my journal and cut it up like the other ones. I swept the pieces into my hands, carrying them gently over to the bed. I rested them on the covers as I pulled my pillow out of its sheet and opened it. My mother thought the pillow had a lot of fluff inside of it. If only she knew. I poured my words into the pillow, quickly zippering it up.

"Dinner," my mother called from downstairs.

"Already?" I asked, but when my father worked late, my mother would make dinner early, sometimes by five like today.

I looked out the window into the girl's house, her room, but she wasn't there. Was she eating dinner early too, and why did she always leave the shade up? Did she know that I could look into her room? Did she care? Maybe she was afraid like I was, and we had every reason to fear.

I opened my door and almost tripped over my brother's foot. He laughed like those kids on the bus and pushed past me. I sighed, moving down the stairs when his words made me freeze mid-step.

"I would kiss every inch of your skin. My pale white to your dark chocolate."

"No," I gasped.

I turned, and sure enough, Patrick had a handful of my words in his narrow fingers.

"Good hiding place." Patrick smiled that ugly smile of his. "Took me some time to find it. I knew you were tearing out pages from your journal and hiding them." I wasn't even surprised. He never respected my boundaries. "Wait till Dad gets home. Maybe, he'll re-educate you." He shoved my words into his pocket. "Like he did with our aunt." He moved past me down the stairs.

"What do you want?" I didn't mean to scream at him, but I did. I had to do something. "What?"

Patrick sighed, pretending to ponder what he wanted. "Your allowance," he said.

"Done. Now, give me my words back." I held my hand out toward him.

Patrick smiled as my hand shook. "I think I'll keep them. For insurance, of course." He moved down another step.

I could have pushed him, but I remained where I was.

"Does she know?" Patrick's gaze cut through me. "Does she know that you love her?" The word, love, an ugly twist on his tongue.

"I don't," I said.

"Of course, you do. I see how you look at her." Patrick bolted down the rest of the stairs. "Freak. Just like our aunt."

My aunt was my best friend. We used to have secret conversations. She would show me little paintings that she did, hiding them in the basement so no one else would see them. I never said a word, but somebody knew. And my father took her away to be re-educated. She was never the same again.

"Dinner, Sadie. What is taking her so long?"

"Maybe, she's watching our neighbor." Patrick plopped down into a chair.

"I forgot the soda. Patrick, can you get it?"

"Sadie, get the soda."

"Patrick, I asked you," my mother said.

"I got it." I walked into the kitchen and grabbed the soda, placing it on the table.

"I own you," Patrick whispered to me.

"What was that, Patrick?"

"Nothing, Mom." Patrick grinned at my mother, and my mother knew his grins.

"Okay. What happened now?"

"Yes, Sadie. What happened now?" Patrick repeated.

I could feel the heat in my cheeks, the tears were not far behind.

My father walked into the house.

"Dad's home? I thought he was working late," I said.

"So did I, and we'll talk about this later." My mother did not look at Patrick. She looked at me.

My father sat down at the head of the table. He looked wiped out.

"Long day?" I asked.

"Yeah. A lot of re-education. Some did not go well, which is why I left early today."

"Deaths?" My mother asked.

I could tell by my father's expression that he wasn't happy that my mother had said that.

"Two wouldn't.... Conform." He looked at Patrick and me. "They just didn't want to accept how society is now, the things that you can't just do." He ate his food. "Have you heard from your sister lately?"

My mother almost choked on the piece of chicken she just put into her mouth. She covered her mouth with a napkin. She coughed and then folded the napkin up, placing it on her lap.

"I just need an update on her progress."

"No." My mother avoided my father's stare. "It's been some time, but I can call her later in the week."

"Tomorrow," my father said. "We have to make sure that she doesn't slip."

"Is it so wrong that she wanted to be an artist?" I blurted, giving my brother the perfect opportunity to out me. He didn't because he wanted my allowance. I knew my brother well just like he knew me.

"Being an artist is equal to being a writer, and we have to control their narrative," my father said. "Otherwise, there would be rebellion, protests, war."

"War?" I laughed despite my fear. "Why would a piece of art or writing create war?"

"Because it changes things, and things are perfect right now. So, no. No art. No books, and if you're going to write," My father pointed his fork at me. "You write what is acceptable. That's the way it goes, or you will be re-educated."

"Would you re-educate Sadie?" Patrick asked. He almost seemed like he felt sorry for me, but then he grinned.

My father sighed. "If she takes after her aunt." He glanced at me. "Then, yes. I must follow the law."

A long silence followed. My dad and brother went back to their meals.

"Sadie, you're barely eating."

"Neither are you, Mom. Can I be excused?"

"Something I should know?" My father laid his silverware neatly on his plate. "Sadie?"

"I had a bad day at school. Okay? The kids called me, fat. Ugly."

"Fugly." Patrick winced as Dad slapped the back of his head. "What? That's what they said. I ride the bus after her, and the kids repeat it. But they don't call me Fugly."

"Go to your room." My father did not have to say it twice.

Patrick gave me a menacing stare and stormed away.

"You may be excused." My father stared at me, but I avoided eye contact with him.

"Thank you." I hurried away from the table.

I was almost to my room when I saw Patrick standing in front of the door.

"I don't feel sorry for you," Patrick said. "Your allowance." I was right. That was why he didn't out me. "Don't forget." He dropped a piece of paper at my feet and walked away.

On the paper was one sentence that read: Will she ever know?

Later on, there was a knock at my door. I was lying on the bed and turned to see my mother walk into the room. I opened my mouth to say something, but my mother held up her hand.

"He found them, didn't he?" She closed the door behind her and locked it. "The words that you are hiding in your pillow."

"How..." I paled, glancing over at the pillow.

"I'm not an idiot, Sadie. I knew what was in your pillow."

"How... How long have you known?"

My mother smiled sadly. "At one point in time, I would have turned you in, but..."

"But?"

"I don't know my sister anymore." My mother sat down on the bed near me. "She's more like a zombie now, disconnected, unemotional. I don't want that to happen to you. So, this is what we are going to do. At midnight, you are going to meet me outside in the backyard with your pillow."

"Why?"

"Just do it, Sadie." My mother touched my face and then moved away from the bed. "If you don't, then you leave me no choice." She unlocked the door and opened it.

"Patrick has my words. At least, some of them."

"I'll get them. Your father went to a meeting. He won't be back until much later, after midnight."

I sat up in the bed. "Why wait until midnight?"

"They don't watch us at midnight. Their surveillance is focused elsewhere, so we should be safe. At least, I hope we will be, and Sadie?" My mother fixed me with a cold stare. "Stop watching her. You don't know her, and she knows, I bet she knows, that you are watching her. All she has to do is report you, and this house will be searched. Do you really want them to come here?"

"No." I shook my head, tears running down my face. "I love her," I said.

"I know, but you can't." My mother left the room.

At midnight, I dragged my pillow outside into the backyard. I expected to see a barrel burning, ready to eat my words. Instead, there was a large, gray fan, and my mother was plugging it into an outlet near the patio.

"When the fan turns on, shake out your words. All of them. Let them fly away."

"Won't anyone know that it's me?" I asked.

"Did you ever write your name on them?" My mother watched me shake my head. "Then, no, no one will ever know that you wrote it. Ready?"

I nodded, opening the pillow, and the fan turned on. I shook out my words. At first, only a few escaped. Then, they all did, filling the night sky like small, paper stars. They lifted up and were blown away, traveling where I could not follow.

"Here." My mother reached into her pocket. She had the words that Patrick had stolen, and she threw them up toward the fan.

The last of my words took flight far away from me.

"We should have burned them," I said.

"No." I looked at my mother in surprise, and she smiled at me. "We lost something of ourselves when we locked the artists and writers away. We need to get it back." She looked up at the sky. "Maybe, now, we will." She touched my face, and I smiled.

I glanced over at the house next door. She stood in the window, watching us, and fear iced over me. But then, she smiled. It wasn't that ugly grin of my brother's or the dangerous smile of that boy on the school bus. It was a beautiful smile.

"She knows," I wrote inside my head.

SKETCHES OF A BOY

EARL CARRENDER

***CONTENT WARNING: ABUSE/DISCRIMINATION OF** child for queer expression.*

The Looks of Him, 1975

Martin stood in front of the mirror and tried to remember what his grandmother told him.

"A light touch," she said. "You want it to look natural, so no one knows it's there," she smiled as she brushed and blended the foundation on his face—the lighter shades to highlight his eyes, the darker shades along the cheekbones and jawline to add shadows. When she was done, he turned and looked closely at his reflection in the mirror. Even he couldn't tell from the looks of him that he had make-up on his face.

"But you'll know," his grandmother winked at him. "Even if no one else does."

When he looked in the mirror his face shimmered, his skin glowed. He looked...

"Beautiful," his grandmother whispered.

As He Was, 1975

Martin's lips were bright red, his eyes darkened with black eyeliner, his cheeks rouged, his nails painted and polished and sparkling. His grandmother would be appalled, he thought. Too gauche, too garish, she would surely say. And—looking in the mirror—he agreed, though, truth be told, he was rather pleased with himself. Until his father barged into the room.

Shocked, Martin's father swung out and slapped the boy so hard that Martin fell to the floor.

"Get up!" he yelled, pulling Martin to his feet, and dragging him across the hall to the bathroom. "Wash it off," his father demanded, pushing Martin's head down in the sink as he turned on the faucet. "All of it! Now!"

Martin grabbed the soap blindly and began to wash his face as his father stood behind him watching. Then he grabbed a towel and dried himself off, tears and all. Any sign of his disobedience, any trace of his indiscretion, all of it wiped away. He could not risk his father seeing him as he was. With a contemptuous grunt, Martin's father left.

He looked in the mirror and promised himself that his father would never see that side of him again.

A Gift, 1976

It was Martin's best friend, Jason, who gave him his first camera—a little pocket-sized Kodak—for his thirteenth birthday. And Martin loved it; not as much as he loved drawing—he now spent hours in the treehouse he once hated, sketching on whatever was close at hand, lost in a world of his own making.

A camera did not offer the same escape; but Martin loved it because it was a gift from Jason. Martin carried it everywhere with him after that day, taking roll after roll of photographs.

"Stop!" Jason whined whenever Martin took his picture.

Changes, 1977

But things changed. The summer before the boys started high school was the summer that things just felt...different between them, or so it seemed. Martin started to notice things—the way Jason smiled, sometimes, at him and stood up for him when the other boys jeered and laughed. It meant so much to Martin—no one else defended him. And the way Jason looked in his tight blue jeans (Martin couldn't help but notice). Martin thought about Jason when he was alone in his bed and felt guilty, touching himself as he dreamed about his best friend, his only friend.

And then it happened.

Walking home, just as they stepped inside Martin's house, they hugged as Jason was leaving and Martin kissed him. For a moment, Jason clung to Martin and kissed him back (or so it seemed to Martin, but, maybe, he was wrong. Was he wrong? He wondered fleetingly); then stunned, suddenly furious, Jason punched Martin, knocking him to the floor.

"Why did you do that?" Jason asked.

"I dunno," Martin said, touching his mouth, blood—warm and metallic tasting on his lips—stained his fingers. "I'm sorry," he whimpered, as Jason loomed above him.

"You don't think I'm..." Jason seemed disgusted by the tears in Martin's eyes. "Fuck! You do, don't you?" he yelled and kicked Martin.

Martin curled over, clutching his side as Jason ran out. "No! Jason, stop!" he yelled after his best friend. "Please stop," he cried.

They never spoke again.

You Just Know, 1978

"When did you realize," his friend, Sharon, asked, "that you were...different?"

"Always, I guess," Martin said without hesitating. "I mean, I've always been..." he paused, trying to form words in proper order. "I mean...Not like other boys. Like, a boy and a girl," he cleared his throat and tried again. "I know it doesn't make sense."

Sharon looked at him, nodding. "Come here," she said and took his hand. They stood in front of her bedroom mirror. "Look," she said, nodding toward the reflection. "It makes all the sense in the world."

What's Hidden, 1979

Ybor City had its own secrets. Ybor, they say, was haunted. Always a feeling of *something* there or of being watched. Folks turned suddenly to find nothing behind them when they would have sworn that they felt or heard someone approaching.

Martin was standing on the sidewalk in Ybor and watching two men leaving El Goya together. He knew about El Goya, the gay bar. He read about it in the *Tampa Trib* when the bar caught fire just before he turned fourteen. Possibly arson. Maybe organized crime. No one talked about it.

He watched the two men as they crossed the street and walked right by him.

Were they friends? Lovers? he wondered. *Had they just met inside the bar?*

Martin drew in his breath and watched them as they walked up to the corner and waited for the trolley. One wore boots, the other wore sandals. Both were deeply tanned and sporting mustaches. One was a construction worker, judging from his clothes—a denim shirt with the sleeves rolled up, the chiseled arms, the chain hanging from his leather belt. His Marlboro cigarettes and buzz-cut hair. Blue bandana hanging loosely from the right back pocket of his faded blue jeans. The other man was some young beach bum, wearing tight cut-off shorts and a white tank top that matched his glaring white teeth. That bleached blond hair and Hawaiian Tropic sheen.

Each of them stood in a comical pose looking like the fucking Village People.

Martin almost laughed at them. It was as if they mocked the masculinity they craved; like they were making fun of those who made fun of them. Little things betrayed them, no matter the clothes they wore or how they cut their hair. The way the beach bum swished when he walked; the way the construction worker flitted his wrist when he smoked his cigarette or the way he put his hand on his hip when they stood, waiting for the trolley. The way they moved too closely to one another as they boarded and took their seat together. And yet—Martin watched as they sat beside each other just before the trolley passed—to want it, to desire that unattainable manhood. To want the thing that hurt you the most and to scorn and reject it at the same time. Martin both pitied and envied them.

Then, there was a man entering the bar that he recognized. It was Mr. Miller, his Art teacher; the one who gave him a copy of *To the Lighthouse*, and a book on Duncan Grant. Those paintings! Like nothing Martin had ever seen! The dancing, swimming, flying nudes, the details cloudy and somewhat obscured, but so blatant, and...well, sexy, that Martin blushed.

Martin stood across the street from the bar and watched, frozen, putting his hands in his pockets. What if Mr. Miller saw him? What if Mr. Miller knew he'd been seen?

Martin often saw, with muted longing, the gay men on the beach that he watched swimming or playing volleyball or simply strolling along as the waves rushed to their bare feet. He watched from across the street as men came and went from El Goya and tried to summon the courage to sneak into the bar for even a few prized seconds before being tossed out. But, just as he stood ready to cross the street, his audacity faded like one of Ybor City's legendary phantoms.

Martin stood and stared at the façade of El Goya. Mr. Miller, his beloved art teacher, was there, inside a well-known gay bar. Martin smiled and turned to run and catch the bus home.

Knowing.

Leaving Home, 1980

Martin was trying to learn about New York; the real New York he saw in the pages of the *Village Voice* that he bought at a local bookstore. Thanks to Mr. Miller, Martin got accepted at the Pratt Institute for the coming fall and he couldn't wait to get out of Florida where, after all, being Martin was a crime. Mr. Miller even managed to convince Martin's parents—almost.

"It's your decision," Martin's father said. "You're nearly a grown man now. But if you go there, you're on your own."

Martin faltered at that. But Mr. Miller insisted. "You have a way out of here, Martin," he said. "You say yes to Pratt. Say yes to New York. And don't look back."

Martin took an envelope that Mr. Miller had given him out of his jacket pocket and showed it to Sharon. She opened it and found a plane ticket inside.

"New York," Mr. Miller smiled at Martin when he gave the envelope to him. "One way."

Post Punk Wonderland, 1980

They were the New Wave. Born of Jack Smith's *Flaming Creatures* and Warhol's *The Kiss*.

They didn't just rise from the ashes after the city burned in '77, they danced in the blaze. They ripped it up. They did their thing. They threw their names up on the walls:

"It's not the SAMO anymore."

They turned on the cameras and let the beat drop right there on the street.

There was Donna sittin' outside the door, Erika doing her hair tied up in a black nylon knot while that blond boy she was always dancing with flirted with some Puerto Rican kid, his press-on nail flashing glittered gold. John Sex was playing

Peter Pan on the second floor at Danceteria, his Lady Liberty hair piled high, the crowd screaming for more...more...more.

Everybody was doing something. Everybody was doing everything. Everybody was somebody on the dance floor.

"Paradise Garage opened the winter after the blackout," Erika said. "Thank God."

"I missed it," Donna reminded Erika.

"Missed what?"

"The blackout," Donna told her.

"I was working the coat check at the Top of the World when it happened," Erika said, "The lights went out about eight o'clock, we lit candles and the champagne flowed. It was a good night," she said, and waved the Gucci watch she still wore in Martin's face. "Fool left this in his coat pocket."

"You didn't!" Martin squealed though it was obvious she did.

"Of course not," Erika lied. "It just...fell out."

The three of them burst into giggles.

"Why didn't you sell it?" Martin asked.

"Girl, you don't sell Gucci," Donna said as if she'd told Martin a thousand times already, "You flaunt it!"

Finding Home, 1980

On Sundays, Martin wandered into Manhattan. He went there the first chance he got after he arrived in New York and every Sunday after. He went to Radio City Music Hall; he rode the Staten Island ferry and took pictures of, "the Goddamn Statue of Liberty," to send home to his friend, Sharon. He went into Nathan's, off Fifth Avenue, feeling like a real New Yorker, not some boy fresh from the orange groves of Florida. He went to Times Square, predictable as that was. The peep shows, the prostitutes and hustlers just like in *Midnight Cowboy*. The signs that advertised *Annie* and *42nd Street*. The homeless man pissing on the sidewalk. The Burger King.

It was everything he hoped it would be.

Baptism, 1981

Martin loved the Lower East Side, where he lived with Donna once he persuaded her to abandon her room at the Jane West Hotel, where survivors of the Titanic were once housed.

"What a dump!" she complained. "Drag queens everywhere and dead junkies being carried out on stretchers at least three times a week," she actually laughed, "But those queens taught me how to do my hair and make-up and how to put on a show. Yes, they did."

"You should give credit where credit's due," Martin told her, pretending to be annoyed. "I taught you everything you know. And that look you got is second hand. My hand." It was Martin who took her to all the right places—Mudd Club and Fiorucci—and changed the way she dressed.

"The world already has one Chrissie Hynde," he told her when he finally convinced her to go blond and "Stop, pleeease, with the ripped shirts and safety pins!"

"Hush, girl," she smiled and kissed him whenever he pouted and pretended to be offended. "You know you're the gay man I always wanted to be."

Getting off the subway at Astor Place on the day Martin moved into their apartment on Fourth and B, Rollerina—one of New York's most legendary drag queens, he later discovered—skated right by him and blew glitter in his face.

Martin felt baptized.

He could walk the streets for hours when he wasn't on the subway to Brooklyn or in class. Days wasted away. Hours at Lucia's (Donna loved the masters, reimagined; American Gothic in Van Gogh's bedroom window; Marilyn peeking behind the Mona Lisa; the Cubist Lady Liberty), or the Circle (Martin loved the light sculptures in the basement there—lightning in a bottle). The jazz blaring from the doorway. Dr. T.F. Chen stood casually in the corner, waving as Martin or Donna greeted him. They grabbed pizza and a cocktail at Arturo's; stargazed at the cappuccino bar at Fiorucci.

"Look! It's Liza," Donna squealed. "Look, it's Liz!"

They shopped at Trash and Vaudeville and plundered the street vendors selling books and sunglasses among the runaways that filled Tompkins Square Park, the music blasting through Martin's bedroom window at all hours; "Love is the Message," blaring out on the streets.

Lucky Stars, 1981

Keith, on the dance floor at Paradise Garage, invited Martin to his studio for New Year's Eve.

Every wall of Keith's studio was filled with art like the walls of a gallery. One wall, in fact, was painted entirely by Keith, in red and black continuous lines, forming a maze of dancing cartoon-like bodies with arms and legs flailing as they flipped and turned in obscene somersaults amid the child-like play of the tumbling figures. On one wall, to Martin's left as he walked across from the door, was a long, beady-eyed worm carrying an Apple computer on its back. In the corner of the wall was a painting of a nude figure, its silhouette covered in white swirls and standing next to the corner was a tall, black woman with short cropped, flat-top hair, also nude—her own body painted in the same white lines and swirls as the figure on the wall so that, though completely naked, she appeared fully dressed.

"I have seen the future," he wrote home to his high school friend, Sharon. "I have counted myself among the stars. I danced among them," he bragged.

"How lucky am I?"

Mr. Incognito, 1982

Keith's friend, Mark, was the first to take photos of Martin. "Look straight at the camera," Mark instructed, aiming the lens at Martin, and shooting the picture: Martin dressed from another time, and yet was also New Wave and thoroughly modern. Francis Bruguière's photos of Sebastian Drost from the 1920's—old and yet modern—spread out around him as he reflected on the pictures that he, himself, reflected.

"Come here," Mark said as he lay Martin on the couch, his back to the camera, his face hidden. Mark pulled back Martin's long, blond hair exposing the dangling earring he wore, moved his leg so that his ass was rounded and full; not a hair on his body, shaved smooth just as Mark suspected it would be. Laying like that, even nude, it was hard to tell if Martin was a boy or a girl.

"These are gonna be great," Mark said, pleased with himself (Martin thought) as he took several pictures. "Mister Incognito."

Martin went to class at Pratt during the day and tended bar at the Lucky Strike at night. Days he wasted away with Keith or Tim or Mark. Then nights at the Garage, Mudd Club or the Funhouse, dancing with Donna.

And life went on.

And on.

And on.

Outbreak, 1981-1982

In early 1981, there were twenty cases of a rare skin cancer called Karposi Sarcoma that doctors, at the time, thought might be caused by using poppers (Martin passed out the first time he used poppers, but he got used to it and learned to love it; everyone was using them, it seemed).

By summer, the outbreak was being reported in the *New York Native* and on page twenty of the *New York Times*. There was speculation, at the time, that promiscuity among gay men was the reason for the recent outbreak in the States.

In April, the following year, there was a fundraiser at the Garage to raise money for all the men taken ill with this new disease. While outside the city lay bitter cold and frozen and still waiting for the delayed spring to come; while all around men like Martin and Tim and Keith were falling ill and dying, Martin and Tim sang and drank and danced just like they had on so many other nights since that day they first met at Nathan's.

They danced that night—there at the Garage filled with a crowd of men, the clock always ticking—while onstage, Evelyn "Champagne" King thrilled the onlookers by belting out her hit songs, "Shame," and "Love Come Down," with nothing but love and joy in her voice. And that crowd of men, their wounded looks lost now, roared out in shouts and applause.

Outside, the city was arctic, dark, and strangely silent, the streets and sidewalks covered in fresh snow—white like hope, like death.

Tim hugged Martin for the last time and said good night.

Disappearing, 1983

Martin was walking up forty-second, in the Spring of '83, when he saw, there on the newsstand, the front page of the *New York Times* read: "AIDS Battle No. 1 Priority."

It felt, strangely, like some final confirmation. There was no denying it if it was on the goddamn front page of the *New York Times*. Not a rare, unknown cancer; it had a name now: AIDS. And Martin already felt his own death inevitable—he knew so many already who were sick by then. Klaus Nomi died that summer. Martin hadn't met him except in passing; only saw him at Fiarucci and knew people who knew him (everybody knew him). But he felt the loss all the same. It was happening all too often—someone you'd always seen around in all the clubs and around the Village and maybe knew, suddenly, just wasn't there anymore. Like Nomi. That voice was now silent, and Martin missed it; and the legend that he was, Martin feared, would likely be forgotten outside of St. Mark's.

Life...and death... infection...fever.

Martin could feel himself disappearing a little more every day.

Feel This Free, 1984

Weeknights he went to the gay clubs—Reno Bar, The Saint, The Pyramid, Paradise Garage. All the clubs on Washington Street. The straight people who came anyway didn't know whether to shit, run or go blind. There were blinding, flashing strobes and the pulse—one pulse, one beat, one heart—of the music. There were shirtless, sweaty, prancing, preening, primping, pimping boys all (well maybe not all) queer like Martin. Bears and Twinks and muscle boys and flaming queens and boys who might not scream, but they yelled a little. And the attitude. The shade. No need to tell you 'cause you already know.

Out there in the world, if it ain't right, it's wrong, but in the bars and clubs it was fucking holy. It was a sacrament and hell yes, Martin got down on his knees and praised Sweet Gay Jesus he was home. He was no longer lurking outside El Goya, looking. He was inside the St. Marks Bath house, and he felt free and unafraid for the first time. And each time he went out he thought: Am I dreaming? And each morning, another sun-drenched boy disappearing out his door, yes, he was disillusioned, but still willing to believe and still willing to return to the bars and the bath house night after night. After all, what else was there?

Wasted, 1985

The doctor said it was measles.

It was not.

Exhausted, feverish, Martin stayed inside for a month, but nothing changed. His face was covered in red marks; dark brown blotches appeared on his chest. Walking from room to room he found himself breathless and collapsing on the sofa. He took to wearing long sleeves and heavy clothing, despite the summer heat, to cover his once translucent skin, now scarred. When he laid down at night, the sheets were soon soaked in sweat and he woke many times, day, or night, to find the bed soiled, the room wreaking of his own waste. He lost weight almost overnight, it seemed, and he joked that he was evaporating.

St. Vincent, 1986

When Donna arrived at St. Vincent's AIDS ward, she was asked to wear a plastic bag before entering Martin's room.

"Like garbage?" Donna yelled at the nurse.

"You'll have to wear this," the nurse insisted, face flush and red, her body stiff and imposing as she stood toe to toe with Donna.

"Like hell I will," Donna refused, turning to open the door to Martin's room.

"You can't go in without..." the nurse screeched.

But Donna, as always, did as she pleased.

"Fuck you," she spat back at the nurse and rushed inside. Keith and Erika followed, both pressing their bodies against the door, keeping the nurse on the other side as Donna pushed a heavy chair that was by the bed over to block the door and keep anyone from entering.

"I'm here baby," she whispered to Martin, who was sleeping, as she sat by him on the bed. She leaned down and kissed him and stroked his hair, ignoring the looks of concern that suddenly crossed Erika and Keith's faces. "I'm here," she said, part promise, part prayer.

The Call, 1986

Martin's mother didn't know who else to call; she called Donna at two in the morning and woke her from a sound sleep.

"Sorry, dear," she cried into the phone. "It's our Martin. He's...he's..." she broke down sobbing unable to find the words.

"I'll take care of everything," Donna assured her. "Don't worry."

Donna called the ambulance, thankful that St. Vincent's was seconds from Martin's apartment. She called for a car; called Martin's mother back and told her she would meet them there.

"Hurry, dear," Martin's mother said.

Forty-Eight Hours, 1986

"It won't be long," the doctor told them. "His kidneys and liver are failing. His body is shutting down."

"How long?" Donna demanded.

"Forty-eight hours," the doctor said. "At best."

Martin was blind by then and could only hear voices—distant, like in a tunnel or a cave. He heard his mother crying, his father giving her comfort. Someone was holding his hand and though he was embarrassed by the sores, he knew were there, he was too weak to pull away.

"Martin," he heard a voice, "Martin, I'm here baby," Donna whispered, and her voice became a mere echo.

Martin closed his eyes, and they were on the dance floor at Paradise Garage. He lived for beauty such as this—lightning in a bottle, music blasting out onto the street and ecstasy at his fingertips.

There was Donna, sitting outside the door, Erika doing her hair tied up in a black nylon knot. John Sex was playing Peter Pan on the second floor, his Lady Liberty hair piled high.

Everybody was doing something.

Everybody was doing everything.

Everybody was somebody on the dance floor.

The music flowed like holy water and bodies of all shapes and persuasions swayed to the endless beat. No echo, no treble, just bass for days, or at least until morning, when Martin slipped away.

-800-

Literature

2ND FROM YOUR RIGHT

JOHNNY FRANCIS WOLF

I was not much to look at.

Sure, my Mom would say *not true*. Happy face, dopey grin,

knees together, socks forever matching, always sitting near the cutest boy.

The photo was taken in 1936, late in the Great Depression (we finally had a decent car), before the last World War.

And if it's not clear that Beau isn't just about the handsomest 19-year-old that ever lived (closest to your right), then I am deluding myself, the photo faded, you are blind, or some combination of that trifecta.

I was to attend University that coming Autumn. He was headed for the Coast.. LA the goal. To try his hand at Acting.

Everyone said he should. Everyone said he looked the part.

From Basketball, to Track and Field, to Football every Fall, nothing corporal he ever endeavored would find him wanting, could rise above his physical prowess. With girls (and others) caving under.

That we became friends — that he didn't espy the pining eyes I endlessly hid, attending all his games and races — yet remained as two best buds — a mystery candied, puzzle too sweet.

—

"I think your Sister likes me."

His grin seemed awry, the white of his teeth skewed to the left.

The field was some distance from the picnic. We found ourselves not talking about September, as was usual. Not speaking of when we wouldn't walk together, like this.

"Am doubtful," I lied, eschewing my competition. "She doesn't regard boys as I.." now tangled in lingual barbed wire, "I... rene and your Cheerleader friends."

Prayed he didn't notice my uninspired recovery.

"I think I'll get fat if I do nothing today, your Aunt's potato salad coming right through my middle," he groused brightly.

Thanking God for Beau's tenuous attention span and, as if on cue — for reading my mind or somewhere lower — he lifted his shirt exposing the tightness that enameled his vigor, held in his brawn.

Pushing it out to mimic a paunch, he invited me to punch him hard, to test the flesh, the muscle neath, for strength and beef and sinewed might. I cooperated wholly and in slow motion, like some Saturday fight we'd seen and talked of 'til Sunday night.

—

Fell about wrestling, tangled in sweat, smelling now of the other's skin, shirts were missing, shoes were doffed, hair askant.

He pinned me down.

Drips from his forehead fell in my eyes. They stung full well. I didn't blink, hoping to collect more.

"I think there's a pond not far," he wheezed, catching his breath, bending in warm — his elbows giving way.

Feigned confusion, as if I hadn't heard the seven simple words he'd strung together quite plainly. My eyes squinted, inviting him near.

"Pond," he exhaled, "I think.."

Was still closer.

And with more fortitude than he'd ever shown with any touchdown pass, alley-oop, or sprint across a finish line, he stood up, grabbed his clothes, and ran to leave such thoughts behind.

Turning round and smiling wildly, he swung his belt above his head and whooped like a cowboy spinning his lasso, stumbling over pants sliding well below his hips.

—

"Where are your things?"

I arrived to see him treading water, middle of the sizeable pond.

"On the rock, by that tree," he pointed.

Having fully re-assembled that which had been personally sundered by our spirited joust, I sat on the stone, shoed and clothed, and watched him play.

From swimming, to floating, to dives off a raft moored to the dock, to pull-ups from a low-hanging branch over the lake, I was not bored by his antics, his self-conscious performance. He gave me a show, the last in real time, before we were off to opposite oceans.

"I might miss you," shaking his fur akin to a dog. His water ballet finally through.

"Quit it," I bluffed, tasting his lake as it landed on my lips.

Naked, he sat by my side.

"Come out with me. Take a year. You and I, a bungalow on the beach. All those starlets in swimsuits and.."

—

I kissed him right then. Was slow motion again.

No one seemed mind. Least, not him.

"Starlets, you say.."

Fighting Book Bans Isn't Enough

Joshua Isard

As long as there are books, people will try to ban them.

Book bans have been around so long that it's hard to see them as anything other than a built-in part of human civilization. Books were banned during the Qin Dynasty, in the third century BC; before and during the French Revolution; and in my home country of the USA, as early as 1637.

They were banned in my high school while I attended, they're being banned now, and they will be banned long after I am gone.

I appreciate everyone opposing book bans. Every year I shop the banned books table at my synagogue fundraiser. One of the best classes I took in college was on banned books. For what it's worth, I will always speak out against book bans, and encourage others to do the same. If people stop speaking out, then the bans will only swell.

But let's be honest, we're not going to stop the bans. So that means we have to do more than fight them. We have to take responsibility for our own reading, for our own minds. Bans mean that there are people we cannot trust, people who have power over what reading material we see. Dissent is a part of fighting that power, but personal action has to go along with it. Without that action, we're doing little more than engaging in a perpetual shouting match.

Taking personal action does not mean buying banned books. When *Maus* was recently banned from some United States schools, I was heartened to see the book jump on to bestseller lists, but this is only a gesture. As much as I like the Japanese phenomenon of tsundoku—which basically means piles of un-read books—that is only an aesthetic thing. Books need to be read to be effective. Buying them, even as that supports living authors whose work has been banned, is not enough. One must read them.

It is very easy for me to say: read banned books. I live in the United States. Here, I am middle class, which for the planet makes me upper class. If there's a book I want, I get it. My local library is spectacular, and I work at a university. I have access to Amazon, ThriftBooks, AbeBooks, not to mention all the free literature available online. Like most Americans, it's not hard for me to acquire reading material.

I also have plenty of leisure time, being a middle class American. Personally, I have less since I had kids, but in the scheme of things I still have a lot.

I would like to think that I follow through on actually consuming the literature that others might not want me to access, so that I can have an opinion on it. I try to be aware that the privilege I have is globally and historically rare.

Still, plenty of Americans don't take advantage of this. I am sure many of those people who recently bought *Maus* did indeed read it. But based on my own stack of intend-to-read books, which currently casts a shadow over the laptop I'm using to type this, I am sure as many did not read it after purchasing it, which makes the purchase little more than shelf decoration.

According to a recent Gallup poll, the average American reads 12.6 books per year, the lowest in two decades. According to the NEA, 45% of adult Americans say they haven't read a book of any sort in the past year. While this does mean we have some avid readers in the USA, it also suggests that there are a lot of people not taking advantage of our access to literature and actively fighting book bans by engaging with that banned material.

Many polls I have read indicate that Americans overwhelmingly oppose book bans. One poll from The Brookings Institution revealed that nine out of ten Americans are against book bans. If that's true, and it's also true that 45% of Americans haven't read a book in the past year, then something like 35% of Americans both oppose book bans and don't read books. That's a good chunk of the wealthiest country on the planet pushing back against bans without taking action to engage with the material in question.

This is particularly jarring when considering that it's so much more difficult around the world to obtain and read the kind of books we take for granted.

In July of 2023, a high-ranking Chinese official was expelled from the party for possessing banned political books and journals. If this happens to people of wealth and power, imagine what happens to the average citizen in possession of similar books. Actually, you don't have to imagine. Just look up the cases of Yalqun Rozi and Gui Minhai, and you'll understand. By no means does it end with those two, or with China.

Iranians can and have been arrested for producing and consuming banned material. In Hungary, a bookshop chain was fined for selling a children's book about a child with same-sex parents. When that same children's book was published in Russia, it was labeled "18+."

The point is that I know it's easy for me to encourage people to do more than fight banned books. If I criticize other Americans for not reading enough, at least I know that the majority of them have the access to banned materials, and that we all have the freedom to consume them.

But not everyone does. And so when I am tired at the end of the day, having coached one kid's baseball team after work and then helped my other kid with long division, I think about Ismail Mashal. He's a teacher in Afghanistan who has given out free books and promoted education for girls and women. He was arrested early last year. Whatever book is on my bedside table, it seems only right to actually read it, no matter how hard it feels like my day has been. Because like all Americans, I can do so and sleep soundly.

Love, The Way God Intended

Ryan David Ginsberg

Content Warning: School oppression/censorship of queer literature.

The administrators of Washington Middle School could no longer sit idly by as the dangers of the outside world crept into their community, threatening their students—both in heart and in mind and in body. Too many events had already occurred around the nation—the librarian in Oregon with the rainbow flag on her front desk, the bus driver in New York who played Kendrick Lamar over the radio every morning, the group of sixteen-year-olds in Ohio with the watermelon charms on their Crocs. They had seen too much to turn a blind eye. They had to be proactive.

They had to protect their kids.

So, they installed security procedures that rivaled any other in the nation. All who stepped foot on their campus first had to go through a multi-tiered security system—teachers, students, parents, administrators. Even the mailman was subject to this high level of security.

And the security only increased inside. Teams of police officers and retired soldiers with constantly loaded guns on their hips monitored the hallways. Cameras were installed inside every classroom, down every hall, throughout the playground, on the gates that surrounded the campus, and anywhere else a potential danger could possibly be. And all potential employees had to go through intense background checks and psychiatric tests before they were even given the chance to interview for a job so near the youth of this great community.

The school had to protect their kids.

Mrs. Estrada was the seventh-grade English teacher at Washington Middle School. But she had never wanted to be a teacher. After watching Michael Phelps win another gold medal as a kid, she had wanted to be an Olympic swimmer. She had once considered becoming an astronaut or a veterinarian or maybe a fashion designer. For two years in high school, she thought going to the WNBA was a real possibility. And at one point in college, sitting in the library at two in the morning, she thought life would have been a lot easier if she had just become a stripper.

But in the end, following in the footsteps of her mother and father and all the other men and women she knew with a medical degree, she became a doctor.

In particular, she was a pediatrician. And she was good at it. She did it for many years. But watching what was happening around the nation, and hearing from her patients about the changes taking place within her local schools, she felt a sudden call to change her profession to education. She had heard her community's cry to protect their kids. And that's what she wanted to do—protect the kids. So, she sent in her application, underwent the required psychiatric evaluations, the intensive interview process, the years of additional schooling and training, and was now well into her sixth year as a seventh-grade English teacher at Washington Middle School.

———

Mrs. Estrada joined the line for security, which was already wrapped around the corner even though school wasn't set to begin for another forty-five minutes. Everyone in line waited patiently. Like her, they were used to these intricate, laborious security procedures. And many of them agreed this was all necessary for their kids' safety.

As she waited, she altered the arm carrying her box of books, occasionally setting the box down to rest her arms entirely. When her turn finally came, she set it on the conveyor belt, removed her shoes, belt, jewelry, and electronics, then walked through the body scanner.

"Clear," said the first security guard, and onward she walked, to a second security guard who scanned her once more with a wand just in case the body scanner missed anything.

"Clear," said the second security guard.

The box of books and the rest of her belongings were also scanned while a third security guard observed carefully. Once the box had reached the other side, yet another security guard grabbed the top book, eyeing it.

"These books received approval?" he asked.

"Yes, sir."

Mrs. Estrada pulled the signed paperwork from her pocket and handed it over. The security guard looked through the paperwork, checking the legitimacy of the signatures from the school board, principal, and state governor. He then compared the title on the paperwork with the top row of books. Everything matched. He handed the paperwork back to Mrs. Estrada, though his evaluation was far from complete, and picked up a copy from the top row, reading the title of the book and its author out loud, along with the description on the back of the book. Nodding approvingly, he removed the dust jacket and studied the boards, then carefully scanned the pages within to ensure they all matched the description he had just read. Again, he nodded approvingly. Lastly, he went through the box, ensuring every cover matched those on the top of the box.

Finally satisfied, the final security guard said, "Clear."

When Mrs. Estrada got into her classroom, she kept the door locked, the blinds drawn, and the lights off. Relying on feel and faint outlines, she made her way to the back table, where she gently set down the box of books. Carefully, she removed each book and set them down in front of her. Each book had upon it a picture of a young boy and a young girl holding hands. Written in big, bold letters was the title of the book:

Love, the Way God Intended.

A raving review from the nation's most popular news organization called the book, "A triumph for American society and future generations."

The story followed the lives of two elementary students who later married and started a family. They came from great, wealthy, religious households that blessed them with wonderful morals no other child around them seemed to have. And every time they found themselves tempted to behave like those around them, they needed only to hold their lover's hand and remember the morality placed in their hearts by their parents and their God. It was a beautiful telling of how God could defeat the evilness of humanity, a beautiful telling of how love could triumph evil, and a beautiful telling of what morality truly looked like.

It was one of only four books approved by the school board to be read by in Mrs. Estrada seventh-grade English class.

As Mrs. Estrada arranged the books on the desks around class, one dust jacket slipped to reveal that underneath it was not actually a copy of *Love, the Way God Intended*, but rather a book called *We Do Not All Love the Same, And That's Okay*—a book that had been banned by her school district and many other districts and libraries throughout the nation for its inappropriate inclusion of same-sex relationships and drag queens and polygamy and other methods of love that did not align with the views of many.

Mrs. Estrada quickly readjusted the jacket to ensure the book appeared like the others. She looked nervously around at the cameras around her classroom, at the little cracks in the window, then hurried to her desk to grab some tape.

As she finished taping the dust jacket to the book, the bell suddenly rang.

Frantically, she opened the blinds, turned on the lights, returned the tape to her desk, and unlocked the door. She forced a smile as she welcomed the class with her usual:

"Good morning and God bless."

———

After the morning prayers had been spoken over the loud speaker, Mrs. Estrada introduced the class to their new book by reading from the script provided her by the school board.

"*Love, the Way God Intended*," she read, "is a monumental novel taking the nation by storm for the morality it strives to return to American households. This story serves as a much-needed blueprint for how love and relationships should look in a society too often deceived by the Devil and his advocates. It is the sort of book that has the potential to wipe away millions of sinful acts before they even occur, the type of book that can change the actions of an entire society, the type of book that comes at the perfect time, delivering the perfect story. It is the book this nation needs to save itself from the..."

The script went on for several more minutes. Afterwards, she led the class in a short discussion about what they thought love should look like and how it should feel and whom that love should be between. She then assigned them a worksheet to help them reflect on that discussion. And as they worked on the worksheet, she walked around the class, making sure all of their answers corresponded with the answer sheet the school board provided her. After collecting the worksheets, she ordered them to open their books to page seven, where the prologue began.

Once everyone had made it to the proper page, she began reading, and they all followed along—except for a certain four who found within not a copy of *Love, the Way God Intended*, like the dust jacket and Mrs. Estrada's instruction implied, but rather an entirely different book: *We Do Not All Love the Same, And That's Okay*. This was not the first time these four students had been assigned a book unlike the others, so they were not surprised to find that their books began on a completely different page and included words that did not match what Mrs. Estrada read aloud to the rest of their classmates.

These students, like their books, were not like the others. They had souls that had been banned from the state their bodies dwelled. Nor did their souls align with the world propagandized in the book that the school board demanded Mrs. Estrada read. In the simplest terms, they did not love in the way God intended. They did not present themselves to the world in the way their politicians preferred. They did not—

The doors to the classroom opened, and in walked three police officers.

"Random search," one of them declared as another stepped up to the nearest student's desk, grabbed their backpack, and dumped out their belongings. The three officers searched through the dumped-out items, finding a pencil box, a notebook, a binder, a textbook, and a lunch pail. One officer sifted through each item in the pencil box. Another carefully investigated every word written upon the pages of the notebook, while the third did the same with the contents of the binder.

Once every item had been evaluated, even the items within the lunch pail, the officers dropped everything back on the desk.

"Clear," said one of the officers. Onward they moved, on to the next student. One officer dumped out everything within their backpack: a loose pencil, a notebook, a pocketknife, a sandwich in a plastic bag, a handheld video game console, and even a handgun. The officers crowded around the table again. One lifted the gun and found it loaded. He rolled the bullets around in his hand, before slotting them back inside the gun, and then placed them back among the items. Another officer picked up the pocketknife and ejected each of the tools—several seemed freshly sharpened. One of these even cut the officer as he fiddled around with the knife.

"Clear," said one of the officers.

Again, they moved on to the next student, repeating the process, ensuring no illegal book, or banned topic existed any-where among the items. They cleared this student, then moved on to the next.

Another half dozen students later, the officers approached the first student who had on their desk a false copy of *Love, the Way God Intended*. The officers grabbed this student's back-pack, dumping out their belongings on the desk.

Among the mess was the hidden copy of *We Do Not All Love the Same, And That's Okay*.

One officer picked up a notebook and looked at the content inside.

"Whose initials are these?"

The student panicked, knowing the initials did not belong to a person of the proper sex. Fortunately, several students at the school shared those initials, many of whom were of the proper sex, so the student randomly selected one and provided their name to the officer.

Satisfied, the officer dropped the notebook to the desk.

"Clear."

All the while, Mrs. Estrada continued reading from the book and the students followed along, even as the officers prowled around the room. Mrs. Estrada's voice was shaky, and she often stumbled over her words, though she relaxed slightly as the officers cleared two more of the students she had provided with illegal reading material.

When the officers poured out the backpack of the final student whose book differed from the others, the book itself was knocked to the floor along with a few other items. As the student reached for it, one officer stopped them. He picked the book up himself, turning it over slowly. It was the same officer who had cleared Mrs. Estrada when she entered the school earlier that morning.

His eyes fixated on a little strip of tape. He did not remember this from his earlier evaluation, or with any of the other books. He asked a nearby student for their pocketknife.

Mrs. Estrada stopped reading. She could not move. She could not think.

Everyone was watching now as the officer cut the tape. He returned the pocketknife to the student and removed the dust jacket from the book, revealing behind it *We Do Not All Love the Same, And That's Okay.*

All three officers drew their guns and aimed them at the student.

"Get down on the ground!"

"Put your hands on your head!"

The third officer turned his gun on Mrs. Estrada.

"Did you know about this?" he raised the book in the air, angling it so she could read the title on its spine.

"No, sir," she said. "You saw the books yourself this morning. They were all correct. I would never allow that sort of—that sort of filth in my classroom."

The officer nodded, then turned to the student on the floor. He pressed his knee into their back.

"Do not resist! I said, do not resist!"

Aggressively, he cuffed the student's hands behind their back.

And as quickly as the officers had barged in, they left, dragging the student behind them.

The class was visibly disturbed—not so much from the treatment of their fellow classmate, but rather from the idea that such a book had been in their presence all this time. They carefully studied their books, ensuring none of those words had somehow managed to jump into theirs. Comforted by their discoveries, they returned their attention to their spilled-out belongings.

"Go ahead and take the next minute to clean up your belongings," said Mrs. Estrada. "We will resume reading in three minutes."

As the students slowly cleaned their belongings—their pencils, their binders, their notebooks, their guns, their lunch pails, their pocketknives, their textbooks, their electronics—and returned them their backpack, Mrs. Estrada hid behind her desk. Tears poured from her silently, she could not let the students hear her, nor the cameras overhead see her.

Beneath her desk, visible only from her crouching position, were several tallies scratched into the wood. Mrs. Estrada took a pocketknife from her own pocket and extended one of the blades. Quietly, she etched one more tally into the wood alongside the rest—now twelve in total—and took a moment to mourn the ones she had been unable to save. Then she thought of the others—the ones she had saved, at least if only for a moment. The ones she had been able to introduce to ideas the state had forbidden.

She remembered why she made the switch to education in the first place:

To protect the kids.

———

Once she had regained her composure enough to continue, she stood and grabbed her copy of *Love, the Way God Intended*.

"Okay, class," she said, her voice slightly shaking, "what page were we on, again?"

"Fifteen," called one student.

"That's right," said Mrs. Estrada. "Please turn back to page fifteen."

Everyone returned to page fifteen.

Except for three, who still had their copies of *We Do Not All Love the Same, And That's Okay* opened in front of them.

ON READING BUKOWSKI TO A BABY

THOM HAWKINS

WE ARGUED
ABOUT READING BUKOWSKI
TO a baby—

She said
Bukowski was dirty—

I said
the baby doesn't have
any context—

Bukowski is just sounds
many of them soothing

like a lullaby.
like lust.

The End of Doubt

Rinat Harel

Censorship of Pro-Palestinian Speech.

An amicable spring sun hovered in the sky, and the late afternoon air gleamed with excitement. A light breeze rose from the surrounding desert, wafting into the amphitheater. Perched on a hillside overlooking the undulating curves of the valley, the five-hundred-seat theater was filling up fast. Spectators of all ages were still pouring in when it was time for the show to begin. We were running late, but the atmosphere was calm and joyful. Everyone, especially the children, was looking forward to this annual celebration, and the surprise finale at dusk. Any minute now!

I settled into my seat in the front row alongside the journalists, exchanging a smile with the gentleman beside me, and feeling a tinge of shyness as the only high schooler among them. I pulled out my notepad bought especially for the assignment and ran my fingers across its velvety cover.

Constructed from the local rockface, the new semi-circle stage was as impressive as had been advertised. The eight Corinthian pillars at the back stood with imposing elegance, supporting an arch that linked the two squarish wings of the theater. Golden sheaves of wheat were heaped in the corners of the marble stage floor.

The column furthest to the right stood erect a mere few feet away from my seat. As I drank the fresh spring air, my eyes swept over the valley, taking in the blue of the sky and the brown of the Judea hills. Small clusters of red roofs glinted in the offing, beyond which the desert sprawled deep into the east.

The crowd was finally settling down as some movement bubbled in the wings. Then two drumming bands of high school boys emerged from either side of the stage, rolling sticks on the snares in short, succinct sounds: Drr-drrrr-drrr-drr; Drr-drrrr-drrr-drr. Waves of cheers rose from the crowd in response; the combined sound reverberated in the nearby hills.

Facing each other, the bands then split into three staggered drumlines each, and advanced in small steps. With one group clad in blue and the other in white, their smooth choreography created a white-and-blue wave that swayed this way, then that, as the boys paced back and forth to the rhythm in coordination: Drr-drrrr-drrr-drr; Drr-drrrr-drrr-drr.

As the drummers exited, around twenty schoolgirls came on stage. Clad in lilac dresses and carrying wicker baskets overflowing with yellow flowers, they sang with ringing voices while arranging themselves in a wavy formation across the stage.

We bring this fruit of the land
For our country, a beautiful bride
Dates, figs, pomegranates, and olives
We carry a branch clustered with grapes
We come from the villages
From the fields …

At the end of the beautiful song, the girls stepped forward and placed down their baskets, forming a line of yellow blossoms, then turned to leave, making way for an adult chorus in white gowns, entering the stage from the right wing. The new group—about thirty strong—laid themselves out in two layers of wide crescents, echoing the shape of the pillars. The audience received them with rhythmic applause.

"Greetings, all," the chorus announced in unison at last. "And welcome to the Harvest Jubilee."

One of the lilac girls took a few tentative steps forward from within the group, basket in hand, and took a few tentative steps forward.

There she stood, between the chorus and the line of yellow baskets.

The crowd looked at her.

The chorus looked at her.

We were all attentive, curious to watch her solo act. From my seat in the front, I could see she was shy, perhaps a bit confused. But then she finally spoke.

"This is the land of milk and honey," she said in a thin voice.

A few people from the front called: "How cute" and "Adorable!"

"We cannot hear you," a man called from a back row.

The girl's mouth moved again but no sound came out.

A gentle voice of a woman rose from the crowd. "Please speak louder, little flower."

Encouraged, the girl gave a faint smile. "This is the land of milk and honey," she repeated with a flushed face, her words ringing loud and clear this time. "But what about the Nakba?"

A long silence followed.

Is this part of the program? I thought with apprehension.

"Hahaha," the chorus bayed in one voice, turning to the crowd. "Did you ever hear such innocent prattle?"

"But ..." said the girl, facing an amphitheater brimming with onlookers.

"Now go ahead little one and join your sisters backstage," the chorus said.

"But ..." repeated the girl.

"What a curious act," some people in the audience murmured.

"Sweet girl," one person in the audience whispered to another. "And what talent!"

"Sentimental claptrap," said the chorus to the audience.

"But ..." piped the girl.

"We had no choice," the chorus began to singsong, looking at the crowd. "It was us or them, us or them."

"But ..." said the girl, her thin voice carried on the light breeze.

"Us or them, ussssss or them," the chorus hissed, swaying their heads from side to side, before turning to the girl. "Now go off and join your sisters." They sounded more insistent now.

Her feet planted in place, the girl did not move.

"A thought-provoking act," some of the audience said. Others seemed confused but a renowned art critic with a booming voice explained that experimental theater can take many forms. A few expressed concern for the child but were quickly reassured. Her confident stance was beyond impressive. Her feet seemed to have shot roots into the marble floor.

I gazed at the girl with growing unease; she seemed small and vulnerable on the large stage, and I was no longer sure hers was part of the act. My seat suddenly felt hard and uncomfortable.

"This theatre is a public venue," someone from the crowd called. "Let the little one speak."

"We made it illegal to mention the enemy's special day," the chorus replied to the person in the crowd. "Three years in prison!"

"And rightly so," a potbellied man from the second row cried.

Some called out in his support; others expressed objection. The act was turning out to be participatory theater—the program had promised innovation and originality, after all. Yet, the heated dialogues didn't quite match the intention of this jubilee. I glanced at the journalist beside me. His brief nod said: we are here to report, nothing more.

"Peace now," shouted a woman behind me, raising high two fingers high in a V sign.

"Heresy, foreign influence!" the chorus barked at the woman.

"Jezebel," the potbellied man snarled at her.

This is a known theatrical method, I recalled: planting an actor amidst the audience.

"Hear, hear," a few spectators chimed in; others shifted in their seats with unease. A few got up to leave, hurrying their children through the aisles.

The light breeze abruptly died, and the air felt stuffy even though we were surrounded by an open landscape.

"Arrest her this minute!" commanded the chorus, stomping their feet and pointing at the woman who still had her hand raised. "Where are the guards?"

More people slipped away. The girl's eyes followed them with sorrow. Twilight was descending; small pools of darkness were collecting in the clefts of the hills. The air stood still, heavy with hesitance.

I glanced around, wondering if I should leave as well. And take the little girl with me.

A few more people stood up with their hands raised in the peace sign.

"If you carry on," the chorus warned, "surely we will be rid of you."

The crowd splintered: some roared, "Arrest these people, arrest them!" while others called "Save the child!" jumping from their seats to climb onto the stage. But they stopped short, frozen in place. Squinting, I saw the spring flowers in the baskets were in fact razor wire painted bright yellow.

"Damnation!" the chorus barked at the failed raiders, their ire gushing into the audience like a sudden gust of icy wind.

The girl, still standing in place, blinked a few times in rapid succession. Shoulders stooped, eyes cast down, she morphed into a shrub of lilac, and her purplish petals began falling to the ground, wilted.

The dusk sky quivered, stretching away in nascent layers of blue and crimson. The whole desert around us was holding its breath.

The public was on its feet now, arguments rising into shouts and yells. A few people turned against each other, fists and all. The air turned sour, tinged with angst. Parents took their children and fled the theater. A panicked young man, the whites of his eyes looming large, stumbled as he turned to escape the mayhem and was sprawled breathless on the ground a few feet away from my seat. I froze in place, unable to move or think.

The chorus remained lined up behind the bare lilac bush that was now bent over a pool of shriveled blooms.

Suddenly, a flock of white doves burst forth from behind the Corinthian pillars, soaring into the sunset. Even amidst the turmoil, all heads turned skyward. All eyes followed the freed birds—white feathers against a blazing-red sky. Our ears filled with the sound of whistling wings. What a splendid finale indeed!

An uproar directed our attention back to the stage to discover the raiders had successfully stormed it from behind, entering through the sloping side of the hill. They celebrated their triumph with wide smiles and joyful dancing.

With that, the chorus took fast hold of the pillars upon which the arch rested, and leaned upon them, some to the right, others to the left.

And the chorus said: "Let us die with the Philistines!" And they bent with all their might, and the pillars fell upon the rebels and upon the people who sat within reach.

It has now been a full year. My arm still hurts at times. The complex fracture might never properly heal, the doctors say. Occupational hazard, they joke. My uncle Dani blames himself for getting me a front-row seat with his journalist friends, but I kept telling him I was glad to have been there, and my arm will eventually heal for sure. True, what was supposed to be a school project didn't turn out as expected; I wasn't allowed to use my report for class. Too violent, the teacher said. But I didn't really mind. Instead, I submitted a paper about camel riding in the Australian desert, inspired by my boyfriend's passion. And then I started this blog after my mom said she loves my maturing writing style. Don't you find that sometimes your mom's opinion is all that matters?

It's time for the Harvest Jubilee again, to be celebrated in an open field this time, away from pillars and stones. Although the authorities have guaranteed that the havoc will not repeat itself. Under no circumstances! they stressed. We shall celebrate our sovereignty and prosperity with no disturbances whatsoever, said the official proclamation in all the media outlets.

For a while, there was a heated debate as to whether last year's performance went badly wrong or was deliberately sabotaged. We never learned the truth. The name of the lilac child was never disclosed, perhaps never discovered, and so the public dubbed her 'Doubt.'

She was a menace of the first order, the media said. A destroyer of hope and tradition. She brought nothing but ruin and deserved to be buried under rubble and blood.

Some rumors suggested she showed early signs of dissent; a few experts predicted that in middle school she would have caused a teacher to lose his temper, turn into an army runaway a few years later, and be involved in worse transgressions as time went by. Others insist to this day that she never existed; her so-called stage appearance, they say, was nothing but a theatrical hoax. An illusion. To what end, they never specified.

'Doubt' has been gone a full year now, and everyone blesses her absence. Quiet has been restored, civil order has prevailed, and her mere mentioning is strictly forbidden.

By law.

The New Librarian

Amy Nielsen

THE POUNDING ON THE door should have startled Stevie, but she'd been tipped off. She took a slow, deliberate sip of steaming Earl Gray. Then she placed the chipped floral cup on its matching dish atop the side table. She picked up her cane but made no attempt at a speedy greeting. The people on the other side of the weathered door were not friends. They could wait.

"Open up, Old Lady. We know you're in there. We've come for the books!"

Her bony fingers unclasped the chain at the top, next the deadbolt, followed by the dial on the patinaed handle.

Two burly uniformed men pushed past her.

"Where are they?" the first one demanded.

The second scanned the dusty living room.

A third, one she recognized, slunk in last.

"Chet, how's your grandmother? Haven't seen her since they canceled Children's Story Hour at the library. What was that, like five years ago?"

"Ma'am, this isn't a social visit," said Second. "Hand them over—now!"

Chet shot her a pleading look.

Stevie brushed the young man's shoulder as she shuffled back to her worn recliner. "I must've misplaced them. Like you said, I'm an old lady. Memory isn't what it used to be."

First pointed a rifle at her chest.

Second shoved a document in her face. "Here's the list. You have until 5:00 pm this afternoon to summon your memory. Or we have orders from the Governor to take you in."

Stevie pushed the rifle away. "Oh, how nice of the Governor to want to see me. I've never been to his mansion. That'll be a nice treat." She crimped her gray frizzy curls. "I suppose I should wash my hair for the visit."

Second slammed the butt of his rifle on the hardwood floor. "Ma'am, this won't be a visit to the mansion. It'll be a permanent assignment to the jail."

Chet broke his silence. "Ms. Stevie, please turn over the books. I don't want..."

First held his hand up, cutting him off. "We'll be back at 5:00. Those books better be in this room in a nice little stack." The trio exited with a slam of her door, Chet looking back remorsefully.

As they'd been instructed, exactly five minutes later, Bennet and Darcy tip-toed into the room. "Are they gone?" Darcy asked.

"Yes, Dears. Come here."

The twins wrapped their arms around their grandmother. They were both trembling and soon the tears came.

"Nana, do we still have to do it?" Bennet sobbed. "I'm scared."

Before Stevie could respond, Darcy answered her brother. "Yes, we do. I'm scared, too. But we have no choice."

Stevie hated that her twelve-year-old grandchildren would be left to pick up the pieces when she was gone. But they'd been raised for this. And someone had to do it. The alternative wasn't an option. She wiped back a tear. "There's not much time. You go on and get your things packed. I still have some preparations."

She hugged them both one more time. Today would be the last day she'd ever see them. They all knew it.

Stevie shuffled down the basement stairs. She pulled the chain on the single light bulb. Then she inserted the key and lifted the hatch on the secret door in the floor and shuffled down those stairs. It wasn't a bad thing this was coming to an end. She was too old for this. Time to pass the torch.

Rows of shelves lined the dark cavernous hallway. She turned on a battery-operated lantern. Shadows filled the walls. She ran her hands down the spines of her beloved books. The banned books she'd secretly guarded and slipped to desperate readers.

<u>My Heart is Hurting by S.E. Reed</u> — the story of a teen girl whose neglectful, sex-worker of a mother abandons her and how other adults and her best friends save her. Stevie remembered how hopeful it made her feel as a teen when she read it. Her own father was forced into sex-work when his job as a drag queen in 2023 became illegal. Even though her father wasn't neglectful, she could relate a lot to Jinny.

<u>Men Unlike Others by Johnny Wolf</u> — a beautiful anthology of poems and stories that capture the human spirit, written by a deep-thinking, people-observing gay man. But his book was banned in 2023, when a conservative-leaning Supreme Court upheld a website developers' lawsuit to not create websites for same-sex couples.

<u>Not in the Plan by Dana Hawkins</u> — an adorable lesbian RomCom about a writer and a café owner. She'd read this fresh and fun book in her early twenties. Months after its release, the Supreme Court reversed its previous 2015 decision and banned the rights of same-sex couples to marry followed by a decision to ban books containing LGBTQ+? relationships.

<u>Worth It by Amy Nielsen</u> — an issue-driven story about a homeless teen who ends up living in a trailer park with an abusive older man who impregnates her. After the aforementioned Supreme Court overturned Roe V. Wade, restricting women's rights to abortion, books discussing abortion were also banned.

Stevie wanted to relish in each story. But time was running out and much was left to do.

She turned off the lantern and ascended the stairs for the last time taking the memories of her favorite stories with her.

Bennet slumped puffy and red-eyed next to his bag of meager belongings.

Darcy stood stoic and poised — ready for Stevie's last instructions.

Stevie dropped her cane and landed in her recliner. She sipped her now room-temperature Earl Gray. "The books are safe. They won't find them."

"How long?" Darcy asked.

Stevie pulled her thoughts together. "That'll depend. When you reach the legal age — vote. It's our last chance. Spread the word. Work grassroots to mobilize other voters. There's strength in numbers."

Bennet shuddered. "Nana, when they pick you up. What happens to us?"

She grasped his trembling shoulders. "Sweetie, the orphanage is safe. I've put provisions in place. You and Darcy will be together. You'll be okay. I promise. The house will be yours when you're eighteen."

The three shared an afternoon meal of egg salad sandwiches and pickles.

Bennet sniffled. Darcy nudged him. "I got you. We got this."

A tap at the door ended their last meal as a family. Darcy stood.

"Wait with your brother. Let me." Stevie used her cane to reach a standing position and opened the door.

Chet greeted the family. "Ms. Stevie. Darcy. Bennet."

"Well, hello, Chet. I was hoping they sent you."

"Wouldn't have it any other way." Chet held out his arm to escort Stevie to his police car.

"Such a gentleman. Your grandmother always told me that."

Darcy and Bennet grabbed their bags and followed the pair out the door.

"Books change lives — definitely changed mine. Thank you for your service," Chet said.

Stevie placed a key in his hands. "Yes, they do, boy. Yes, they do."

He led her to the car's front seat, while Darcy and Bennet huddled together in the back seat.

As the house disappeared in the review mirror, Darcy whispered, "I guess this means I'm the new librarian now."

The Termination Bureau

Ryan David Ginsberg

Content Warning: Violence/murder of children (one line).

A baby lay peacefully asleep in an incubator. It had been wrapped gently for hours in a cozy warm swaddle. But now, as morning slowly shone in upon the city of Sarasota, the swaddle around the baby loosened, stirring it awake. At first, it only fussed a little. Kicked around a bit. But then it began to cry.

This baby had just recently gained the strength to lift its head, though only for a second or two before it fell back to the white pillow of its incubator. Everything around the baby was white — its blanket, its onesie, its cap. The clock on the wall, the light fixtures, the sign above the door that read 'The Incubator'. Even the nurse who came to his incubator was dressed in all white. Her blonde hair showed through the bottom of her white cap. Her bright blue eyes focused in on the baby.

Humming softly, she placed the crying baby on her lap. She held a bottle to its mouth, and it began to suckle. Soon, it was fast asleep again. The nurse returned the baby to its incubator and carefully swaddled it. She grabbed the baby's chart from below the incubator and checked her watch, marking the time on the sheet, with the ounces of milk consumed, and signing her name 'Susan'. She put the bottle away and moved over to Baby No. 234, checking its diaper. Dry. Nurse Susan made a mental note to return in another hour or so, then moved on to the next—whose diaper was not quite as dry.

As she cleaned Baby No. 235, another baby nearby began to cry.

"I got it," said another nurse, coming over with a new bottle.

"Thank you, Nurse Tina."

Nurse Susan wrapped the dirty diaper in a plastic bag and tossed it into the waste department on her cart. She then took a clean diaper and placed it on the paper. A few incubators over, another nurse changed a different baby's diaper. She was an elderly lady, the oldest of all the nurses in the Incubator. She was the one each nurse turned to for motherly advice. Their eyes met and they smiled to one another warmly.

"Nurse Joyce, how are you doing?"

"Oh, just wonderful, dear."

"Any big plans for the weekend?"

"Yes, actually. My grand daughter is turning 4."

"Is that right?" interjected Nurse Tina. "I remember when little Annie was just born."

"They grow so fast," said Nurse Susan.

Just then, the door swung open. All eyes turned to the man walking in. His stature cleared most of the doorway. His thick brown hair had been meticulously brushed to the side. Even his mustache had been combedto a tee. His white uniform looked freshly pressed, down to the creases in his pants. The golden badge upon his chest glimmered in the light. A slim baton was tucked into his belt on his left; a handgun was holstered against his right.

"Officer Tommy," The nurses straightened.

"I have room for three more," Officer Tommy said to no one in particular.

Her heart fluttering, Nurse Susan gathered three babies and their files at random onto her cart and wheeled them to Officer Tommy.

"Here you go, sir," she said, "three babies ready to go!" She gave Officer Tommy a curtsy, brushing a few loose strands of hair behind her ear.

"Thank you, miss," said Officer Tommy with a wink. Nurse Susan couldn't help her smile growing. "You're welcome," she said softly as he opened the door leading back to the room he had entered from. A room completely white from floor to ceiling.

The nurses walked up to Nurse Susan's side.

"That man is such a hunk," said Nurse Joyce

"He's a real hero," said Nurse Tina.

Nurse Susan nodded. Then they each let out a deep, wanting sigh.

———

Against the back wall of the White Room stood twenty-six podiums. Like the walls, these podiums were painted daily with a fresh coat of white. But as the working day progressed, if one looked close enough, they would several faint drippings of a red substance upon them.

Atop each podium was a tray about three feet in width, enclosed with thick, bullet-proof glass — though the front of the trays remained open. All had a baby on them. Except for three.

Officer Tommy located these empty podiums and placed a baby atop their empty tray.

The collective sound of twenty-six babies crying was piercing. But Officer Tommy was used to it by then. He had worked in that particular office for several years and many more years in an office in Alabama, so he hardly even noticed the noise anymore.

Once he had confirmed that all the babies were securely on a tray, he collected their files from the cart and sat behind his desk on the opposite side of the room. He took his thermos of black coffee and had a small sip. The coffee was lukewarm, but he preferred it that way. It was a sign of a hard day's work.

He opened the file of the first baby and carefully looked over its information: a birth certificate, some information on the baby's birth parents, an application for termination, a couple of recommendations, an approval letter from the Moral Advisor, a signed Declaration of Release, the results from the baby's examinations, and so on.

Once satisfied, he moved on to the following file.

As Officer Tommy looked over the files, he could see the Waiting Room full of patients both young and old through the window on the eastern wall. Each patient had their reason for being there that day, all rehearsing those reasons in their heads as they waited their turn.

Whenever the door to the Waiting Room opened, the room went immediately quiet, every whisper hushing. All eyes turned toward the door, at the secretary standing there, hoping their name would finally be called—wanting nothing more than to get this horrible, regretful day over with.

"Jocelyn Adams," said the secretary.

"That's me," a nervous voice said.

A thirteen-year-old girl stood. Her big, pregnant belly nearly knocked over the little kids playing in front of her. She stepped over a couple of babies as she made her way to the door.

"Excuse me," she said, "excuse me."

The secretary looked her up and down disgustedly as she watched this little kid approach her.

"Mmm," she said, "follow me."

And so, Jocelyn Adams followed her to the back. The door closed and the Waiting Room once more filled with whispers—this time about the pregnant little girl.

Officer Tommy concluded that all the paperwork was in order. So, he stood and made his way to the safes across the way, twelve in total, one for each Officer on staff. The safes were lined up just below the window looking into the Waiting Room.

For a moment, Officer Tommy studied the faces inside. The tears, the pain, the hopelessness, the nervousness—the shame. Then he waved with a smile. But the patients did not wave back.

Still with a smile, Officer Tommy knelt before his personal safe, entered his combination into the padlock, and opened it carefully. He looked through every gun inside before choosing his favorite.

Then he filled his magazine with 26 bullets.

The secretary showed Jocelyn Adams to Office No. 3, where inside sat the Moral Advisor assigned her case. He was a tall slender man, an old man, with a thick mustache as white as his skin.

"Sit," he said, without looking up. His voice was deep, commanding, and everything but welcoming.

Jocelyn sat in the chair across from him. She grabbed her application from her ripped-up backpack, setting it gently on the table. The application took all last night for her to fill out. She had done quietly, with her room lights off and only the light from her phone to guide her.

The Moral Advisor drew the papers closer to him. He placed a pair of half-moon reading glasses over his eyes.

Jocelyn tapped her toes anxiously as she watched him flip a page. She wiped sweat from her brow with her shirtsleeves. A minute later, he turned another page.

Her head started to pound. The fetus swayed inside.

A few pages later, the Moral Advisor stopped suddenly. He removed his reading glasses and looked up at Jocelyn.

"It seems," he said, "you have neglected to get the signature from the man who has impregnated you. According to the law here in the state of Florida, 'A pregnant girl or woman is not permitted to sell her baby without written permission from the man who impregnated her.' I am afraid I cannot approve your application."

"But sir," said Jocelyn, "you see..."

She stopped. A tear rolled down her cheek. She averted her eyes from the Moral Advisor, whose judgment was piercing her skin.

She found a nice piece of carpet below to focus on instead.

"You see," she continued, "the man who impregnated me is... well... he... it was my father. And he refuses to sign."

The Moral Advisor grabbed the handbook from the shelf behind his desk. He flipped through the pages with familiarity. When he found the page he needed, he turned the book to Jocelyn and pointed at the seventh line on the left page.

As she looked at the words, the Moral Advisor rehearsed them from memory.

"It matters not who the man is — whether he be a blood relative, a rapist, a liberal, an atheist, a retard, or all of the above — if he is an American citizen, then it is his right to choose what becomes of his unborn child; the woman he impregnates is simply the carrier of his property, not the owner or decider of what happens to it."

Jocelyn looked up at the Moral Advisor stunned.

"Is your father an American citizen?" he asked her.

"He is," she said numbly.

"Well, in that case," said the Moral Advisor, taking his red stamp and slapping it on the front page of her application, "your application has hereby been denied by the state of Florida. And as the law requires for an impregnated woman, your baby must be carried to term and taken care of until the age of eighteen, or else, you will be sentenced to life in prison for the destruction or neglect of another man's property."

"But sir!" Jocelyn cried. "I cannot raise this child." The pounding in her head worsened. The fetus no longer swayed but rocked.

"Then you should have thought about that before you went and got yourself pregnant, my dear," said the Moral Advisor, standing up from his chair.

"I didn't ask to get pregnant!" she screamed.

"Miss, I have other patients to see."

When Jocelyn refused to move, he grabbed her by her shoulders and shoved her out of his office, along with her backpack.

Then he returned to his desk and pressed the button that called his secretary:

"Hold my next patient" he said. "First, I must make a call."

Officer Tommy got into position in front of the first podium. He lifted the ocular lens to his right eye and ensured the baby's head was in sight.

According to the documentation, this particular baby had been placed into the care of the state of Florida by a married couple who attended the same church as Officer Tommy. In their application, they stated that, after many nights of prayer, it had been revealed to them that God had not willed this baby to be part of their family after all, and that God had told them it would be best to instead sell it to the state, so that it could go to wherever it was it was God willed it to go.

The Moral Advisor assigned the case, someone who just so happened to believe in the same god as the patients believed in, approved this application almost instantaneously.

"God's will be done," the Moral Advisor wrote in the notes.

While the biological parents returned home after the birth of the baby, the baby remained in the hospital for several weeks, where the state of Florida ran multiple examinations on it—blood tests, DNA tests, eye tests, and so on — to determine any statistical likeliness that it would grow up to be a helpful servant of the state.

Every baby sold to the state went through these same tests. As a result of these tests, most were sent to various facilities around the state or sold to private organizations around the nation. Those that tested high in intellectual potential got sent to academies that specialized in science, technology, and weaponry. The babies that tested high in muscular potential were sent to academies that specialized in physical labor. The babies testing high in loyalty and obedience were often sold to private organizations.

But every now and then, a baby failed to test high in any significant category and was determined statistically useless to the state, the federal government, and all private organizations.

This — the baby born to Officer Tommy's church-mates — just so happened to be one of those babies.

Officer Tommy blinked away the thoughts of his fellow church-goers. Again, he focused on the baby across from him. He exhaled slowly, emptying his lungs, steadying his body, then held his breath as he pulled the trigger.

And the crying decreased by one.

In the alley behind the Termination Bureau, Jocelyn Adams grabbed a metal hanger she had hidden before going into the Termination Bureau. She had hoped she would not need to use it. She had hoped the Moral Advisor would hear out her predicament, that her application would be approved despite the missing signature. She had hoped...

But she had no more hope left to feel.

She had to use the metal hanger.

So, she hid herself against the wall, in the shadows, away from the cameras, and carefully untwisted the hanger. She pulled the metal wire into a straight line. She looked around one last time. No, there was nobody near and no cameras in sight to catch her.

She carefully took off her pants, followed by her underwear. All the while leaning against the dumpster, she closed her eyes inserted the wire inside herself in the same forceful way her father often entered her. Even through the pain and discomfort, she continued to force the hanger deeper, just as she had seen in the videos she had studied the night before.

Tears poured down her cheeks as she scrambled the hanger to the left and right, up and down, side to side, until blood began to ooze out of her and onto her hand.

She dropped the hanger, falling to her knees. The blood continued to flow. She cried out in pain and guilt and sadness and hopelessness.

After all twenty-six targets inside the White Room had been terminated, Officer Tommy carefully disassembled his gun and returned it to his safe. He closed the door and locked it.

He looked through the window into the Waiting Room. Just about all of the eyes were on the drops of blood behind him. He smiled and waved, then turned back to his desk. He grabbed twenty-six report forms, filling them out one at a time.

Ten minutes later, all were completed. He placed the forms in their folders, stacking them in a neat pile, and tidied up his desk. With another sip of lukewarm coffee, he brought the pile of folders to his secretary.

They shared a joke about this and that. He drank some water. Entered three dollars into the vending machine for a bag of chips, which he pocketed for later.

Then he strolled back to the Incubator, whistling.

"Nurses, I am ready for the next group."

It took no more than five minutes for police cars to fill the alleyway behind the Termination Bureau, for as soon as Jocelyn Adams left his office, the Moral Advisor called to let them know an act of murder was likely to be taking place in the alleyway. He told them to hurry, that there was still time to stop it, still time to save a life — though the life he was concerned for was only of the unborn; a life already started meant nothing to him, for it meant nothing to the state he worked for.

After all, the state of Florida no longer permitted the sale and purchase of born persons; only the unborn were allowed to be sold and bought in their holy state.

Jocelyn had yet to pull up her pants when the police arrived. She was just lying there in a pool of her own blood — crying. The officers didn't bother to locate her missing pants. One Police Officer took her arms and roughly put them behind her back as his partner put his knees into her side.

"Stay down!" they yelled at her.

"Stay down!"

One aimed his gun at her head just in case she refused to listen. He kept his finger on the trigger. When she had been cuffed, they dragged her to the nearest car and threw her into the backseat, leaving behind a trail of blood.

With sirens playing in the background, Nurse Susan made her way around the Incubator as Officer Tommy watched her and her fellow nurses from the doorway to the White Room, which became less and less white as the day went on.

Unwritten

Mitra De Souza

Despite my best efforts, the library's plush velvet armchair could no longer cradle my lanky pre-teen extremities. I closed my worn copy of *Moby-Dick* and stretched my legs, imaging how the sailors aboard the *Pequod* must have felt in their cramped quarters during their hunt to destroy what they believed was the enemy. When the acrid scent of smoke pricked my nostrils, I froze.

The Saviors were coming.

Riding on white horses and wielding flaming torches, they left no village untouched. In hushed voices we called them what they really were:

The burners.

Miss V stood motionless by the library's front window, clutching the pendant that hung from her neck, her knuckles white against its deep purple hue.

I rose from the cushion and approached her. "How far are they?"

"I imagine they'll be here soon." Her voice remained calm. Too calm.

"What do we do?"

She faced me with tight lips, the light in her eyes diminished.

"We need to do something." I hurried to the door and locked it. I threw my weight into the bookcase nearest the large glass window, but it held firm against my juvenile attempt to protect us.

"Joshua, come away from the window." Her voice was sharp. "I need you to do something. Come quickly."

I ran to the table in the back of the library where she stood wrapping a leather-bound book in a piece of cloth. She tied twine around it, once vertically and once horizontally, knotting it in the middle.

"I need you to take this for me. To keep it safe. Do you understand?"

I nodded.

"It's the most important book in the entire library."

I swallowed and steadied my hands to receive it. "What book is it?"

She ushered me to the back door. "Quick, you must leave now. Promise you will keep it safe. Get as far as you can from here and hide it."

Before I could reply, she squeezed my arm and sent me out the door. If I had known it would be the last time I laid eyes on her, I would have stopped to imprint the etches in her face, the warmth of her scent, the wisdom in her eyes. But the burners drew close, so I hid the package in my coat and ran into the darkness without looking back.

The night sky glowed with an unnatural orange, and ashes rained from the sky like the first winter snow. Barking dogs and angry yells sounded from the distance as I sprinted along the edge of the forest, inhaling smoke and pine. My worn shoes pounded on the unforgiving ground; my pulse throbbed in my neck. The path to my house veered left, but home wasn't safe. The only problem Father had with the burners was that they wasted "good kindling." Instead, I headed into the forest.

Despite the darkness, I found my way to the small cave where I once sought shelter. When Father had taken me on my first hunt, I had wept over the dying fawn. He forced me to take the final blow to help me become "a man," but I vomited in the bushes and ran away sobbing. I spent the rest of the day hiding in that cave until I thought Father would have forgotten his rage. He didn't.

Aside from the library, the cave was my only refuge. I crawled inside and rested my back against the damp wall, gasping for breath. When my breathing slowed, I took the package from my coat and cradled it in my arms. The twine was so tight I would need to cut it open, so I searched for a sharp stone. The yelling and barking grew louder.

Miss V had told me they train the dogs to track paper, ink, and glue bindings — scents of the enemy.

I tore through the soft earth with rigid fingers until I had a space big enough for the book. I placed it in the hole, still wrapped in twine and fabric, and buried it. After marking its location with two stones, I ran home.

For most of the night, sleep escaped me. Thundering hooves echoed in my ears long after the burners had retreated. Thoughts of Miss V flooded my mind, and my tense muscles refused to relax, as if yearning to spring from the mattress beneath me. Despite squeezing my eyes shut, Miss V's countenance haunted me. Her dark eyes called to me as the library stood engulfed in flames of judgement and fury. I pulled the quilt over my head and shuddered in the darkness.

The next morning an eerie stillness filled the air. Not even the birds dared warble from the old oak tree. Hazy sunlight filled the room where my siblings lay sleeping. I arose and dressed, determined to finish my chores before breakfast. Once I had fetched water from the well and polished Father's shoes, I set off to check on Miss V.

When I reached the town square, a mob had gathered where the library once stood. Now only piles of ashes and smoking embers littered the ground. I gasped as I recalled the countless times I had found comfort between its walls — where every story was a friend that understood me. The one place I felt whole had been reduced to ruins. Time stopped as the surrealness of the devastation sunk in. Not here. Not my library.

Not Miss V.

My body trembled as I searched the crowd, my chest too tight to breathe. That's when I saw her — a stranger in the crowd clasping a pendant, her eyes vacant. Miss V's pendant. Its deep purple gemstone glistened in the broken sunlight, the golden key a reminder of unlocked worlds. I moved towards the stranger, my face asking the question I dared not speak. She shook her head as tears streamed down her face.

For days I moved through time like a ghost, going through my daily motions while feeling dead inside. Wake, chores, sleep, wake, chores, sleep, trying not to draw Father's wrath. At night my dreams were haunted by fire-breathing horses and snarling dogs, after which I would wake to damp, salty cheeks, and the smell of scorched paper in my nostrils.

Until one night when I dreamed of the book I had buried. Like a seed, it had grown into a garden full of books. Books hung from vines like delectable pieces of fruit and sprung up like wildflowers in all directions. As soon as I picked one book, another grew in its place. That morning, I got up early and rushed to the cave.

It must have been my childish sensibilities, but I half expected to find a book garden when I approached the cave. Instead, I found the two stones, unmoved. After pushing aside the stones, I dug through the earth with my bare hands until I reclaimed my buried treasure. As I clutched it to my chest, my eyes stung. *The most important book in the library.* I used a sharp stone to cut the twine and carefully unwrapped the book. Its burgundy leather cover was embossed in gold. I turned it over in my hands, caressing the smooth cover and rigid spine.

After a moment I took a deep breath and opened it.

Inside, the title page piqued my curiosity. It was blank. I turned the page. Another blank. Then another and another. I thumbed through blank page after blank page before slamming it shut and throwing it in the dirt.

Miss V had tricked me.

I clenched my fists and screamed into the empty forest. My scream descended into a wail from deep in my chest, broken by jagged sobs. *I should have stayed. I could have helped her.* I beat the wall of the cave until my knuckles were raw and I collapsed to the ground.

She did it to save me.

She knew it was the only way to make me leave. She had saved my life. I glanced at the book lying in the dirt, shame burning my cheeks. But what was my life without her—without books?

I bent over to pick up the book and the last page fell open, exposing a handwritten note.

The most important story is the one you'll write.

As long as we keep telling our stories, they can't win.

- Miss V

Grief silenced me as the years passed without her — without the library. But over time, the realization that my silence sustained their victory weighed on me. I had to tell my story. For Miss V and for those who told theirs.

And so, I did.

-900-

History
&
Geography

THE CARCASS OF LIBERTY

WRYANN TRISTHAN A. BENITEZ & LESTER N. LINSANGAN

"The reason was justified"
But with millions of people who died?
It seemed like he was a villain
It was revealed like how light shines through a curtain
A leader, a dictator, and an artist.
He was a fine man with a twist
His vision was once clear
Then he started to kill everything he holds dear
Now he is seeking for revenge
For the root of his bloodline, he's trying to avenge
He had the plan in the palm of his hand
Having all bow before his command
His lead was influential
Power is always essential
And that? Is something simply exponential

For someone with those credentials

The cause was for good, noble even

But the actions that followed were something you couldn't be-

lieve in.

Wiping out a chunk of humanity

I guess it got to his sanity

But was it justifiable? Was his reason really true?

Regardless, his resolve was already through and through

Defending for your home turf is something we can't fight

But his ways are what made him into dark than light

Don't actions speak louder than words?

Let alone thoughts and intentions, it was completely absurd

His words influenced how we looked at the world.

One against all made him feel caged, in a corner all curled.

Didn't even reach old age

Trapped in his own cage

It just hit him like a truck

You could say he ran out of luck?

A noble man indeed

Tried to save the land he was born in, right under his steed

But in the end, nobody from either side won.

Only temporary peace was won. Soon enough all of it will be

gone.

But upon consideration, were the victors questioned if they told

the truth?

Or was it all just half-truth?

To be the one true victor, you have to be morally correct;

Rather than being immorally correct and morally incorrect.

Castaways

Rebecca Linam

"I live on Esperanto Street," said the old woman. "Eighty-seven Esperanto Street."

The taxi turned to the right. "Eighty-seven Esperanto Street," repeated the driver in a strong accent. "My brother also lives here."

His dark hair and dark skin told her that he wasn't a native German.

The old woman nodded slowly and gazed at the houses as they drove by. The windows were closed with the outside shades pulled down tight. *Surprising for such warm weather,* she thought. *Normally, the city would have every window open, taking advantage of the pretty weather.*

"That'll be fifty euros," said the taxi driver.

The old woman gave him fifty-five since she was in such a good mood. Taking her purse and a plastic bag full of personal items, she stepped out of the taxi and looked up at her house.

The first thing she would do was open all the windows and air it out.

The taxi drove off in the direction of the local brown coal mine.

The old woman pulled her house key out of her purse. For five long years she had battled cancer and won. Somewhere in the middle of it all, she had fallen and broken a hip. Chunks of time seemed somehow lost in a fog, what with the chemo and all... but, no matter—at least she was finally home again.

She put the key into the lock and...

...nothing happened.

"Did my children get the locks changed?" She tried to force the key. "Probably thought I'd wait around in that nursing home forever. I'll ask Beate for my spare key." Beate lived next door and always kept an eye on things.

However, Beate's windows were closed with the outside shades drawn tight, just like so many other houses in the village. The grass stood at least half a meter tall.

"She's probably traveling somewhere," said the old woman. "As soon as I get my door open, I'll call her grandson and tell him he should mow the lawn."

Looking down the street, she wondered at the lack of cars and people. Normally, children were coming home from school this time of day, some riding their bicycles and others running behind playing freeze tag. The bus always ran every half hour.

"Strange," the old woman said. "It's so quiet."

However, she knew everything was fine because suddenly the church bells rang out in the distance. Every day at noon, they tolled across the village.

Maybe the employees at the church will be able to help me get into my house. She made her way through the quiet village to the church's door.

The door was locked as tight as her own house.

"What's going on here?" the old woman exclaimed.

Everyone had free access to the church; it was always open for prayer. Then again, maybe today was the annual May children's festival out in the fields. That would certainly explain why children weren't storming down the sidewalks after school.

She walked back to the information board in front of the church to check the location of the children's festival, but the only thing there was a homemade poster protesting the mining of brown coal.

"Brown coal," she said. "Maybe they've all gone out to the mining site to protest again. In that case, I'll just go to the grocery store and get a bottle of water."

It didn't take long to get to the small grocery store, what with the lack of cars, bicycles, small children, and dogs. Yet, when she pulled on the door, she found that it was deserted.

Then it dawned on her. "It's practically a ghost town!"

Where were the people, her neighbors, her friends? She pulled on the door to the grocery store again and then hurried to the printing store next door—closed. She went down the block trying every door, but they were all locked up tight.

Suddenly, the old woman shivered there in the hot sun. This had happened once before during the war.

"They ran us out," she whispered. "They took us all to that labor camp."

She glanced briefly at the numbered tattoo on her wrist.

Back then, the same thing had happened. The streets were empty because everyone had been forced to leave.

"Even though I was Catholic... just because I had Jewish blood."

The old woman walked through the streets aimlessly. No one remained here, just like that other time. The silence was so loud that the old woman began to weep a waterfall of tears that almost blinded her.

"The poor children!" she cried.

Back then, she had been a child of eight. She had never forgotten the biting hunger. Her own children had never known such hunger. The minute they had said "hungry," she had immediately given them something to eat.

But... who was guilty this time? Here in the village, there had only been one Jewish family. Was it the Catholics this time or the Protestants or maybe the atheists? The old woman went to the nearby bus stop and sat down.

This time she had been spared.

This time.

How many more times would it happen that people got run out of their homes? Where would they be taken this time? Would they be forced to work themselves to death like last time?

Sometime later, a police car turned the corner and slowly made its way to the bus stop where the old lady sat, tears still streaming down her face.

"Can I help you? Is everything okay?"

The old woman stood up immediately and took a step back. She didn't want to go back to the labor camp. She would rather stay in that nursing home. No, she would rather die than go back to the constant hunger and the biting cold of the winters in the camp.

"Don't be afraid," the policeman said. "I'm not going to hurt you."

Finally, she found her voice.

"I-I-I-I-I-I wanted to go home, but my door won't open," she stammered. "And everyone else is gone. I can't even ask my neighbor for my spare key."

"Don't worry," the policeman said. "What's your address?"

"Eighty-seven Esperanto Street. I've lived there for seventy years."

The policeman stepped out of his car and walked her down the street toward her house. "You're one of the last," he said. "Most of the others have already gone."

Did she dare say it? Should she say out loud what she hadn't said that other time?

"Driven out," she whispered. "They were all forced out of their homes."

"Forced is a little exaggerated, don't you think?" the policeman said. "Most of them went willingly."

She stopped in front of a rose bush that hadn't been pruned in years. "Willingly?"

The policeman nodded. "This is your house, right?" He pointed to her front door. "Let's ring the doorbell first." He pressed it firmly.

"But no one's home," the old woman insisted. "I've been away for so long, and my children have been watching over the house, but they're away now —"

She was interrupted by the front door opening. There in her very own house stood a woman with olive-colored skin wearing a tan headscarf. Behind her, she noticed that her large oak dining table with its six chairs was missing.

"What's going on here?" she cried and pushed her way into the house.

Much of her furniture was missing. Only the IKEA coffee table that her grandchildren had bought for her eightieth birthday still stood in the sitting room, and who was this woman in the headscarf? Had her children hired a cleaning lady without her consent?

"But my children promised me that they would look after the house," she whispered. They had done that until two weeks ago when they had traveled to New Zealand for a ski trip. They had probably thought she would be content to stay in that nursing home forever; she'd never notice if they sold a few pieces of furniture here and there.

The policeman stepped inside the house, and the woman in the headscarf shrank back into the kitchen.

"But you sold your house, right?" the policeman asked the old woman.

"No!" cried the woman. "My children were watching over the house while I was sick. They paid all the bills, everything! This is my house!"

Suddenly, she stopped.

The woman in the headscarf stared at her from the kitchen door with scared eyes. Two small children stood behind her, peering out at the old woman. One of them looked up to his mother and asked something in a language that might have been Arabic.

The policeman looked at something on his cell phone. "But here it shows that you sold your house last year. Don't you remember signing a contract for it?"

The old woman tried to think. Yes, she had signed many documents — papers about cancer and hip operations, therapy contracts, hospital authorizations, and nursing home forms.

"Why would I sell my house?" the old woman asked. "I've lived here since — since the war ended."

The old woman pointed to the newcomers in her kitchen.

"What are they doing here in my house?"

"They live here now," the policeman said.

The old woman teetered over to her remaining coffee table and sat down on it.

It was just like last time. After the war, they had finally made their way back home. Everything looked the same, but a new family had already moved in. "We've been here for years," they had said. "This is our house now."

She and her family had traveled all over and finally ended up here in the tiny village of Morschenich where they had gotten jobs on a local farm.

And here she was seventy odd years later with a policeman telling her that this strange woman in the headscarf now lived here — in her very own house.

"Most of the residents have already moved," the policeman continued, "so we've been using a few of the vacant houses for the refugees who've arrived. Most of them have already moved on to other parts of Germany, but a few still live here."

The old woman had heard a lot about the refugees from Syria in the news... but why had her children sold her house without telling her about it?

"Why did everyone leave?" the old woman asked quietly. "Because of the refugees? Were they driven out to make room for them?"

"Not at all," the policeman answered. "Surely you've heard of the brown coal deposits here in the area? There's brown coal underneath Morschenich. They're going to tear down the village and mine it out soon." He sighed. "Never mind that we have enough renewable energy thanks to all of the windmills."

Suddenly, she understood. "So, they really did run the people out of their own homes," she whispered. "But this time they did it with money, not guns."

The money that her children had gotten for the sale of her house was probably there in her bank account, but that still didn't change reality. She would have to move on because her house no longer belonged to her. Her gaze rested on the refugee family in the kitchen. She had been in their shoes before, un-wanted and scared in a land so far from home.

And now she was old and tired. She didn't want to travel anymore, but at least she could do one thing for another family of refugees. She stood up and slowly made her way out the front door.

"Where are you going?" the policeman asked.

"Back to the nursing home."

Cherry Bomb

Eric Diekhans

Alabama, 2024

T-Rex and me are kings of four square. It's the perfect game. Symmetrical, my dad likes to call it, whatever that means. Four players, a square divided into four parts. Bounce the ball from one square to the next. Hit a line, let it bounce twice, or knock it past the square and you're out.

After recess, we tromp back inside sweaty from the sun, shoes sticking to the bubbling asphalt. Ms. Wheeler waits just inside the door, stiff as a flagpole, flashing us the stink eye because we didn't have time to towel off in the restroom. Library time comes right after recess and we aren't about to miss it.

"Line up," she orders. "Inside voices. Recess is over."

Our class jostles for position until we form a line. Ms. Wheeler frowns over her glasses like she thinks this is boot camp instead of third grade.

"Class, follow me."

T-Rex is in front of me so I can't see ahead as our line shuffles down the long corridor to the other end of the building. His real name's Turner, but I call him T-Rex because he's the biggest kid in our class.

Classrooms bustle as we pass their doors. Kindergarteners hunch over Petri dishes, bug-eyed behind the lab goggles Ms. Vanderkolk hands out so they feel like real scientists.

Ms. Walker waves to us from the reception desk. She always looks like she stepped out of a Disney Channel show. Mr. Kelp's office is tucked behind the reception area. He sits at his desk and leans on his elbows as he listens to a woman in a short green dress and green tennis shoes. Her back is to us but I guess she's someone's mother. She waves a finger at our principal like she's about to poke out his eye. Mr. Kelp nods, his face scrunched up and serious. I strain to make out the lady's words but Ms. Wheeler keeps our line moving. Library is only twice a week and we don't have time to mess around.

Besides the cafeteria and auditorium, the library's the biggest room in the school. The ceiling is so high it hurts my neck to look up. Tall windows stretch across one wall and give a nice view of the playground and our four square court. But my favorite part of the library is the brick fireplace. Mr. Wilcock, our old librarian, said they used to light a fire to keep the room warm, but that was like the 1800s, before even my sister Isabelle's time.

Mr. Wilcock retired last year. He didn't look that old. Maybe he was just tired because he seemed grumpy toward the end, always complaining about the ignorant people on the school board. One day we showed up for library and he was gone.

Ms. Gretchen is the new librarian. Gretchen isn't her last name but that's what she told us to call her. She's young, just out of library school or wherever they teach you how to put pictures in the right folder and tell kids to shut the drawers gently, please.

Besides the fireplace, the picture drawers are the coolest thing in the library. They take up most of the room, except for the looking nook with beanbag chairs and little tables where you can stack the pictures you've already looked at.

The drawers are humongous. Even T-Rex can't stretch his arms from one end to the other. They're stacked two high in big metal cabinets. The drawers slide in and out like they're on greased tracks. Signs on the outside tell you what's in them but they only have numbers that you have to look up on the computer. T-Rex and me never bother. We like to explore the drawers like we're hunting for buried treasure.

T-Rex likes sports, football especially. He knows exactly where to go: 796. I usually head for the 900s because I love history. My fingers tingle with excitement as I grab the silver handle and pull open the drawer. The sight of all those pictures divided by subject into plastic folders is almost as good as Christmas morning. A label on the corner of each folder has another number that tells you what's in it. Today, I'm not looking for anything in particular. I'm here to explore.

I pick a folder toward the far left and slide it out of the drawer. It's stuffed with black-and-white and color pictures. I slip one out at random. A grumpy-looking guy with wavy black hair wearing a white turtleneck stares off to the side. I flip the picture over to the label on the back. *James Monroe, 1758-1831. The fifth president of the United States and the last founding father to serve as president.*

Bla-bla-bla. The label goes on for a few paragraphs, but I slip it back in and pull out another picture—*Richard Nixon, 1913-1994, 37th president.* I've looked at the presidents' folder a few times before, and it's still boring.

One corner of the label's coming up so I press it back down. The labels peel off, which Ms. Gretchen says we're not supposed to do. That's her job. Sometimes, while we're looking through the drawers, she sits at her desk and prints out labels from her computer. I asked her once if those were for new pictures.

"Sometimes," she said. "Or sometimes I change the labels because the school board wants them to say something different."

I didn't get that, at least with history. It's already happened. What's to change?

I slip the presidents back in their folder and return it to the cabinet even though you're supposed to let Ms. Gretchen do that. I pull open the 300 drawer. Usually there's something interesting here. I close my eyes, run a finger down the row of folders, and pull out one at random. The label reads 323.

I slip out a black-and-white photo. In it, a fireman sprays four people with a hose. They're crowded in a doorway and I can't see their faces well. Maybe they're hot and he's cooling them off. I flip the picture over to read the description but there's no label. Sometimes they fall off so I look through the folder, but don't find anything. Maybe Ms. Gretchen missed this one. I should tell her.

I choose another picture. This one's in color. A Black lady holds a little girl's hand. They're standing on a sidewalk. I squint at the sign above their heads. For some reason, the words are blurred. I like puzzles so I stare at it for a minute until I figure out the second word is ONLY. I turn the picture over to see if I'm right but again, there's no label. Weird.

"Okay, children," Ms. Gretchen calls from the front of the room. "Pick your favorite picture and we'll meet in the story circle to talk about them."

This folder's really got me curious so I carry it to the looking nook, but all the seats are already taken. T-Rex's butt sinks into a red beanbag chair and he's got two photos of football players in his lap. He's a huge Packers fan so~~and~~ I'm guessing they're Aaron Rodgers and Brett Favre, his favorite quarterbacks.

I wave him over but he pretends not to see me. I don't blame him for not wanting to give up a comfy chair. After I jump up and down and wave some more, he finally crawls to his feet.

I tuck the folder under my arm and head toward the tall metal shelves that line the back wall. They're too narrow to hold the picture folders. When I was in first grade, I asked Mr. Wilcock what they were for. He tucked a pencil behind his ear and followed me back to the shelves. His eyes held on the bare brown metal like they were something special. "The library doesn't have a use for them anymore. Somebody's supposed to pick them up but the administration's wheels turn slowly and I'm not likely to see them gone soon."

His face turned all sad then and he put a hand on one of the shelves. "There used to be a lot of truth here. People didn't like that. It made them uncomfortable. Pictures are better because you can make them say whatever you want."

That was the last time I talked to Mr. Wilcock. I still don't understand what he was talking about. Now he's gone but the empty shelves are still here.

I drop cross-legged onto the carpet and lean back on the cool metal. T-Rex plops down next to me. "Check this out," He shows me a picture of a bunch of football players piled on the ground and a ref signaling a touchdown. "Ice bowl, 1967. Bart Starr won the game on a quarterback sneak."

I hand him a photo from my folder. A young Black woman and a white woman are sitting in a diner drinking milkshakes. The white girl must have gotten vanilla or mint by mistake because she looks like she's about to throw up.

"So what?" T-Rex says.

"Turn it over."

He flips the picture over. It's blank like the rest.

He shrugs and hands it back to me. "The label must have fallen off."

I hold up the folder. "They're all like that."

He grunts. "Weird."

"Sharing time," Ms. Gretchen calls from the front of the room. "Bring a favorite picture you found. Hurry up, everyone."

T-Rex and me hop to our feet, folders in hand. I'm burning to know what my pictures are about. When we get to the front,

Ms. Gretchen is sitting in her rocking chair in front of the fireplace. The other kids circle her on beanbags, chairs, or the floor. Everyone has a picture, excited to hold it up and read the label on back. If I'm going to ask my question I need to jump in quick, so I pull a random picture from the folder. It shows a young woman in grandma glasses getting fingerprinted by police officers.

"Who would like to go first?" Ms. Gretchen asks.

I wave my picture in the air before anyone else can even open their mouth.

Ms. Gretchen smiles. "You're eager today, Joel. Show everyone your picture and read what it says on the back."

Our class swivels to see the photo as I hold it up. "It doesn't say anything, Ms. Gretchen," I say. "There's no label on back."

"Look in the bottom of the folder. Occasionally, the labels come loose."

I shake my head and hold up the whole folder. "There's no labels on any of these pictures."

Ms. Gretchen scrunches up her face. "Bring it up here and let's see."

I snake through the other kids. Ms. Wheeler, who stands off to the side, gives me a look like I just let out a loud fart. I pass the picture to Ms. Gretchen. She glances at it and her pale skin gets even whiter.

"Oh," she says, "these were on my desk waiting to get board approval for new labels. Somebody must have put them back accidentally."

Ms. Gretchen holds out her other hand. "Give them to me and I'll take care of them."

My hand twitches like it wants to obey but I grip the folder tighter.

"Who is that lady and why's she getting arrested?"

Ms. Gretchen glances at the picture again and the other kids crane to see too. "That's Rosa Parks," Ms. Gretchen says. "She uh…" She stops. Maybe she doesn't remember what the lady did wrong.

"She was arrested because she didn't want to change seats on the bus," Ms. Gretchen finally says.

I scratch my head. I figured maybe she shot somebody or held up a bank. "Why was that against the law?"

I like Ms. Gretchen, really I do. But right now I don't have a good feeling about her. For one thing, she doesn't look like a grown-up anymore. She shifts her eyes like a kid who's been caught in a lie.

Ms. Wheeler makes her way through the kids on the floor towards me. She accidentally steps on Catie Stafford's hand. Catie squeals but Ms. Wheeler doesn't even look down as she snatches the folder out of my hand.

"You should trust what Ms. Gretchen says and not ask so many questions," she snaps.

Ms. Wheeler is always saying we should ask questions if we don't understand, so why does she look so mad?

The whole class is staring at me and I want to run and hide. But like always, T-Rex has my back. "That doesn't make sense," he says. "Why would you get arrested for sitting in the wrong seat?"

Some of the other kids nod. Ms. Wheeler glares at T-Rex and shakes her shoulders like a bird rustling its feathers. "You each have assigned desks in our classroom. Suppose you came in one morning and Elena or Sarah were sitting in your seat? You wouldn't be happy and it would cause a disruption. That's why rules are made and we must all follow them."

Ms. Wheeler's words make sense, I guess, but it still seems wrong that somebody would go to jail for something so little.

I raise my hand but don't wait for Ms. Wheeler to call on me. "But if Rosa Parks' picture is in here she must be a celebrity. How'd she get famous for sitting in the wrong seat on a bus?"

Ms. Wheeler snaps to attention like somebody pulled the fire alarm. "Library time is over." She claps her hands twice. "Line up!"

After school, T-Rex and me hang out on the playground. We can usually get up another game of four square, but the other kids brush by us and head to the basketball court. We stand in opposite squares and bounce the ball back and forth, neither of us in the mood for a game.

"What was up in library today?" I say. "Ms. Gretchen and Ms. Wheeler acted like I'd found dirty pictures in the folder."

T-Rex catches the ball and bounces it a couple of times on the pavement. "You threw a cherry bomb," he says.

"Huh?"

"Like when we're playing four square and some kid doesn't like being called out. He throws a cherry bomb to mess up the game."

T-Rex lifts the ball over his head and slams it into my square with a loud slap of rubber on asphalt. I try to grab the ball but it flies high over my head and rolls to the gym door—a classic cherry bomb.

I walk over and pick up the ball. T-Rex waits in his square, but my stomach's all in knots now. I start to drop the ball back in the big blue barrel where we're supposed to return playground equipment. I change my mind and drop-kick the ball. It sails high in the air, hits the running track, and rolls into the grass.

Maybe sometimes throwing a cherry bomb's a good thing.

FALSE STORY

NICOLE SMITH

Instead of teaching
wrong from right
we are more concerned with teaching
that which paints white in the best light.
We clutch our pearls
at the horrific truth,
we share a doctored narrative
That is beyond obtuse.
Lies were told,
debts need paid,
for every action that allowed
racism to pave the way.
Things need to change,
remorse needs to be shared,
so as a nation we can heal
in hopes the next generation can be spared.

Lit Matches

Christopher DeWitt

Logan carefully watched the building in the near distance, its dark profile slightly limned by ghostly blue moonlight. He'd been doing so for thirty minutes. There was no movement at all until he felt a stirring at his side.

"Clear, boss," Potts whispered in his gravelly voice.

Logan marveled again at how such a big man could move so stealthily.

"Like a shadow," Potts grinned as if reading his mind.

The motel had been abandoned for some time. The room they chose testified to that. Peeling wallpaper, filthy carpet, and a thoroughly disgusting bathroom.

The two men exchanged looks.

"Beats the great outdoors," said Potts with a shrug. Then, under his breath, "The freeze your nuts off, ground hard as granite great outdoors."

Logan plopped down on the sheet-covered couch.

"Gotta do it, Potts."

"Pulling rank on me, boss? Nice."

Logan tilted his head toward the hulk of angled metal in the corner that was a cot.

Potts let out an exaggerated sigh, then sat on the cot. He smiled broadly as it groaned menacingly. "Just like Grandma's goose-feather bed."

That's why every mission needs a Potts, though Logan, smiling back at the huge man. *Nothing fazes him. He could go on these trudges endlessly.*

"Made good time today. We earned it."

"Make sure to put that in your report to the Curators, boss–" Potts caught himself, propping his M4 carbine against the wall. "Sorry."

Logan stared at the swirled patterns on the carpet, those still peeking out through the years of grime.

"Grooms wasn't your fault." Potts removed his field jacket, laid it across the springs of the cot. Then after a pause, "Neither was Anna."

Logan shot him a look. Potts stared back at him earnestly. "It's done. But when it comes to Grooms I've got your back. Anna, now? Well, that shit's entirely on her."

Logan held his gaze, then his eyes became distant.

"I failed, Potts."

Potts set his elbows on his knees, nodded his head, as if he knew what was coming.

"Even if we get back with the package. The Curators were clear on the mission. This book is vital. We have to secure it."

"Hell, Chief, that's why they sent the best."

"You just don't do it, Potts. You don't lose a fellow Archivist. I'll be reassigned. At the very least. It'll be the end of field work for me."

Potts held his head down.

"We still have our orders, Logan."

"We do. Grooms and... Anna... won't affect that. Can't affect that."

"Damned straight." Potts looked up at him. "We will get that book, boss, as sure as the Earth turns."

Logan woke to the soft, familiar pattering sound of rain. He rose, went to the door, and carefully peered out, down into the courtyard of the motel. A jungle of weeds surrounded a small pool and jacuzzi, empty save for a muddy puddle collecting at the debris-clogged drain. A hopeless, rusty chain link fence attempted to defend its perimeter. A battered sign dangling from the gate stubbornly proclaimed *Closed Until Further Notice* in faded lettering.

I'd say so, thought Logan.

For a moment he pondered the remnants of what had passed for commerce from back before it all came down. Before the war.

He scoffed in quiet disgust.

Potts was impossibly crammed into the confines of the cot. He had made do and was inexplicably sawing logs.

Logan decided to leave him to it as long as possible. The tantalizing notion of hot coffee sprang to mind. They could get away with a small, open fire this far out from the city. He could use it. Potts could use it.

Potts came heavily down the outside stairs leading to the courtyard, a meaty hand running over his half-bald head, his ever-present M4 slung over his shoulder.

"Damn, boss," he said. "Aren't we being extravagant today."

Logan smiled thinly, handing him a steaming tin of coffee.

"Just shut up and enjoy it."

"Can do," said Potts quickly, smirking mischievously.

They sat silently enjoying their coffee, the day coming to life around them, with birdsong, and soft wind rustling leaves on the ground. Logan had forgotten how sweet the desert air could be after a morning rain.

"I've never been this far west before," Potts' gaze drifted beyond the open end of the courtyard that faced the old highway. Something that sounded like a crow called mournfully in the distance.

Later, with the rising sun at their backs, they marched to the western horizon.

Sunlight reflected sharply from the glass of the tallest buildings in the clear desert air, their first glimpse of the cityscape.

Phoenix, in what was formerly known as the state of Arizona, now known as The Southwest Neutral. Some people put "Quadrant" at the end of it. Some people put "Zone." Neither mattered to Logan.

"Looks bigger than I thought it would," said Potts, "I don't know why." His grey eyes carefully scanned the sky above the buildings. They couldn't be too careful. If someone was in control of the city, they could still have aircraft, though unlikely.

Logan examined the city through his binocs.

"Don't see any checkpoints from here."

They trudged on. Phoenix had become an open city toward the end of the last of the wars, which seemed kind of a miracle to Logan. There weren't many of them, but most were in the Midwest or the Deep South. It wasn't so much that none of the factions wanted to control them, it's just that none had energy left for it, worn out like bloodied heavy-weight fighters after fifteen rounds. Logan knew, though, that these were the places to where subversive scum gravitated. Like those they now hunted.

An hour later they had reached the outskirts of the city, coming in from the southeast. Logan was relieved, but not surprised that they had seen no traffic, autos, or aircraft. Operating them was extremely expensive, parts almost impossible to come by and fuel was as precious as diamonds since the refineries had all shut down, not to mention the wars consuming ghastly amounts of fuel. It was also why the Archivist's long "trudges" had become increasingly necessary, thought Logan wryly. Driving vehicles cross-country would draw far too much attention.

Maybe Phoenix is not so much open as it is dead.

Potts hefted the sling of his M4 and adjusted his field jacket. "Look like a Neutral, do I?"

"Neutral enough," Logan said, checking himself over as well.

Logan adopted an even more confident gait – a practiced attitude that had served him well in both neutral zones and occupied. They received the usual careful and wary looks when they finally did come across some people. Logan mused that by now most people were used to almost everyone carrying weapons on them, for quick use, if necessary, especially in an open city. He noted that there were still signs of some civilization and order, markets and shops were open here and there, even for clothing, shoes, etc. Impossibly, as if it were a monument to lost causes, there was even a used car lot with banners exclaiming *Best Prices in the Neutral Zone* and *Let's Talk Trade-Ins*!

Good luck with that, pal.

Potts stopped at a stall and casually bartered for some fresh fruit. They stepped aside to an area where there was less foot traffic and Logan bit into an orange. The sharp tang of the orange peel assaulted his taste buds with a delightful sting.

"Peel and all, huh?" said Potts squinching up a sour expression.

"Waste not, want not," replied Logan with a shrug. He couldn't remember the last time he had an orange. The juice spilled out, covering his chin, soaking his beard.

Potts happily munched on a plump tomato. "Where to start, huh?"

"It's a big city. They know what they're doing."

"Yep," said Potts, his eyes carefully studying the growing number of shoppers.

"Let's hope this contact of theirs is dependable. We're going to need an assist here."

They both scanned the surrounding buildings with expert eyes as they walked further into the city. Long experience had taught them that eventually, something would tip them off. Signage, postings, or flags may indicate a meeting place or rally point for subversives. That is where it would be, Logan was sure of it. Especially something as particularly dangerous as this book was, if the Curators were correct. And they almost always were when it came to something this serious. If they were to restore the Republic, such books must be stamped out, forever.

It was early in the search and Logan didn't really expect to detect a tell so soon. These people might be extremist lunatics, but they were no fools. Like the Archivist Corps themselves, they had learned from their mistakes and had refined their methods and tactics.

And then there had been Anna.

She had given the enemy aid and comfort. Treason. Treason to the Republic. She had jumped ship, "Gone west," as they now said of people who deserted. Not only deserted but joined the ranks of those who would topple what was left. Bring it down forever, to be replaced by... what? A mercilessly ravenous system that would oppress the people for countless agonizing centuries until it could be righted again? Logan always thought of himself as a strong, resilient man, but the very thought sometimes made him shudder.

They had trudged well into the heart of the city, what had been the government district, according to some of the signage still left. This is where they would find their local contact, they had been told, and it was indeed a prominent location: The former state capitol building.

Logan and Potts kept their distance and stared at the legislature building from across the large park sprawling just before it. The huge gun batteries from the old battleship named for the former state loomed in the foreground, no longer menacing, having been defaced with many years of neglect and graffiti.

"Look at that," muttered Potts finally. "The place is defended like the friggen Alamo."

Logan examined the fortifications through his binocs. "Yeah, that was a defeat for the defenders, you know." Concertina wire seemed to go on for miles around the place. There were even machine gun nests, every hundred feet or so, some of them possibly dummies. He spotted a few observation posts, as well. There were at least two men on the roof of the main building with scoped rifles, on either side of the large copper dome that dominated the building. The statue of Winged Victory still stood defiantly atop the dome, as if daring any would-be attackers.

"Sure doesn't look so neutral, does it?" said Potts.

"No flags or symbols. Unusual for these warlord types."

"We're sure that's where he's coming from?"

Logan let the binoculars drop "We're sure."

"Got it, boss," Potts shrugged slightly, sat down, and rested his back against a low concrete wall. After a moment, Logan did the same. He reached into one of the expansive pockets of his field jacket and pulled out a small package of jerky. He handed a piece of it to Potts, whose eyebrows shot up with delighted surprise. "Been holding out on me, chief?"

"Nothing to get too excited about. It's not real meat."

Their contact arrived shortly after midnight. He matched the Curator's description perfectly. A short, compact man with close-cropped hair and a serious, absolutely-no-bullshit demeanor. The Curators had been very firm as to his reputation: Infallible. His information had literally never failedthem.

"Kelly," he said to them curtly, by way of introduction."It's not far." He turned and walked away.

Logan and Potts exchanged looks. A man of few words and all business, as advertised. Logan appreciated and respected that. He also appreciated that Kelly was risking a lot, being ensconced in the head quarters of a regional warlord. Most of their type were particularly vicious and thus were known to do particularly monstrous things to spies and informants. People like Kelly were, naturally, highly valued by the Republic.

After walking carefully through the mostly deserted streets for about half an hour, Kelly stopped and hunkered down behind a low stone wall, peering over it. He stared at a squat building about thirty yards away. A dilapidated sports arena lay just beyond it. *Arizona Veterans Memorial Coliseum* read the faded sign. Tattered remnants of what was once the Arizona

State Fair were scattered around it. Once cheery signage and flags flapped sadly in the desert night's breeze.

"Lightly defended, if at all," said Kelly. Logan looked at him carefully. Hard not to doubt a man you have literally just met. Logan steeled himself to fully trust the judgment of the Curators.

"Ingress on the north side of the building. Password is 'Cato.'

Logan and Potts stared at him. Kelly frowned a little, the first time his expression had changed since they had met. "It's a reading. You should have been briefed." He looked them both over. "You'll pass for locals, don't worry about that."

He started to turn to leave. Logan put a hand out, holding him up for a moment. "A reading?" He ignored Kelly's glare.

Kelly shrugged. "They figure it's safer for them than trying to print copies. Makes our job easier, I guess."

Logan nodded, and Kelly left. Logan and Potts watched the building for a few minutes, then made their way to it, cautiously watching the building and their surroundings.

"I don't like this," Potts muttered.

Logan's mind raced. What next? Observe for a while longer or go in and see what this "reading" was all about?

Decision finally made, Logan made it to the north side of the building, Potts on his flank. A murmuring of voices could be heard from inside. Logan knocked on the door. There was a brief rattling sound. The door opened slightly with a metallic creak. A man with fierce, dark eyes peered out at them.

"Cato," Logan said.

The man blinked, inspected Logan for a moment, then looked past him and examined Potts. There was a tense pause.

"You're too early," the doorman finally said irritably, and started to close the door.

"Look, Logan said, using his best reasonable tone, "We've come a hell of a long way, just for this. Just need to take a load off, for a bit." The doorman disappeared for a moment, then the door creaked further open. "It's starting soon enough anyway, I guess," he grumbled. Potts gave Logan one of his patented shrugs and a look that said, 'That was easy!' and they stepped inside.

A few bare lightbulbs lit the interior of what looked to be something of a small warehouse. The vague smell of stale hay and animal dung had permeated the walls. A sign announced *Maricopa County 4-H Clubs Welcome You!*

Folding chairs had been set up near a small dais that Logan assumed had once been used for livestock ribbon presentations and auctioneers. There was a small office in a darker corner of the warehouse. A little light seeped through the office's window. They could hear a soft voice coming from the office, alternating with another voice that had a tinny quality to it.

Someone is communicating on a Ham radio, Logan thought. *More intel for the Curators.*

Logan sat down on one of the folding chairs with a groan, exaggerating his weariness.

"Thanks, friend," he said to the doorman. "Been looking forward to this."

The doorman nodded curtly, still serious and wary. He went to the office, and the conversation on the radio ended abruptly. Logan could hear the doorman speaking softly to someone. After a moment, he reappeared, with someone else right behind him. Logan could not quite make out who it was at first. Until they came into the center of the room.

"Son of a bitch," Pott's voice was a low growl.

Anna.

Logan stared in disbelief. *Anna the traitor.*

Anna stopped in her tracks as Logan stood. The doorman stopped, looked at her, then at Logan. "You know these guys," he said. It was not a question. He stepped aside, his hand reaching behind him.

"I wouldn't," said Potts evenly. Quietly and with great economy of motion, he had already unslung his M4 and held it at his hip, the barrel aimed squarely at the doorman, who slowly let his hands drop to his sides.

Logan's mouth was dry. He was trying very hard to hold down his rage. He had been betrayed before, but this was like a rusty spear through his very soul.

"I'm sorry about Grooms," said Anna. Then, her voice trembling slightly, "God knows I am."

Logan's hands formed into fists.

"Just give it to us," he said.

Anna stared at him, her eyes shining.

"You're going to have to kill me, Logan."

"It's not worth it, Anna. Give us the book and none of that needs to happen."

Anna tilted her head up slightly, defiantly.

"That always happens, sooner or later. Doesn't it?"

"You're not getting out of this," said the doorman. "A lot ofpeople are going to be here soon."

"A whole lot of threatening going on," said Potts, menacingly.

"A very wise man once said that there are plenty of ways to burn books," Anna said, "And the world is full of people running about with lit matches." Logan stared at her, waiting. "Is that really what you want to be, Logan? Just another lit match?"

Logan shifted his stance, reaching to his hip, slowly unbuckling the strap holding his .45 in its holster.

"I don't have it, Logan."

Logan's eyes had not left hers.

"Please, Anna."

The warehouse was very quiet. A soft ticking sound could be heard on the metal roof. It was beginning to rain.

"In Congress, July 4, 1776," said Anna suddenly, her voice strong and resonant. The doorman shot her a startled look. "The unanimous Declaration of the thirteen united States of America, when in the Course of human events, it becomes necessary for one people to dissolve the political bands which have connected them with another, and to assume among the powers of the earth, the separate and equal station to which the Laws of Nature and of Nature's God entitle them..."

Anna stopped, raising her hands at her sides, her eyes wide and earnest.

"Should I go on?"

"Oh, God," Potts said, his voice low. "She doesn't have the book."

"She *is* the book," said Logan. His hand still rested on the butt of his pistol.

"Like I said, Logan," she said, "You're going to have to kill me."

After a moment, Potts shifted his feet, the barrel of his rifle shifting slightly from the doorman to Anna.

"You call yourselves *Archivists*," said Anna. "I always thought archivists wanted to preserve things, not destroy them."

Logan flinched only the slightest bit, tried to steady his breathing.

"You can't burn an idea, Logan," said Anna, her voice firm with resolve. "Many have tried. But you'll have to kill *us*. You'll have to kill all of us. Because I'm not the only one."

"Well?" said Potts to Logan, after a moment.

"Potts, we're not doing that," Logan said quietly. "We're not murderers."

The murmur of a crowd reached them from the locked door. Without taking her eyes from Logan's, Anna said, "Let them in."

Potts lowered his carbine reluctantly, then slowly slung it back onto his shoulder. The doorman walked to the door.

Logan let his hands drop to his sides, looked down at the floor, took a deep breath. People started to filter in, most of them armed. They quietly took their seats, the chairs scraping slightly on the concrete floor.

"You're welcome to stay, Logan," said Anna, "and hear the rest of it. It might just change the world. Again."

Logan turned and made his way to the back of the room. Potts joined him, his face darkened with anger and frustration.

Potts stared at Logan, as serious as Logan had ever seen him, seeing a sad regret in his eyes.

"That's it, Logan. You know that, right? For you it's the end."

"You're wrong, Potts," Logan replied, his gaze not wavering from Potts'.

"This is the beginning."

The Last True Story I Will Ever Write

Anonymous

Content Warning: Veteran war experiences.

I

I am the son of an Army Officer. We are stationed in Germany at the height of the Cold War. I live, go to school, and spend most of my free time exploring every inch of the Army base I live on, Benjamin Franklin Village, or BFV. It was built in the late 1940's to house the families of the thousands of Soldiers required to both keep the peace inside Germany after World War Two and defend the country from the Soviet Union during the Cold War that followed. It was here, in the mid-1970's, that I was introduced to the complicated issues of race, class, socialism, fascism, war, the power of history, and the lasting impression of a first kiss.

At that time, BFV had become a one-year layover for Soldiers transitioning from Vietnam to wherever they called home back in the States. U.S. Soldiers are still being spit upon back home. Not in Germany. Many Soldiers still have time to serve under the terms of the draft. A disproportionate number are Black, from low income, mostly urban areas. The White Soldiers are mostly from rural, low-income areas. The two cultures do not mix. A significant number of these conscripted Soldiers have come to Germany with an addiction problem formed in Vietnam. It is a volatile brew that I was blissfully unaware of until one afternoon. A young Black Soldier had been self-medicating a bad case of what we now call Post Traumatic Stress Disorder. The very high Black Soldier climbed into an M60A1 tank and drove out of the motor pool and past my family's apartment building causing a big stir on base. It wasn't unusual to see tanks, it was unusual to see one zig zagging down the street. He didn't get far. He was still on Post when a White Military Policeman, a Sergeant, shot him dead. BFV was locked down tight as a drum to keep the place from erupting into violence. As crazy as it sounds, this wouldn't be the last time a Soldier stole a tank and went on a rampage in Mannheim.

My father told me this is the Army. There is no White or Black, there is only Green. I had Black friends in school and on my block. I knew there was Black and White, but I understood what my dad was saying. There is no place for racial distinctions in the Army. But there was room for class distinctions. And sometimes those overlapped with race.

Officers weren't conscripts. They didn't live where married senior enlisted men lived. And the Staff Sergeant and above didn't live near the barracks where junior, single, or unaccompanied, enlisted Soldiers lived. They didn't socialize in the same clubs either. Outside of the job, my father didn't see his men. I only saw them together running in formation past me on my way to school. I went to class, played sports, and had fist fights with the sons of all ranks. Initially I didn't see the difference, but I understood that they existed. That the rules were sacrosanct and inviolable and necessary. Officers led these men into battle. These men would fight the Vietcong or the Russians and some would die because of the orders they received. There couldn't be fraternization that created resentments or the perception of favoritism. Over the 40 months my father was stationed in Germany, I gradually became part of the Officer's son's clique. We didn't fraternize with the sons of enlisted men either.

At the end of our time in Germany, my father took a long leave of absence. We traveled to the beaches of Normandy, where I saw the Nazi fortifications and imagined the horrors delivered upon the men storming the beach. We went to Dachau Concentration Camp where other horrors of the Nazi regime took place against people they simply declared inferior, sub-human, and undesirable. It was evil. Pure evil wrapped in a populist fascist wrapper that equated right with Aryan and Nationalist. It was tangible evil that leapt from the pages of my history books into standing buildings, medical centers performing ghastly and barbaric experiments on living people, gas chambers, and the ubiquitous ovens to efficiently erase the existence of those exterminated. This atrocity was over, and these building served as monuments to remind generations of Germans to never let it happen again.

Next, we took a train from West Germany across East Germany and into West Berlin. We went to Checkpoint Charlie, looked over the Berlin wall. In that moment, I understood evil not as history, an academic exercise, not as a religious construct, but as a tangible thing that existed here and now. I could see it happening just over the wall. I decided on that spot, that the thing I wanted to be, more than anything else, was a Soldier. I wanted to be an Officer, like my father. I wanted to be at the pointed tip of the spear where I could fight this cursed evil.

My last day of school my teacher asked me what I had learned during my time in Europe. I wanted to condense it all into something I could say in a sentence, but the truth is it will take me the rest of my life to process all I experienced in those years. Instead, I said, "I want to be an Officer in the United States Army where I can defend the world from the Soviet Union." Her eyes welled with tears. She bent down slightly and kissed me on the lips. She said, "God bless you." I fell in love with a fourth-grade teacher that I never saw again.

II

I am a Navy Intelligence Officer attached to a Naval Special Warfare Group operating in Colombia during the early days of the War on Drugs. My mission is to conduct Covert Reconnaissance and occasionally Direct Action (military speak for blow things up and kill people). The targets I have been assigned are at all points of the production and distribution network providing America's favorite recreational drug, cocaine. I spend most of my time in country "down range". Basically, the jungles, rain forests, and river valleys of a country at war with itself and with us. It is here, in the early 1990's, that my ideals about socialism, fascism, and "war" are tested. It is in a drug stash house that my best friend will die. It is in a Cleveland cemetery that I will hear the hollow echo of Taps and realize how truly alone I am in the world.

I washed out of Basic Underwater Demolition/SEAL training with a broken collar bone. I was promising so I could have come back and tried again. While I healed, the Navy sent me to Intel school. Virginia was a long way from San Diego. It was closer to home, not that it mattered. Going in the military after college was expressly against my parent's wishes. So, with nobody to talk to, I reunited with my college girlfriend. Upon completion of my school, I was assigned to a ship that was proceeding directly to an overhaul in Boston, Massachusetts. I would get married, knowing that I was making a mistake. I began to question all my choices. It was in that moment when fate intervened and I was offered an assignment to Doral Florida, at U.S. Southern Command, I would be on loan to a Special Warfare Group to help identify the sources of cocaine, the methods used to export the drug, and the structure of the organizations. I was good at my job. I was recognized for it and offered a coveted slot on one of the "down range" (the guys in the fight) teams. Of course, I went.

Before I left Florida, I naively thought of the war on drugs as a legal matter. It was really another front in the Cold War. Marxist Communists formed an organization called FARC in Colombia and waged a civil war against the American aligned Colombian government. FARC and other Marxist groups used drug money to fund their war. In response, Right Wing death squads, under the aegis of the Colombian government waged a terrorist war against the Marxists. They also used drug money to help fund what the government would not, attacks on Catholic Priests and nuns with socialist sympathies. Into this mess I was dropped, learning as I fell.

The first time I was ever shot at, I had been in country for a few weeks. We went on patrol with Judicial Police. We all knew we would be walking into an ambush at some point. Everyone in Colombia was paid by the cartels. Someone had told the bad guys exactly when and where to expect us. When the shooting started, I didn't realize I was being shot at until pieces of trees and leaves near me disintegrated. Without a thought I hit the deck and began shooting back. It ended without any casualties on either side.

A few nights later, as I retrieved film cannisters from the trail cameras we set up to monitor shipments of cocaine to a small airstrip and warehouse, I heard movement and took cover in the high underbrush. I saw the dark shape of a man walking straight at me, as if he knew exactly where I was. But as he got closer, I could see the path he was following. I could see and hear the clanking of his AK-47 rifle slung to one side. He wasn't being careful or quiet, which meant he probably wasn't a Soldier. I drew my combat knife. At the last moment, as he literally stood above me, I thrust upward with all my strength. The eight-inch blade of my knife penetrated just beneath his chin and crushed through his palate into his brain. The wound was fatal, but my body did as it was trained. I pulled down hard on the knife turning it so that it slashed across his throat and severed his larynx and carotid artery, As I stabbed into his chest, he was already falling, and the tip of my blade chipped on his sternum. As I lowered his still living body to the ground, I could see his eyes go wide and then vacant. I had killed a man, in the dark, without a conscious thought or a sound. When I got back to the Team, I could see by the red light that I was covered in black blood. I vomited on the spot, then debriefed what had happened. Before dawn, the Team Leader called in an airstrike on the warehouse and drug lab we identified. We spent the whole day moving to an extraction point, then flying to our temporary barracks in the dark. I was now one of them, the Operators.

My best friend was my Swim Buddy at BUD/S. His team relieved my Team in a rotation that happened every few months. We had a couple of days together to bring the new guys up to speed, and then we took off back to Florida. Those would be the last days I would ever see Jim alive. He would be blown apart by a booby trap, what we call an Improvised Explosive Device (IED). His Team was assaulting a stash house, where packaged cocaine was kept before it was delivered to a plane or a boat.

I flew down to escort his body back to Andrews Air Force Base. I identified his remains at Mortuary Services. Then flew with him back to his hometown of Cleveland, Ohio. His pregnant wife and toddler son met us plane side as we loaded his coffin into the waiting hearse. Linda insisted upon seeing Jim one last time. The mortician and I both advised against it. There could be no open casket. But Linda insisted that she be able to see her husband to say goodbye. The Mortician did his best to make what remained of Jim presentable. I escorted Linda into the closed room. Stood beside her, both of us weeping over what was left of Jim. When she began to tremble, I held her up and stood beside her until she could bear no more.

As we walked away from the casket Linda turned to me and said, "Kill them all."

I don't think we ever spoke again.

I returned to my hotel room that night alone. Some Team guys had come for the funeral, but my wife had refused to come with me. She said she just couldn't do it. Couldn't stand to see the pain in Linda's eyes or his parent's eyes. And because I couldn't imagine not being there, and I couldn't drink with the guys tonight and function tomorrow, I was profoundly alone. In the morning at his wake, I told his parents what a hero their son was. I told them about our invention of combat volleyball to some amusement. When I thought this pain could not get worse, I heard my Skipper eulogize my best friend at his gravesite, heard the Tridents pounded into his casket, the present arms, and the report of the salute, and the hollow haunting notes of Taps played by a bugler, and I hurt so bad, I went numb.

I took every opportunity to go back down range. Used any excuse to go out with the Teams for an eyes-on assessment. And I got very, very good at hunting people who didn't want to be found and killing or capturing them or putting Operators or bombs on target. And as I lost my humanity, I thought, I wanted to be the tip of the spear. Now I am. I wanted to make the world safe from evil. I wanted to ensure that neither Communism not Fascism would ever again emerge to kill millions. I guess that's what I was doing. But I'm not sure. The wall came down. It's more complicated than that. It's messier than that. There is a new kind of horror in the world. A new, tangible evil. A religion married to a totalitarian ideology, committed to destroying America. I am going to the Middle East. I am going to Southwest Asia. I am going to meet them on their land, and I am going to kill them. It turns out, they had the same idea.

III

I am a Paramilitary Operations Officer in the Special Activities Division of the Central Intelligence Agency. It is the third year of Operation Enduring Freedom. I am in a medevac Blackhawk helicopter having sustained a traumatic brain injury during an assault on a Haqqani Network leader's hideout. I think, "Am I dying." I am wrong. I am not dying. My face is paralyzed where my fifth cranial facial nerve has been crushed by my broken jaw and fractured skull. My shoulder is dislocated. My armor and clothes are saturated in blood, some of it is mine. A medic is giving me oxygen and has put in an IV. He is cutting off my clothes trying to find where the all the blood is coming from. I am occasionally unconscious. Somewhere in my mind I know this can't be more than a thirty-minute flight. I remember the flash and the bang of a grenade before I breached the left corner of the broken wall. Then I feel the thump of something hitting my helmet and white noise, then pain, rough handling, and a helicopter.

I've been in this fucking shithole of a country from the beginning. Often alone or in small groups amongst these people who switch sides before battles trying to comprehend what motivates them and how they work. Why they embraced Osama bin Laden's suicidal mission, and why they cannot be compelled to reason by military threat or economic incentives. I've called more fire missions, air strikes, and Special Mission Group Direct Action than any other guy in this fight. I am probably responsible for more deaths in this country than Smallpox. I wanted the call sign "Reaper" but every derivative of that was taken by one aviator or another with a small fraction of my body count. But look who is fucked up now.

Me.

I am carried off the Blackhawk and into a triage area. A lot of information about me is being shared over me as I try to follow along. I am badly concussed, and my brain is getting stuck on things I think I understand but I'm missing the rest. A nurse tells me I am going to be alright. It sounds like I am not alright. The guy lying across the room from me is absolutely, positively not alright. I am going into surgery. Count back from 10. 9. 8....

I have had shrapnel removed from the left side of my body and my right elbow. My broken jaw has been wired back together. My shoulder has been reset. I am ready to fly to Landstuhl, Germany with a bunch of guys who have been lucky enough to survive this shit show, but unlucky enough to get holes punched in them, or limbs torn off, or badly burned, or any of the million ways to get miserably fucked up in war. I am not confined to a bed, so I take a seat on this C-17 "Patriot Express." I cannot eat the box meal, because I cannot chew, so I have a few cans of meal replacement shake. It's all I will eat for a few weeks.

I have a terrible headache. I try to sleep but between the irritating stiches and horrible dreams I can't get more than a few minutes at a time. I realize I haven't been able to call home. I haven't spoken to my wife in more than a week. She must know that I am coming home. The chocolate shake is better than the vanilla. I need to acquire more chocolate shakes. Now that's the kind of simple problem I can deal with right now.

I am checked out in Landstuhl. The hospital is full of guys returning home. My stiches are removed, which will make a big difference trying to sleep. Tomorrow I am flying into Andrews AFB. God, I hoped I would never be there again. It is midafternoon when I arrive. There are no families waiting out here in the December cold. Inside there is nobody waiting for me. I'm not military so I have few options. A Sergeant at the desk agrees to drive me to the Metro to Vienna and then I hail a taxi to my home in Northern Virginia. I get there about 4 PM. I let myself in the unlocked back door. My dogs seem confused but happy to see me. I walk upstairs to my bedroom to find a guy folding laundry and putting it away. I have seen him before. He is an IT guy who works with my wife. His name is Rick. He looks like he's seen a ghost. My concussed brain puts it together. He lives here now. Those are his clothes he is folding and putting in my dresser. I reach out to shake his hand. She's your problem now, I think. With my jaw wired, that's the best he is going to get from me.

I go back downstairs. I get my keys to my car and my wallet and a coat from the closet, and my SIG pistol from the gun cabinet. I text a friend my situation and drive to his place. We hug. I try to drink whiskey through a straw. It's too harsh. I resort to red wine. That works. The next days are a blur of doctor appointments, finding a lawyer, showing back up for work. Finding out that I have been replaced on the "in country" team and consigned to a desk. I report my impending divorce to security. It's a red flag for my clearances. I'm asked to write a report on the last four months and three days I was down range. Busy work.

In the days that follow I am haunted. My dreams are of bodies tangled in barbed wire as they attempted to escape Communist East Berlin. Of Jim, torn apart, lying as best he could be arranged in his coffin. Of a village in Central America where the children had all been hung from the rafters of a schoolhouse like macabre ornaments and the nun who taught them had been crucified to the wood floor, raped, and then shot in the face by members of a right-wing death squad. I dreamed of searching the rubble of a house I ordered a drone strike on. I needed to find the body of my target before locals stole his remains. In the dark I recall stepping on a severed arm of the son of the target... The target's body was there too, pulverized. I dream of every bit of carnage I had seen on three continents. It ran like a highlights reel, re-edited each night to remind me of something I missed the night before.

When drinking failed, I tried reading myself to sleep. I read anything and everything I could get, so long as it wasn't about war. My friend's bookshelf had quite a collection of what I thought of as classics. I read John Steinbeck's *Of Mice and Men*. Then *The Great Gatsby*. Then, *To Kill A Mockingbird*. My friend called it his banned book collection. As a practicing Buddhist, possessions didn't mean much to him, but the knowledge that others didn't want you to have, that was priceless, thus the collection.

I made it to *Fahrenheit 451* before we got into nightmare territory again. Then I bit the bullet, so to speak, and read *1984*. Coincidentally, that was the year I graduated High School. I voted for Ronald Reagan in that election, an unpopular choice on my college campus. Here I am, reading the book 1984 in 2004, and Ronald Reagan has just died. I wasn't immediately certain how I felt about that. Even though he was the President when that horrible wall came down in Berlin and the evil Soviet Union collapsed, I had still fought in the wars that lingered long after the Soviet Union was dead. Wars he started. Some ideas transcend death. These books I was reading proved that. Heinlein had died in 1988; Steinbeck in 1968 and Fitzgerald in 1940. But their ideas had proven to be dangerous into the 2000's and beyond.

I read that a new book had been banned in some places. *The Kite Runner* told a complex story about Afghanistan, a place I did not want to revisit, even in a book. But I read it none-the-less and found myself horrified by the new perspective. Vengeance, no matter how deserved, was never going to change that country, or any other. Neither was a campaign for hearts and minds. The best option was isolation. The next was extermination. Neither was feasible or humane.

In 2004, half the resources I had used to prosecute the war in Afghanistan, a war that most American's will never fully hear about, had been pulled out to fight a pointless and bloodier war in Iraq. Meanwhile, every day came evidence that the war on drugs was a failure. The price of cocaine had not risen a dollar per gram from 1984 to 2004. Jim's life was in vain. Linda's vengeance had been in vain. Nothing I did changed anything except the players and the game got bigger and bigger as I became irrelevant.

A new commanding General promised to fix what his predecessors fucked up in Afghanistan. Instead, he made new mistakes. More Afghans died. More Americans died. Iraq became a meat grinder as a civil war broke out in the middle of our occupation. My people were now in two wars. I had been lucky not to lose anyone since the Balkans, but that luck ran out the end of May 2004. A star was chiseled into the marble wall and blackened as is the tradition at Langley. His sacrifice was acknowledged at a private, highly classified, memorial. Nobody would know what he accomplished beyond the people who already knew. Nor would they know that before he died, his Iraqi captors drilled holes through his kneecaps and his fingertips and his testicles before finally drilling a hole in his skull.

I resigned in June and moved to Florida. I had nothing more to give to a cause I no longer understood. I tried to reconcile with my wife. It lasted two more tortured years and then we were done. Rick moved to Florida, and still lives in my old house. I met an incredible woman who accepted a very broken version of me. It was then that I sought help. I needed it.

The Agency reminded me that what I knew and experienced was classified and if I disclosed it, I would be subject to prosecution (thus explaining why I am vague about some things herein and why I don't share my name). I tried therapy anyway. Eventually I met a psychiatrist who recommended a banned treatment, 3, 4-Methylenedioxymethamphetamine, also known as MDMA, Molly, or Ecstasy. Because of taking this banned drug, I lost my Top-Secret SCI clearance and could no longer do the thing I was best at. I was also functionally cured of PTSD. Banned knowledge proved to be so effective that a decade later, the FDA called MDMA a "Breakthrough" drug in the treatment of PTSD. Soldiers and First Responders were enrolled in trials of the drug and 80% of them were cured. In 2024 MDMA may be removed from Schedule 1. And all I think is how many people had to die, or go to jail, over a drug that is a miracle cure. Did all that mayhem and murder stop one twenty-year-old kid from rolling at a rave? What is the problem with a drug that at worst makes you want to dance and fuck and cuddle, and at best saves lives?

Michael Pollan's book, *How To Change Your Mind* wasn't banned. In 2018, the idea that psychedelic drugs had therapeutic benefits was perfectly acceptable. But ideas about marriage equality, gender, orientation, and minority representation which had gained traction in the prior decade found an angry reception in 2016 as a counterculture wave of right-wing, neo fascism swept the country and exploded in 2020 with an insurrection at the Capitol and a failed coup attempt.

Today, I don't recognize the country that I willingly risked my life for. I don't know how we devolved from the aspirational Constitution that I swore and Oath to uphold and defend to the emergence of a Nazi-like cult of personality headed by a game show host that was impeached twice, indicted four times, and faces 91 felony counts. I don't know how Reagan's Morning in America morphed into Trump's American Carnage. I don't know how a man convicted of fraud and found liable for sexual assault is still a viable candidate for the Presidency. In my darker moments I sometimes wonder if that hit to my head really did kill me and this is the hell I deserve. But then I meet people who have no business living in hell and I know this isn't it. Someday soon, if we don't take this seriously, my story will be banned knowledge too.

I said, "Fuck."

I critiqued America. I insulted the Fuhrer. My narrative may not belong on the same shelf as *Fahrenheit 451*, after all, this isn't a work of brilliant fiction but merely a record of a life committed to sanctioned murder. But I hope you recognize the ideas, however misguided, that brought me to this place where death or banishment are not as frightening as the loss of our democracy.

I have this last true story to tell. I didn't separate my ego from my ideals and so I came to believe that what I did was good because *it was done for a good cause* and others shared my delusion. But even the cause is suspect now. This isn't a confession. I don't believe that anyone can give me absolution. Your condemnation makes no difference either. I ask for something harder to give because it requires actual work on your part. I want you to understand. To place yourself in my boots, smell the cordite and the sickly-sweet smell of rotting meat that gets into your clothes, and to really understand what this moment in time portends. I want you to separate your ego from the cause and realize that much of what you might believe is a lie a' la *1984*. The hidden information isn't hidden at all. You've just banned yourself from it, allowing people who don't want you to understand the meaninglessness distinctions of race and class and gender and orientation, and who is really a Communist and who is a Fascist and why both alternatives are shit. Anyone who wants to divide you from your family or friends over any of these differences is as evil as Hitler and as ruthlessly greedy as Pablo Escobar.

If I offend you, don't look for me. If you mean me harm, remember what I am and that you won't be the first person to try to kill me and fail. You will just be the next person to die trying and there is no glory for either of us in that. If you want to wish me well, read a banned book. Take MDMA or Magic Mushrooms with a guide and find out who you are and aren't. If you think I make sense, realize that I'm not a politician, I'm a killer. So don't ask me to run for office. Do it yourself. This

Republic must mean as much to you as it does to me, or all hope is lost. - Anonymous

Author Bios

EJ Masters (SHE/HER) IS a seventh-year public school elementary Library Media Specialist in Oklahoma. She has presented sessions at the Oklahoma Library Association and Mountain Plains Library Association's conferences on topics ranging from state book awards, giving book talks, the purchase and promotion of 2SLGBTQIA+ books for all age levels, and self-censorship in the library. She believes in accessibility, advocacy, and equity for all in public education and library services. EJ lives in Oklahoma City with her spouse Danny, her dog, and her cat.

Lorie Wackwitz is an author, editor, publisher, and filmmaker with lead editor responsibilities at two independent presses. She coaches writers from multiple continents, elevates stories of hidden voices, and plants evergreen trees by the thousands. Lorie writes from her island cottage in northern Michigan where her family maintains a private nature preserve.

Jane Hartsock, J.D., M.A. is the Director of Clinical and Organizational Ethics for Indiana University Health, the Co-Director of the Scholarly Concentration in Medical Humanities at the Indiana University School of Medicine, and an Adjunct Assistant Professor of Medical Humanities at the Indiana University School of Liberal Arts. She holds a B.A. in English (creative writing), an M.A. in Philosophy (bioethics), and a J.D. and has published and presented at national and international conferences on the use of fiction to develop ethical sensitivity. She resides in Indianapolis, Indiana with her husband, two children, and one poorly-behaved, but well-meaning Irish Terrier.

Erica Duarte In 2001, Erica graduated from the University of Denver with a degree in Psychology. After working numerous jobs, she joined the Peace Corps where she taught English, traveled, and finally landed in Tennessee. She now works for the College of Fine Arts at Tennessee Tech and is on the board of directors for a small local theater company. Erica is married with two rambunctious girls. At home, she loves having lots of pets, reading lots of books, and writing lots of stories, especially those that embrace shades of gray.

Amanda Hayden is the current Poet Laureate for Sinclair College and an award-winning Professor of Humanities, Philosophy, and World Religions. Her debut poetry collection, *American Saunter*, inspired by backpacking and traveling across the U.S., is forthcoming by FlowerSong Press in Fall 2024. *Old World Wings*, her second poetry collection inspired by her European travels, is forthcoming by Wild Ink Publishing in October 2025. She lives on a windy little farm with her partner, daughters, and many furry rescue babies including two goats, seven pigs, and an incredibly special, blind, three-legged "angel in a dog suit" Vinny Valentine.

You can find her site at https://windychickenpoet.com/

Vi Putrament is a writer, editor, and translator born in Warsaw and raised in New York City, specializing in science, folklore, fantasy, and magic. She's also a language editor for an astrophysics journal based at the Paris Observatory and writes science fiction and fantasy in every rare speck of spare time.

Melissa R. Mendelson is a horror, science-fiction, and dystopian author. She is also a poet. She has been published by Sirens Call Publications, State of Matter Magazine, Altered Reality Magazine, Transmundane Press, Owl Canyon Press, Wild Ink Publishing, The Horror Zine, and The Yard: Crime Blog. She is the author of a self-published sci-fi novella, *Waken*.

She is also the author of the prose poetry collection, *This Will Remain With Us* published by Wild Ink Publishing.

You can find her site at https://melissamendelson.com/

Ester Marquez possesses a unique combination of analytical and creative talent. She is presently enrolled in the Bachelor of Secondary Education with a Mathematics Major at the Nueva Ecija University of Science and Technology. She displays an extreme fondness for literature, showcasing her versatility and commitment to personal growth. Ester aspires to challenge boundaries in the world of poetry and highlight the unexpected parallels between patterns and the rhythm of words.

Lester N. Linsangan is a Filipino writer and educator. He graduated with a degree in Bachelor of Secondary Education at Nueva Ecija University of Science and Technology (Got the highest score of 99% in the final teaching demonstration); earned his Master of Arts in Education at the College of the Immaculate Conception (with honors); obtained his 4-year course in ecclesiastical education at the Institute of Religion, and finished his Doctor of Education at Wesleyan University-Philippines (Cum Laude) Additionally, Dr. Linsangan wrote three literary books entitled Litera, Il Vento Sotto Le Mie ALi, and Rendezvous and served as co-author, anthologist, and reviewer for numerous titles.

Kim Plasket enjoys writing horror, paranormal, and romance. She has various stories in different anthologies of varying genres, such as *The Thrill of the Hunt: Cabin Fever (Thrill of the Hunt Anthology Book 6), Scary Snippets: A Halloween Microfiction Anthology,* and *Blood From a Tombstone Volume 2: Fear*

She released her debut novel this past year, called *The Forgotten Ones.*

Maribeth Juraska, Ed.D. debuted in the world of ISBN numbers with selected poetry pieces in American Poetry Anthology (Vol. VIII) published by the American Poetry Association. Her work has been published in online zines and indie publisher anthologies. Dr. Juraska has earned an Ed.D., M.S.Ed., and B.A. in English, and is a former Professor/Director of Teacher Preparation. She has published and presented research in multiple areas of K-20 Education, including assessment, candidate field experiences, & educational psychology; as well as in her favorite subjects: Diversity and Social Justice. Currently, she dabbles in creative writing (working on a chapbook), and spends other free time scoffing at cold winters and decaf coffee.

S.E. Reed lives in the south and writes strange, haunting, real stories of people and places along old highways. Winner of the 2024 Florida Book Awards and the 2024 Paterson Prize for Books for Young People. Additionally, she's been nominated for a Pushcart Prize and won honorable mention twice in L. Ron Hubbard's Writers of the Future Contest. Her short stories have been featured by The Writer's Workout, SEMO Press, Parhelion Lit, The Writers' Co-op, Wild Ink Publishing, Hey Hey Books, and Tempered Rune's Press.

You can follow her at www.writingwithreed.com.

Eric Diekhans' fiction has appeared in *Etched Onyx* and *Jelly Bucket* magazines, and the collection *Unforgettable* (Walkabout Publishing). His screenplays won the Chicago Screenwriters Network and Illinois/Chicago Screenplay competitions, and he is the recipient of an Illinois Arts Council Fellowship in Screenwriting. Diekhans received a BA in Comparative Literature from Indiana University and an MA in Film from Northwestern.

Kelly Webber is a proud graduate of the University of Maryland's library science program. Before entering the library world, she earned her BA in English literature and taught literacy in a variety of contexts, from reading with preschoolers to assistant teaching for an undergraduate linguistics course. Her first experience working in libraries took place in a beautiful (and possibly haunted) public library. She now combines her passions for libraries and education as a school media specialist in her home state of New Jersey.

Her website is kellywebberbooks.com.

Thom Hawkins is a writer and artist based in Maryland. His work has appeared in *Always Crashing*, *Encephalon*, *Excuse Me*, *The Fieldstone Review*, *Gargoyle*, *Linked Verse*, *Oyez Review*, *Pocket Lint*, and *Poetry Box*. His video art and drawings have been displayed at exhibitions or in performances in Baltimore, Philadelphia, and New York. Thom has also appeared with the Baltimore Improv Group, Ignite Baltimore, and on The Stoop Storytelling podcast. Thom holds a Master's degree in library and information science and is at work on a PhD in the latter.

Wryann Tristhan A. Benitez is the youngest among the Grade 10 students at the Nueva Ecija University of Science and Technology—San Isidro Campus. He is the President of the Laboratory High School student council. He believes in the words of a certain Chef Gusteau that "Anyone can cook."

Caleb William D. Catalan is a 16-year-old Grade 10 student at the Nueva Ecija University of Science and Technology—San Isidro Campus. He's part of the Boy Scouts of the Philippines and has also co-authored and produced four poems for the book "Ourania's Orrey of Imagination." Additionally, he believes in the words of Tony Stark: "Contrary to popular belief, I know exactly what I'm doing."

Amy Nielsen spent twenty years as a youth librarian sharing her love of books with young readers. Daily immersion in story took root and she penned her YA debut, *WORTH IT*, behind her circulation desk. Amy is the proud parent to four humans, one pup, and has more grandpups than she can count. When she's not reading or writing, Amy, her family, and at least two canine co-captains in mermaid life vests can be found boating the waters of Tampa Bay.

Dana Hawkins is a caffeine-fueled, queer mom from Seattle, WA. When not chasing her children, dog, or spouse around the house, she spends her time writing uplifting, sparky, queer love stories.

You can find her site at https://danahawkins.com/

Riley Kilmore earned an MFA in Writing Popular Fiction from Seton Hill University in 2022. Her award-winning poetry and short fiction have appeared in numerous anthologies. Her debut novel, *Shay the Brave*, a middle-grade fantasy, is available from Wild Ink Publishing. A twenty-year veteran of the fire service, Kilmore has leaped from airplanes, sailed the world, been a cop, and braved the life of a homeschool mom. She resides on a sequestered mountainside farm in south central *Pennsyltucky* with one horse, one cat, a dancing goat, a beer-guzzling hound, and her husband of 36 years.

Miranda Huba is a playwright, director, producer, and performer born in Canada, now living in New York City. In NYC, her work has been seen at The Incubator Arts Project, HERE, Horse Trade Theater, Dixon Place, Magic Futurebox, the Silent Barn, and Madame X with Lauren Rayner Productions. Her work has been translated into German and has received German language productions at the Kleines Theater in Salzburg, Austria and Theater Tiefrot in Cologne, Germany. A reading of her play ***Grounded: A Play is Six Airports*** was presented at the inaugural Wuppertaler Literatur Biennale in Wuppertaler, Germany. Her play ***Dirty Little Machine*** was produced in London, England as part of the 2018 Vault Festival produced by Zut Alors Theatre. She holds a BFA from the Simon Fraser University School for Contemporary Arts.

Maria Juweyn Liwag is a third-year English major for a Bachelor of Secondary Education with a strong desire for poetic words that reflect her wild, make-believe imagination. She is currently a dedicated writer at her campus publication, mainly focusing on feature articles and literary pieces that kick her untamed and savage thoughts. She has been in consecutive press conference competitions ever since her elementary days ignited the fire in her heart to discover a new world of her own through romanticized words and symbolic lines.

Abigail F. Taylor is an award-winning author from Texas. When she's not writing, Abigail spends her time in nature, practicing aikido, and cross-stitching. She lives with four cats, two small dogs, and one sassy rooster. You can follow her on her website abigailftaylor.wordpress.com.

J.K. Raymond received her Bachelor of Arts in 1995 from Fontbonne University. J.K. is a chronic illness warrior, or "spoonie", who recast herself as a writer in her forties when her health forced her into a sedentary lifestyle. Published at the age of fifty-one, J.K. Raymond's debut novel *Infinite Mass* was released by Wild Ink Publishing in December of 2023. J.K. has the most amazing safety net in her tiny world, a family who keeps her rolling in laughter while selflessly helping her to continually heal. Her husband of twenty years, Matt Houser, her two sons,

Aidan and Jace, her mother, JoAnn, and her grumble of pugs, Lollie, RueRue, and TukTuk.

Bruce Buchanan has been a professional writer for more than 25 years, as both an Associated Press award-winning newspaper reporter and, currently, the senior communications writer for an international law firm. He is the author of two previously published books and his debut YA fantasy novel, *THE BLACKSMITH'S BOY*, is coming soon from Wild Ink Publishing. He lives in Greensboro, N.C. with his wife, Amy Joyner Buchanan (the author of five published books), and their 17-year-old son, Jackson.

Demi Michelle Schwartz is an author from Pittsburgh, PA, represented by Michelle Jackson at LCS Literary. She holds an MFA in Writing Popular Fiction from Seton Hill University, along with BAs in Creative Writing and Music. Currently, she is an intern at Wild Ink Publishing, the host of Literary Blend: A Publishing Podcast, and a freelance fiction editor through her independently-run services, Amethyst Ink Editorial. When Demi isn't busy in the publishing industry, she's chasing her music dreams as an award-winning songwriter and recording artist.

Helen Z. Dong is a Chinese-American author, product manager, and game writer. In 2018, she received a regional Silver Key for her writing in the Scholastic Art and Writing Awards and her first indie game, *Wake Up*, was released in July 2024. Since 2022, she has been sharing her writing journey on social media to over 12,000 followers. She currently resides in Seattle where she spends time reading, playing video games, and watching cartoons with her cat.

———

Katie Mahood lives in Central Pennsylvania where she enjoys spending time in nature with her husband, three children, and two dogs. While she embraces the ease of technology for many facets of life, she does occasionally wonder about the broader implications of dependence on artificial intelligence.

———

D.S. Lerew grew up in Millersburg, Pennsylvania where she spent her summers reading, stargazing, and walking along the Susquehanna River. She currently lives in Dillsburg, Pennsylvania with her husband, two teenage sons, and black lab, too far away from the river to enjoy walking along its banks, but still able to enjoy books and stars.

D. S. Lerew has written a poetry chapbook called *Stars in a Jar*. As Leta Hawk, she penned the *Kyrie Carter: Supernatural Sleuth* series, which includes *The Newbie, School Spirits, The*

Witch of Willow Lake, An Uneasy Inheritance, and *Dandelion Souls.*

Jacque Vickers is a writer and arts enthusiast who graduated from Newtown High School of the Performing Arts. Her writing has been published in Anthology Angels 2023 anthology: Hot Diggety Dog! Tales from the Bark Side.

Some short plays she has written have been performed at various short play festivals.

Jacque lives in Sydney, Australia.

Victoria Holland is a Pushcart Prize-Nominated Author for her work in *I'm Not the Villain, I'm Misunderstood,* as well as Lead Anthologist for *The Carnation Collection.* She has also published in multiple other collections including *Into the Mirror* and *The Magical Muse Library Vol. 1, 2, & 3.* She is a romantic, daylighting as an activist, and moonlighting as a witch and healer. Victoria lives in Massachusetts with her family, her lovely friends close by, and one day with many allies (of the plant and furry variety) she can name after her favorite characters.

Shaelynn Long is a former dirt road kid from Michigan and current small-town English instructor. She has previously published *Fury's Fate*, *Ache*, *Blur*, *Work In Progress*, and *Dirt Road Kid*, as well as appearing in a previous Wild Ink anthology: *The Carnation Collection*. Shaelynn can usually be found with her nose in a book and covered in Corgi fur.

You can find her site at https://www.shaelynnlong.com/

Earl Carrender is a poet and writer who lives in Indianapolis. He earned his BA in English at Marian University and his MFA at Butler University. His fiction and poetry have appeared in The Kurt Vonnegut Memorial Library Journal, Punchnel's, Clever, Scissors and Spackle and BullshitLit among others.

Johnny Francis Wolf — Homeless the better part of these past 10 years, Johnny Francis Wolf surfs friends' couches, shares the offered bed, relies on the kindness of strangers — paying when can, doing what will, performing odd jobs.

Of late.. Ranch Hand his favorite.

From NY to LA, Taos and Santa Fe, Mojave Desert, Coast of North Carolina, points South and Southeast, back North to PA, hiking the hills, and looking for home —

considers himself blessed. Wait. Did I hear he's found such a home, with rug and bed and pictures on the wall, in Key West?

Johnny can be found most nights on facebook.com/wolf.johnny

Joshua Isard is the director of the MFA Program in Creative Writing at Arcadia University. He is the author of many short stories, essays and articles, as well as the novel *Conquistador of the Useless*. He lives outside Philadelphia with his family.

Ryan David Ginsberg is a writer of poems, short stories, and novels. His first collection of short stories, "The Crumbling of a Nation and Other Stories," is out now. He is the father of three beautiful dogs—Brother, Midas, and Shadow—and the husband of one beautiful wife, Teresa.

Rinat Harel holds bachelor's and master's degrees in fine art and studied creative writing at Emerson College, where she received the 2015 Nonfiction Award. She holds a Ph.D. in Creative Writing from the University of Exeter in England, the fruit of which is a collection of interlinked stories that revolve around life in Israel, home/homeland, war, the Holocaust, and intergenerational trauma. Her writing has been published in various literary magazines and won several awards.

You can find her website at: http://rinatharel.com

Mitra De Souza has loved to write for as long as she can remember. In elementary school, she used to tape her short stories to the back of her chair for her classmates to read. She is drawn to stories that encourage people to view the world from a new perspective. Her debut YA novel, *The Fragile,* was released with Wild Ink Publishing in July 2024. Mitra resides in San Diego County with her husband, two kids and two big rescue dogs who think they're still puppies. Her favorite banned book is Jay Coles' *Things We Couldn't Say.*

Rebecca Linam lives in Alabama. She studied in Germany, which was inspiration for this story. Over fifty of her short stories for children, teens, and young adults have been published in magazines and literary journals.

Find her on Twitter @rebecca_linam or on her website at www.rebeccalinam.com

---

Nicole Smith is an advocate for mental health and body acceptance. She lives just outside of Pittsburgh with her husband and daughters. Recently, she was published in the Pennsylvania Bards Western PA Poetry Review 2023. If Nicole isn't writing poetry, you can find her with her nose in a book.

Christopher DeWitt lives in Phoenix, Arizona, with his wife Christine, son Alex, three dopey but lovable dogs, and a weird, vegan cat. When he isn't writing and reading, he is exploring the beautiful and sometimes eerie Superstition Mountains and the haunts of Tombstone. He also occupies his free time trying to figure out if his house, built practically on top of old western mines, is as haunted as The Copper Queen Hotel in Bisbee, Arizona. (It is.) A United States Air Force veteran and licensed pilot, he loves anything that flies or is launched into space, and earth-bound racing machines.

Devil Preacher – Tales of the Mystic Empire, his novel of the early American West, is debuting through Wild Ink Publishing in 2025. Along with *Lit Matches*, in UnCensored Ink: A Banned Book Inspired Anthology, he has another upcoming short piece, *The Eye of Sucuri*, in the anthology Tenpenny Dreadfuls: Tales as Hard as Nails